THE SPARROW'S FALL

by Fred Bodsworth

THE SPARROW'S FALL

FRED BODSWORTH

DOUBLEDAY & COMPANY, INC.   GARDEN CITY, NEW YORK

DOUBLEDAY CANADA LIMITED   TORONTO, ONTARIO

God sees the little sparrow fall,
It meets his tender view;
If God so loves the little birds,
I know he loves me too.

God made the little birds and flowers,
And all things large and small;
He'll not forget his little ones,
I know he loves them all.

Maria Straub, 1874

⋘⋘⋘ Chapter 1 ⋘⋘⋘

IT HUMPS NORTHWARD five hundred miles from the precipitous, rock-cragged shores of Lake Superior to the flat and muddy seacoast of Hudson Bay—a big and lonely land of bog and forest, as diversified within as the contrasting coasts that mark its extremes. It is a land of clashing contrasts, too, in its nurturing of the life that depends upon it —a benign land sometimes, amiable, even indulgent, but at other times a cruel land of perverse hostility.

The first hundred and fifty miles lift abruptly from Lake Superior, a rugged terrain here of worn-down mountains carved by rivers that tumble steeply to that greatest of inland fresh-water seas. In this southern region there is a sporadic network of roads and railways, a spattering of lumbering and mining towns; but to the north beyond, for the remaining three hundred and fifty miles to the tidewaters of Hudson Bay, there is forest and bogland broken only by a sprinkling of Indian settlements that cluster around the fur-trading outposts of the white man. There are no roads here, not even foot trails of any extent, for much of it is bog too soft and spongy for foot travel in summer, and buried deeply by snow in winter. It is reached from without only by aircraft; within, it is traveled by canoe along its lake and river waterways in summer, and by dog sled and snowshoe in winter.

The foresters know this forest as taiga, the great boreal-forest formation that spans the subarctic zone around the world. To the south are the deciduous, hardwood forests of the temperate zone. To the north, beyond tree line, is the arctic tundra where no trees can grow. The taiga—in most places hundreds of miles wide—is the transitional forest empire between.

Here the rounded silhouettes of the temperate zone's deciduous hardwoods change to a ragged skyline of spire-like conifers, because the subarctic summers are too short for most trees to throw off leaves and grow new ones every spring. Thus the taiga is a forest mainly of needle-bearing evergreens. There are a few deciduous trees in this austere land, hardy birches and poplars, but it really belongs to the resilient and needly spruces, defiant trees, trees girded by nature to clothe a land where few others can survive.

It is a harsh land, too, for the wild ones that live here, because each year they must survive a winter seven months long when much of the taiga foodstuff is locked beneath snow and ice. There are two great tribes of taiga dwellers—vegetation eaters and protein eaters, the hunted and the hunters. The vegetation eaters, builders of the protein on which the hunting ones must live, are the mouse hordes, snowshoe hare, beaver, moose, and caribou. The hunters are mink and otter, fox and wolf, and in that region where the great Severn begins its contorted passage to Hudson Bay, the *Atihk-anishini*. For the *Atihk-anishini,* too, are a part of their land in that vital, intense, interdependent way that only primitive people can belong to the land on which they dwell.

The mice are sweet and tender, but too small to be a man food. Beaver by midwinter are sealed up and unreachable beneath ramparts of ice and frozen mud as impenetrable as steel. Moose are here, but rare in the *Atihk-anishini* part of the land, because there is little of the tender, young hardwood forest that follows fires and makes the best moose range. Hares are here, but their numbers fluctuate in cyclic highs and lows as disease resistance waxes and wanes, and sometimes, when epidemics strike, there may be one or two winters when the hare runways are empty and the *Atihk-anishini* snares catch nothing.

And the caribou are here, known to another people in another land far beyond the sea as reindeer, known in this land as *atihk*—sweet meat, tender meat, eagerly sought meat, the winter staple of the *Atihk-anishini,* the Caribou People. These are woodland caribou that live in small groups or alone, not the Barren Ground caribou that flow in massive herds across the treeless tundra farther north. The woodland caribou are here because most of this is old forest that has not felt the devouring scourge of fire for centuries, and thus the caribou lichen that needs a century to attain its fullest growth is spongy and deep on the forest floor. It is branched and coral-like, white, not green, and from a distance can look like snow. Where it remains undisturbed by fire long enough, it lays down a springy, interwoven carpet six inches thick that is a major fodder of this subarctic land.

Unlike the moose that are winter browsers of the tender twigs of young forests, the caribou are lichen grazers and need a forest with the shaggy dishevelment of age upon it. And because the caribou are ground feeders, snow is their scourge. In a normal winter they can dig through the snow for the lichen their bellies need, but when the snow is deep, the caribou roam far to seek out the thin and weak spots in the land's snowy armor.

At long intervals one of the cyclic lows of the snowshoe hare coincides with a winter of deep snow that scatters the caribou far and wide from their usual ranges. And thus, two avenging forces of nature interact to bring a time of famine to the hunters of the taiga.

This one is such a winter in the country of the *Atihk-anishini*. This winter it is a cruel land. Because the hares are gone; and the snows lie deeper than any *Atihk-anishini* remembers, so the *atihk* are gone; and now the belly-squeezing hunger is also gone. Because the hunger is no longer hunger. It is the insentient numbness of starvation.

Chapter 2

THE DAWN WAS BECOMING a gray smear on the canvas tent roof when the cold wakened Jacob Atook. He could tell from the tingling chill on his cheeks that the green birch logs he had put in the little tent stove to hold the fire overnight had burned themselves out. Somewhere outside he heard a spruce tree crack like a rifle shot in the strangling squeeze of the cold.

He rolled over toward her, automatically holding the *atihk* skins and plaited rabbitskin robe tightly around his neck to keep the warmth of the bed from escaping. In the pallid light he studied the face beside him, and a shiver came that wasn't from the cold. For it was a face that had been beautiful and young and full two months ago, one month maybe, because it was getting hard to remember; but now, though beautiful still, it was shrunken, taut, angular . . . old. And the accusing shiver of guilt pang came again, for it was he who had made it that way.

He didn't want to awaken her, but his hand moved slowly, compulsively, down to her waist and under the heavy woolen underwear, and then his fingers spread tenderly over the round, hard belly. Fully awake now, he waited with all his senses focused sharply in that one trembling palm. For a long time there was nothing. The chill spread in him, tightening, squeezing. His hand moved back and forth across the tight, warm skin, seeking, hoping. And then he felt it—a fluttering electric throb, a faint stirring of the life within.

She awoke and smiled. The eyes were dark, large, with the narrowing of the corners that was the mark of their race's distant Oriental origins, but the whites still had their luster and flashed like sunny snow.

"The little one moves," she murmured. "Did you feel?"

"Yes, Niska," he whispered, smiling with her now, "the little one still moves."

"They say the ones that kick in the belly are always boys."

"Yes, a son." For a moment Jacob felt a glow of pride and joy at the thought, then his smile fled, and the chill came surging back.

She fell asleep again immediately, and his gaze lingered a long time on the hollowed cheeks and the ridges where her jaw and cheekbones seemed on the verge of bursting through the brown skin.

Finally he tucked the bedding skins underneath her, so that he could slide out of bed without letting the cold in, and got to his feet slowly, warding off the dizziness that came each morning now if he rose too quickly. He pulled on trousers over the thick woolen underwear in which he slept, then two sweaters, the knitted tuque for his head, the moosehide moccasins, and finally the massive *atihk*-skin parka with its brown and silver fur inside. His breath hung like white smoke before him as he stooped beside the stove. Outside, another tree cracked with the frost, and the sound told him that in the white man's way of gauging cold it was forty below or colder outside, and at least zero here within the tent.

There were still a few red coals hidden in the white ashes of the stove. He cut shavings and arranged them carefully over the red eyes that glowed feebly on the stove bottom. His hands startled him. The backs of them were ribbed like coarse corduroy, and the fingers were long and gaunt, making it appear that there were more than four on each hand. He blew the shavings into flame and added wood, and the fire crackled suddenly with a leaping orange brilliance.

Jacob took one of the fire-blackened cooking pails and stepped to the tent entrance. He pulled on his moosehide mittens and drew the hood of the parka over his head. The dizziness hit him momentarily when he stooped to lift the canvas flap and hunched through, but his head cleared as soon as he straightened up again outside. There was a hollow dug in the waist-deep snow before the tent, and he climbed its trampled steps until he was standing on the snow surface above, his head higher now than the ridgepole of the tent. Then, in the dimness of the dawn, he paused there, throwing the parka hood back from over his ears, all senses—eyes, ears, nostrils—probing with their primordial hunter's instincts the brittle stillness of the new day.

Carrying the ax and cooking pot, he stepped out through the screen of spruces that hid the tent, then he stopped again, and his eyes spanned the stark flatness of Little Ninkik Lake beyond. But he did it from habit, not from hope. There were no new game trails etched on the snow; he had known there would not be. It had been three months since the last *atihk* passed down the Little Ninkik. Jacob looked back toward the spruce forest that crowded down darkly behind the tent. His ears and nostrils strained, but no sounds or scents came; there was only the sharp pinch of the cold air momentarily freezing the nostril hairs with each breath. The forest was dead. The famine would stay until *seekwan,* the spring, could roll back the armor of ice and snow and liberate its imprisoned life.

He walked down the path to the water hole; the snow trail here was packed hard from frequent use, so he didn't need snowshoes. The ice on the lake was almost as thick as the span of Jacob's two arms, but the snow on top of it was only half the depth of that back by the tent in the wind shadow of the forest, because here on the lake the wind swept much of the snow away. He stepped down the pit in the snow, chopped out the night's new ice, and dipped up a pail of water.

Back in the tent the inside air was warming from the fire. He put water on for tea and then he gazed at her, stealthily at first until he was sure she still slept. There was a sharp pinch of pain in his throat, as the pinch of the cold air had been in his nostrils outside.

It would have to be today. He had waited too long. Much too long. The *Manito* who had spoken so clearly early that winter had not spoken now for a long time. He had forgotten they were there.

Jacob hunched beside the soot-darkened stove. Periodically he added wood from the pile at the front of the tent, opening and closing the stove door quietly so as not to awaken her, for there was peace in sleep and only pain and fear in the long, fretting hours of waking. A couple of times she murmured and tossed restlessly on the bed of balsam boughs, and each time Jacob watched, holding his breath like an ice lump in his throat until she settled again.

Even with the saucered cheeks and the too-big, slightly bulging eyes and the tangled hair, he thought, she was beautiful.

The dawn advanced, and the opaque light of a new day filtered wanly into the tent. The water boiled, and he opened the food box and took out the tea tin. Carefully, his hands trembling a little, he poured a thin sprinkling of tea into one palm and dropped it into the bubbling pot.

She awakened then.

"There's still flour to thicken it," she told him. "The last sack, by the door. Don't use too much."

"We'll save it," Jacob said. "We won't thicken it today."

It was a practice of the *Atihk-anishini,* when there was no more lard or baking powder for making bannock, to use the last of the flour as thickening in their tea. But Jacob and Niska had not even had flour now for more than a month. In her delirium she had forgotten.

Instead of flour, he had been using lichens and scrapings of the soft, white inner bark of birch and poplar, the latter a starvation food his people knew as *oseepan,* to give the brew some belly-filling body. But he wondered if it was worth doing, because any food-bearing saps the bark had contained earlier in the winter had long ago been evaporated by the long dry weeks of withering cold. All it seemed to accomplish was to put a bitter scum on top of the tea.

But he added a big double handful and let it boil with the tea. And it must be helping, he insisted to himself. Because they were still alive. And the little one, the *keekish-kawasso* in his round, warm nest in Niska's belly, was still alive, too.

He took a mug of the brownish brew to her. The steam from it had a sharp smell that had been unsavory at first, weeks ago, but in the time since had become familiar and stoically accepted. Niska raised herself slowly onto an elbow and began sipping from the mug, and if she realized that it wasn't whitened and thickened with flour, she gave no indication. It was too hot; she put it to cool among the balsam boughs that carpeted the bed end of the tent, and then let herself sink feebly again onto the bough mattress. Jacob sat beside her, blowing his own mug to cool it. She smiled up at him, but the skin of her face was so shrunken and tight that she seemed incapable of holding it, and the smile disappeared quickly.

"Niska," he began slowly, "I'll have to leave you today. Here alone. We've waited too long. The *Manito* doesn't hear your praying. There won't be any more fish in the nets until the ice goes. It won't do any good to put the snares out, because the hares are gone, the grouse are gone; the wild ones, they are all gone. I must go for the *atihk*. East up the Ninkik first, to the land where it is only a trickle in the forest. Then, over to the Mahkwa, and north down it until it becomes a big river in the land where the forest is thin and the trees are little sticks. . . ."

"Jacob," she interjected, "the Mahkwa . . . the Chee-choos are there. And Taka will be looking."

Jacob stopped abruptly. He saw the alarm on her face.

He stared at his feet and tapped one moccasin slowly against the other.

"It's the only way," he said impatiently. "It's the only river near us that leads out into the land of little sticks."

"Will you go around their camp without letting them see you?"

He considered it briefly, then hurried on, as if the interruption had not occurred. "Yes, I'll go down the Mahkwa and out into the little sticks. The *atihk* will be there, Niska. Out on the bog barrens where the snow is always thin. They always go there when the forest snow is soft and deep, because there are few trees there to stop the wind, and it packs the snow hard, and the *atihk* can move without sinking to their bellies. The lichen grows better there, too, because the trees don't shade it, and the *atihk* can move easily on the hard snow to find the spots where the snow is thinnest and the digging easiest to reach the lichens underneath."

He paused for breath and glanced down at her, but his eyes shifted quickly away before he could go on.

"I should have shot the *atihk*, the big one that was here on the Little Ninkik when the winter was young. But we were getting fish and weren't hungry then, and Father Webber's *Manito*, who sees even the little sparrow fall, said don't kill it, Jacob, because killing when you don't have to is a bad thing."

Jacob was staring into the brown whorl of his tea mug. Then his eyes came up sharply.

"Sometimes I think it would have been better if Father Webber had never come to the *Atihk-anishini*."

Niska frowned. "Why?"

"He came to tell us that if we sin we go to the hell place. But I asked him once if we would have gone to the hell place if we sinned before he came, and he said we couldn't go to hell then because we didn't know the sinning was sin. So it would have been better if he had never come and told us. Niska . . . do you think the *Manito* might have been wrong when he told me to let the *atihk* go?"

"Father Webber says when you hear the *Manito*'s voice inside you, it's never wrong."

"I don't know. Sometimes now I'm thinking that Father Webber doesn't know all. We are *Atihk-anishini*. We have to hunt. We have to trap so there will be furs for credit at the post to buy flour and things we need."

"Father Webber doesn't hunt," Niska said softly, "and his *Manito* takes care of him."

"But Father Webber is not an *Atihk-anishini!*" Jacob replied. "He doesn't have to hunt because he has credit at the store. He buys cans and the white-man meat there. I saw him doing it."

He saw the tight little lines of worry come to the corners of Niska's eyes, and he was sorry, but he had to go on.

"But anyway, Father Webber didn't tell us not to hunt, it was only his god who told us that. And I know why. The *Manito*'s hymn says he sees even the little sparrow fall, and he loves them all, and if he's sad when just a sparrow dies, he must be sadder when one of his big ones like the *atihk* or the moose dies. That's why he told us not to hunt the *atihk*. And Niska . . . I think the *Manito* was wrong."

"Jacob, don't say that! He'll hear!"

Jacob's eyes dropped. Then he frowned.

"He doesn't hear your praying, so how does he hear me?"

"He hears."

They were silent for a long time. Remorse flowed over Jacob Atook in a chilling wave.

"I'm sorry," he said finally. "I know the *Manito* is never wrong. I did right to let the *atihk* go when he told me to, but it wasn't right to wait this long to start the hunt for another. I should have gone long ago, but I thought the *Manito* would put fish in the nets again as he did before. I didn't know the fish could sleep so long. I don't think the *Manito* knew, either. But a wise hunter would have known. Your father, Joe, would have known. So would Taka Cheechoo. They'd have known that when the rapids on the Ninkik froze, the fish in the lake would sleep and not wake again until the ice is gone. They'd have gone for the *atihk* long ago, when the rapids first froze. They'd have gone out into the little sticks if they'd had to, and they'd be back by now, even from the little sticks they'd be back. And if I'd done the same, there would be meat in our bellies right now, and more in the cache outside. And maybe the *Manito* would be sad, and maybe he'd be angry . . . but we wouldn't be hungry."

His eyes dropped away from her. He was plucking moodily at the balsam boughs of their bed.

"I'm not a good hunter, Niska. Even when the dream spirits warned me that the fish all slept, I waited. Maybe the *Manito* was telling me to wait, sometimes it's hard to hear what he says. I didn't want to leave you alone with the little one. But I've got to now. There's nothing else. It's ten days back to the post where the store food is, and you're too weak for that, even if I could draw you all the way on the toboggan you're too weak for that."

"You *are* a good hunter, Jacob."

He faced her now and forced himself to look into the dark round eyes. They were hurtful eyes, because they gazed at him with a pinched, frail smile, and in this bitter winter of failure he had not earned the pride and love that their smile conveyed. It is hard for a hunter to admit incompetence, but harder still when his wife pretends not to know.

"The flour . . ." He wanted to say it quickly, but his tongue was heavy. "There's only tea. The flour is gone."

"It was a dream, Jacob. I know the flour is gone."

Now he sat for a long time with his eyes squinting and cracked lips pressing together, while an agony of struggle filled his mind. Finally his head jerked up. He spoke with a husky quiver in his voice.

"I'll stop at the Cheechoo's camp! I'll tell the old one, Nellie, that the *keekishkawasso* moves a lot now in your belly. I'll ask her to come and bring food and stay here with you until I'm back with the *atihk.*"

His eyes were down again; it pained to say this thing, to admit he must beg for food from the ones who were enemies.

Her smile went instantly. He saw the tremor on her lips.

"But Taka . . . all winter he'll have been looking. And what if Taka comes instead of Nellie?"

"It's a big family, Taka has a lot of young brothers and sisters," Jacob said slowly. "Taka . . . his father and mother, too . . . they'll be out hunting all the time this winter to keep everybody fed . . . maybe out in the little sticks. There'll only be the old grandmother on the Mahkwa taking care of the kids. . . ."

Jacob hoped it was true, and hoped that Niska would believe.

"But Taka *might* be there. They'll be bringing back meat whenever they get it."

"I'll spy out the camp first. I'll make sure Nellie is alone with the young ones."

"Maybe Nellie won't come."

"She will!" Jacob declared. "When I tell her your food is gone and a little one has started to kick in your belly, she won't think about anything else. She hasn't been the *Atihk-anishini* midwife all this time without learning to put mothers and babies before everything else. She's bringing her third generation into the world now. She brought us in, both of us, the first one to hold us in her arms. So maybe she *is* Taka's grandmother, but she's our second mother, too. And she'll remember."

"She'll have to leave a note saying where she's gone."

"She can't write. . . ." His voice raced on to lure her thoughts away. "And the *atihk* that I'll bring back from the little sticks will put milk in the breasts, Niska, for the little one when he comes."

Niska wasn't that easily diverted.

"Nellie will tell the older children where she's going. She'll have to."

"I'll speak to them. I'll tell them their grandmother has gone somewhere else."

"But when she goes back afterward . . . she'll tell Taka then where we are."

His fingers toyed with the tea mug. The pain built in him—not a hot pain of anger, but a chilling one of despair.

"Niska, there's nothing else to do! And maybe we won't

have to worry about Taka then. I'll be back with the *atihk*. There'll be proof for your father that I'm a good hunter." His voice hurried, drawing her on. "I'm going to pull the net out of the lake and bring it in, because it won't catch any more fish. I'll bring much wood into the tent, and leave a pile of ice chunks outside so that you won't have to go down to the water hole."

She raised herself onto an elbow, and the hand that reached for the cooling tea mug trembled. She didn't speak. She didn't smile again.

❀ ❀ ❀ ❀

When he had drunk a second mug of the brew and his stomach was rumbling with the unaccustomed weight of it, he went outside and stepped into the snowshoes. He took up the ax and strode down the familiar trail and out across the lake ice. His head was clear now, there was no dizziness, and he moved with a vigor and intentness because for the first time in many weeks he was responding to a firm decision, not just waiting and hoping. Hope was gone. He was going this time to bring in the net, not to look in it for fish.

The breeze was gentle, but the air it moved was so cold that it stung his cheeks like a dog whip. The vapor of his breath froze quickly in tiny white beads on the thin and scraggly beard of his lower lip and chin, so that the hairs pulled with little tugs of pain when he moved his mouth. It was hardly a beard, only a kinky fringe, for it was characteristic of his race to have little facial hair; he would shave it off back at the Wapanishee post in summer in imitation of the white man, but here in the winter camp in the bush he let it grow.

He chopped the new, blue-green ice out of the hole, then took off his mitts and began pulling in the net barehanded, folding its white twine on the snow. The mitts dangled on their neck string that went up each sleeve and across his shoulders under the parka, a device that prevented losing them and kept them always ready for quickly putting back on again. He worked with bare hands so as not to wet the mitts, for they were the only pair he had, and every few seconds he had to put his foot on the net and hold it while he dried his hands quickly on his parka and jabbed them down the front of his trousers to warm them against the bare skin of his crotch. The net folds on the snow froze rigid in seconds.

There was a tugging on the net when he came near its end. Now he pulled rapidly, his heart thumping, not stopping to warm his hands, and the cold water stiffened his fingers until they wouldn't bend. He went on clawing the net in with fingers that were like spikes and could no longer grasp, until he saw a flash of silver down in the dark blue depths of the ice hole. The tugging on the net grew stronger and the net began whipping back and forth, knifing circles on the water surface. Now his fingers were frozen hooks, clawing frantically at the twine meshes. The toothed snout emerged, and his fingers hooked a gill opening and flung it out onto the snow, where it slapped violently for only a few seconds before it was encased with ice.

He plunged his hands down the front of his trousers to thaw the frostbite out of them, and as the fingers tingled with the returning warmth there was another cheering warmth tingling through his body, for he gazed and he saw that the pike was not big, but it was enough to feed Niska several days. And it was the first fish the net had produced in what would add up to a month on Father Webber's calendar back at Wapanishee.

The rest of the net came easily, for there were no more fish. When the anchor rock came up and all the net lay on the snow, he dried and warmed his hands again, put on the mitts, picked up the fish, and bundled the frozen board-like folds of twine under his arm. He went back to the tent.

"Niska, pike in the net!" he shouted. Then he couldn't stop the voice from making the lie that the heart yearned to say. "A big one! Enough until I am back from the little sticks with the *atihk*. You'll have food now even if Nellie Cheechoo doesn't come!"

But he dropped the fish and net in front of the tent without going inside. One small fish changed nothing. He must still go to the little sticks, and there were acts that a hunter starting a hunt must first perform.

So he went around to the rear of the tent where a bulging bag of dried *atihk* hide hung from a tripod of poles. It contained the skull and shoulder blades of an *atihk* that had been killed by wolves down the lakeshore back in the time before the winter began.

≪≪≪≪≪≪ Chapter 3 ≪≪≪≪≪≪

THAT AUTUMN NIGHT Jacob and Niska had been awakened
by the howling of the pack, for the hunt was near, and the
howls carried sonorously on the still, cool air. Then they
heard the outburst of clamorous yapping that signaled the
wolves had made a kill.

Jacob slipped out of the tent at dawn before Niska was
awake. He went down the rocky shore and had little difficulty finding the kill. The wolves were gone. It must have
been a small pack, for much of the carcass remained uneaten, to which they would return the following night. It
was an old *atihk* with antlers small from age and teeth
worn near to the gums, for it is the way of wolves to take
the old and crippled ones whose role in life is done. Jacob
cleaned the skull, and he rolled it, the shoulder blades, and a
few of the other bigger bones in a large piece of the hide
and took them back to the tent. With a little tugging of
guilt and uncertainty, he cut three poles, raised the tripod,
and hung the bones high up in their bag of skin where the
wolves and foxes couldn't reach them. Niska watched,
frowning.

"Father Webber says there is only one spirit," she murmured. "He says it's wrong to worship other spirits."

"We're not going to worship it," Jacob reasoned with her. "I'm putting the bones in a safe place where they can't be harmed, so the *atihk*'s spirit won't be angered and warn its brothers to go away. The *Atihk-anishini* have always done this. There must be respect for the bone spirits or the hunt will be bad."

"Father Webber says there's only one spirit, the Holy Ghost, the *Manito,* not many spirits as the *Atihk-anishini* believe."

"I know," Jacob answered patiently, "but I don't think the Father is sure, because sometimes he talks about three spirits, God the Father, God the Son, and God the Holy Ghost. And if there *are* three instead of one, maybe there are more that Father Webber doesn't know about. Father Webber has never lived like this in a winter camp in the forest, so how can he be sure that the *Atihk-anishini* spirits are not here, too?"

Niska's lips pouted prettily, but she had no answer.

"I'm sure Father Webber's God is the most powerful spirit," Jacob went on, "but he's far away in the place called heaven, and the forest spirits are many and near. And maybe many weak spirits close by could have more power than one stronger spirit far away."

He hung the bone bag on the poles with a nagging doubt. He didn't want to offend the *Manito,* but he didn't want to risk offending the spirit of the dead *atihk* either, by leaving the bones—the dwelling place of its spirit—where the wolves and foxes could eat them. He listened carefully for the

Manito's voice inside to tell him if he had done wrong. And no voice came.

✦ ✦ ✦ ✦

It was then that the soul-searching had begun, and the sparrow hymn was a dominant part of it. Father Webber had said so much about the *Manito* and his Jesus that much of it was vague and elusive now in the dim and pained recalling. They tried to remember whether Father Webber had said anything about hunting, and they couldn't be sure he had, but the sparrow hymn had spoken for him. And in the end they concluded that if the *Manito* loved the sparrow, he must love the *atihk,* too.

So when the first snows came, Jacob began the hunt with a pained disquiet chafing his heart. And when he found the *atihk* trail at the lower end of the Little Ninkik, Jacob wasn't surprised to hear the *Manito* speak. It came in the hushed stillness of the evening as Jacob stood by the tracks in the thin snow and made the plans to begin following the trail at dawn for the chase and its kill.

"Jacob, you have the fish," the *Manito* told him in the clear, strong voice that came from inside.

The prints in the snow were round and large, almost as wide as Jacob's spread hand. It was a big buck, perhaps three hundred pounds of meat.

"You have the fish. You do not need the *atihk,* too."

Jacob didn't go back in the morning. He let the *atihk* go.

He wasn't sure whether the *Manito* wished him to cease all hunting, but in any case, that was its effect, because while he waited in questing indecision for the *Manito* to speak again, the long cold and the deep and paralyzing snows came.

Snowfall followed snowfall with persistent succession until in the forest clearings, where there was no wind to pack or thin it, the snow lay deeper than Jacob's waist. When he walked upon it, supported by the snowshoes, his head was high among the branches of the spruces. In his twenty-two winters Jacob had never known a deeper snow. There were no thaws to melt the surface so that it could refreeze and form a supporting crust. The forest snow remained soft and fluffy, and even the broad snowshoes sank almost to knee depth in it, making every step an effort; but out on the open lake where the wind could sweep the snow, reworking and packing it, it was thinner and hard in the way that lake snow always is.

Thus, when Jacob finally gave up waiting for the *Manito* to tell him he could hunt again, there was nothing left worth hunting. The *atihk* had moved out of the heavy-forest country into the land of little sticks. The snowshoe hares, normally unaffected because their broad foot pads could support them on any snow, were diminished instead by the cyclic upswing of the disease that was always among them. They had become so scarce that the effort required to hunt them demanded more energy than the eating afterward could replenish.

So Jacob had missed his opportunity to build up a winter meat supply when he let the early winter *atihk* go. The fish were the last to disappear. For a month now, even they had been gone from the nets. Until today.

Yet one small fish was no reason for hope. And now, with the net pulled from the lake and the decision made at last to go to the little sticks to hunt the *atihk,* Jacob stood under the tripod behind the tent gazing at its suspended bag of bones. He knew what he must do before the hunt began, and he hoped that Niska would not disapprove.

He lowered the poles and untied the bag. But he would get some of the fish cooking first, so he left the bag outside and went into the tent for a cooking pot.

"A big one," he told Niska again. "I'll leave half for you, and take half for myself to eat until I find the *atihk.*"

He took the pot back outside. He scaled the fish and cut it into chunks, and it filled the cooking pail because he put everything there, the guts, the head; only the scales were thrown away.

"Your half is in the pot buried in the snow at the door to keep it frozen," he called.

He took two chunks inside and started them boiling in the pail in which he had previously made the tea. While he waited for the fish to stew, he chopped firewood and carried armloads of it into the tent, piling it near the door. And while he worked he thought of the bone bag that still lay outside the tent door, and he feared what Niska might say when he brought it inside.

When the fish was cooked, he prepared a portion for Niska on one of their metal plates, breaking it into small pieces so she wouldn't be able to tell how small it was. While he ate his own, he glanced repeatedly at the belly mound that Niska's wizened body was feeding, and his own stomach was a yearning plexus of hunger, but he left half of his share in the pot where she would find it when he was gone.

He acted quickly now, fearing further waiting. He

stepped out and grabbed up the bag of *atihk* skin, took it in, and emptied the bones with a clacking rattle onto the tent's packed earthen floor. He gazed sharply at Niska; the fish meal, their first flesh food in weeks, had brought an animation back to her face and she was watching closely, silently. He took one of the flat, triangular shoulder blades and placed it on the top of the stove. Niska lifted herself slowly from the bed, she came to the stove and crouched beside Jacob, and he knew now that she was not going to object. Together, silently, breathing hard, they watched the bone as the frost began to thaw out of it, darkening it, flecking it with jumping little beads of moisture. Niska's hand dropped to her side and sought Jacob's. It was thin, bony, and cold, and it trembled. As the bone dried and whitened in the heat, small slivers of meat on it charred and began to smoke. He could hear the breath rasping in her throat; she was as anxious as he. She was squeezing his hand, and he was surprised at the strength still in it.

The bone cracked with a sharp, abrupt snap. Niska jumped. Jacob studied the crack quickly. It was wide and long, running almost the full length of the bone.

"It points north," she whispered.

"I knew the *atihk* were north," he said. "Out in the land of little sticks where the snow is thin."

"Jacob," she whispered again, "Father Webber says the bone spirit doesn't know and doesn't point to where its brothers are."

Jacob turned and his eyes squinted and his lips frowned.

"Father Webber is not an *Atihk-anishini,* so how does he know what the bone spirits can say? And his *Manito* doesn't tell us where the *atihk* are."

"He tells us more than that. He tells us to pray."

"All right, we'll pray, too."

They lowered their heads. Jacob could feel a little whirl of dizziness as he did so.

"Put your hands together, Jacob, and close your eyes."

"I know how to pray!"

"*Manito,*" she murmured, "give Jacob your *manitokay* to kill the *atihk*. And tell Jacob where to go. In Jesus Christ's name, amen."

They raised their heads. The tent roof snapped in a sudden gust of wind.

"It is *Manito* speaking in the wind," she said tensely. "It blows north. He is telling you the *atihk* are north."

"The bone told us that already."

"Anyway," Niska said, "he agrees with the bone. He doesn't say something else. Put it back in the bag, Jacob, and hang it back on the poles so the spirit of the dead one won't be angry and tell the other *atihk* you're coming."

Jacob studied the crack in the caribou bone for a long time before lifting it off the stove with a stick and laying it on the ground to cool.

"It's a long crack," he said. "It means the *atihk* are far away."

"I know," she answered quietly, "but I have half the fish, and Nellie will be bringing more." Then she added, almost inaudibly: "But, Jacob, you'll make sure just Nellie comes."

"Yes, just Nellie!" But the voice that spoke so firmly was a sham, and he wondered how he could stop Taka from coming, too, if Taka was at the Cheechoo camp when Jacob arrived. Taka had to be away on a hunt.

He took the bone bag out and hung it again on its tripod of poles. As he did so, his mind was calculating. It would take him two days to reach the Cheechoos on the Mahkwa, and he wasn't sure how much farther it would be from there to the land of little sticks. Another two? Then two more for the hunt, and four to return. He was counting on his fingers. It came to ten. Yes, it must be no more than ten. The fish, and the *oseepan* he would leave, would last her that long, even if Nellie didn't come.

In the next couple of hours he cut more firewood until the pile inside the tent was shoulder high; then he cut still more, piling it outside, for he would be tired after the hunt and wouldn't want to cut more firewood immediately on his return. He gathered many pails of the *oseepan* bark and lichen; then he chopped ice chunks from around the water hole and carried them up to the tent door where she could reach them easily to melt for water. When it was finished, he went back into the tent and began preparing for his own hunt.

There were few preparations to make. The Cheechoos would surely have food that Nellie could bring for Niska, but they would probably have none to spare for him—and might not give him any if they had. So on the hunting trail he would live as meagerly as the animals he hunted. Into a packsack he put the canvas tarpaulin that he had carried for overnight shelters on the trapline early that winter before the *Manito* spoke. He put in a cooking pot and a mug, an ax, a thirty-two-round box of ammunition, and the extra pair of woolen socks which was the only clothing he had that he was not already wearing.

The good bedding he left for Niska; for himself he took

an *atihk* skin—their most worn one—and an old plaited
rabbitskin robe so thinned with age that they had not even
been using it here in the tent camp. He gazed at them,
deliberating; it was all he could take from Niska, but it was
not enough. So now he gathered up the empty flour sacks,
and he cut the seams, opening them flat, and sewed them
hastily and crudely into a tick as large as a blanket. Now
he went out, and he spent a long time cutting balsam boughs
and filling the tick with the feathery tips. When he was
finished and had sewed up the end, he had a soft, insulating quilt as thick as the breadth of his hand. It was too
bulky to go in the packsack, he would have to carry it
separately.

The last few pounds of tea that remained in the food box
he also left for Niska. He considered taking their spare ax,
in case he broke the other one, for there was little likelihood
of Niska's wanting it, yet she might, and an ax when
needed was vital, so he left the second ax behind.

He shouldered the carrying sling of his old Lee-Enfield
rifle and carried the packsack and flour-bag tick outside.
He lashed the pack and tick roll to the toboggan—back of
center for the easiest hauling. The load was light; he could
easily have carried it on his back, but he would need the
toboggan for hauling back the *atihk* meat.

Niska stood shivering in the tent door, watching silently,
her lips pressed thin and white, her belly showing round
and full even under the bulky parka. When he was ready,
he looked at her. And the day was suddenly night in a
blinding anguish of remorse and despair. His world reeled,
and in the Stygian midnight of his tortured mind there was
only one glaring image, luminous and mocking against

the somber, muddied backdrop of his vision. It was Niska, hollowed-cheeked, all sharpnesses and shadows, starving, because the *Manito* had told him not to shoot the *atihk,* and now he had waited too long to begin the hunt for another.

His vision cleared. The tent, the gray-ribbed sky came back. Niska was still there.

They were not a demonstrative people, but now the love seethed in him like a rapids in flood, and he took her in his arms and kissed her good-by with a mingling of harshness and tenderness that the *Atihk-anishini* rarely displayed toward their women. He held her close for many seconds. Her belly was hard against his own. Her lips were dry and cold. Then, gently, he pushed her away.

"Stay in bed, Niska. You'll use less strength that way. Nellie will be here in two or three days." But he knew it would be four, because the Cheechoo camp was a two-day journey away—fifty or sixty miles in the measuring scale of the white man. It was near midday now, so even if he hurried, it would be the second day before he reached it. And Nellie was old, it would take her two full days to get back here; she wouldn't do it in a single day as a young one like Taka might.

He turned away, his vision misting again until he could hardly see the snowshoe harnesses to strap them on. Then he spoke once more.

"Your half of the fish . . . leave it frozen in the pot that's buried in the snow." She would not discover that it was a small pike—four pounds, perhaps—and that he was taking none for himself, until long after he was gone.

He put his head through the sling and threw the rifle

around onto his back. He flung the toboggan drawrope over his other shoulder and across his chest and leaned forward into it. The toboggan creaked on the dry snow. He stopped once, and turned and waved. Then he entered the screen of spruces that he had left standing in front of the tent to hide it from anyone passing on Little Ninkik, and he headed out onto the lake ice without looking back again.

≪≪≪≪≪≪ Chapter 4 ≪≪≪≪≪≪

IT IS ALL ONE LAND, but not a land of uniform oneness. The taiga is a mosaic of many forest patterns—patterns molded by fire and glacier and by the sedimentation of prehistoric seas.

That part of it that runs northward from Lake Superior to Hudson Bay has two distinct and very different regions created by its hidden foundations—the bedrock underneath. For three hundred miles north from Lake Superior the foundation is Pre-Cambrian rock—crystalline granites two billion years old, the roots of an ancient mountain range, with a humped and rugged topography that ensures good water drainage from its overburden of soil. The remaining two hundred miles to Hudson Bay is underlain by a bed of limestone deposited by Paleozoic seas of four hundred million years ago—a low, flat country that impounds its water and releases it grudgingly into a sluggish flowage toward the Bay.

On maps that record such things, the Pre-Cambrian region is known as the Canadian Shield, and the sodden limestone-based plain beyond as the Hudson Bay Lowland.

Ten thousand years ago, a brief interval in the geologist's dimensions of time, all of this rock lay depressed like a great saucer under the gigantic burden of a continent-wide glacier one to two miles thick that had crept southward across it. Under a weight of such magnitude even the earth's rock crust had to yield, and here it was warped downward eighteen hundred feet below its preglacial level.

Climate changed. The ice burden melted back northward. But for a couple of thousand years, a Hudson Bay greatly enlarged by glacial meltwaters, and by the depression of the land around it, extended some two hundred miles inland from its present shoreline. During that period of submergence, the silts of that older, larger Hudson Bay settled in a thick and compact layer onto the limestone base of the Hudson Bay Lowland. Thus, when the water receded and the coast crept northward, it left behind a capping of clay on the underlying rock which still cups the land's surface waters, letting little of it seep away—one more impediment to the languid drainage of a land too flat to keep its water on the move.

Jacob Atook doesn't know this ancient story of his land, even though it is a story that has shaped the lifeways and history of his race. He doesn't know the geologists' labels for his land—Canadian Shield and Hudson Bay Lowland. Yet in an empirical and much more practical way he is thoroughly aware that such a division exists. For the geologic foundations of the land shape the forests that grow upon it, and Jacob Atook knows the forests well.

In the Shield country where he lives, the waters of the land are always moving, for there is a good network of lakes and rivers to carry it away. Here the trees grow strongly, flowing in a green sea up and down the hills and valley slopes, because the surface water here enriches the soil without staying to drown it. The foresters call it closed-canopy forest, because the trees grow close together and their branches interlock and screen the sun from the forest floor. It is mostly spruce forest, and here and there are the white, springy mats of ground lichen on which the caribou feed, so it is good caribou range, though not the best, because the ground-matting lichens grow richest where sunlight reaches them.

Where the Shield slopes down to the Hudson Bay Lowland, however, the forest alters dramatically; in fact, over large regions it virtually disappears, because this is a drowned and sodden land too wet in most places for trees. Here, across an area eight hundred miles east to west and two hundred miles north to south, the water trapped by the land's flat clay bottom lies in a great shallow, stagnant sea clogged with sphagnum moss—that lush and irrepressible plant colonizer that thrives in the cold, acid wetlands of the subarctic wherever nothing else can grow. Well adapted for living in a watery world, it can even grow as a floating mat on the water's surface, if there is no bottom ooze within reach of its seeking rootlets. It is the subarctic's slow but indomitable converter of water into land, for beneath the green living surface layer, the dead growth of earlier sphagnum generations sinks and builds up and compacts itself into a constantly thickening layer of peat which fills the water basins beneath it. When the peat and sphagnum mat has become too solid for further expansion downward or laterally, it humps upward to form hummocks, aided by the heaving action of winter frosts. Thus, some thousands of years after the sphagnum filling began, mounds begin to appear above water level, to dry in the summer sun and form islands on which other plants can oust the sphagnum and pioneer a new plant community.

There has been another process here creating islands of dry land on which plants and trees can grow. As the bedrock has slowly lifted in its recoil from the weight of ice it once carried, shifting the Hudson Bay shore northward, the receding waters have left behind a striking record of the land's marine ancestry—the gravel ridges of ancient beaches abandoned by the retreating sea thousands of years ago. Each one a hundred feet or so wide, often many miles long, they parallel the shore of modern Hudson Bay like series of curving railroad embankments, linear oases of dry land in a vast and boggy sea. The oldest of them are more than a hundred miles inland today, conspicuous relics of the seacoast that once was there.

Even in the driest regions of the Hudson Bay Lowland, more than half its area is still a network of open ponds or lakes, or vast stretches of soggy, treeless sphagnum bog. But wherever the land lifts a foot or two to give drainage, the hardy spruce and that other needle-bearing tree of these northern boglands, the tamarack, will grow. They grow invariably along rivers where ice shove and flooding have pushed up levees and the streams have cut down below the surrounding water table and thus drain water from the bordering banks. They grow on the ridges of the ancient, abandoned beaches. And they grow on the frost-heaved islands of peat—sometimes just a single tree on an island a few feet across, elsewhere a forest miles in extent where major heaving and drainage have occurred.

But the bog waters underneath are never far from the spreading spruce and tamarack roots. It is cold water, for peat is a good insulator, and ice often lingers until mid-summer a foot or two below the surface, sometimes reducing the growing time to a period as brief as two months. And it is water sharp with the accumulated acids of plant decay. Because of the water's coldness and acidity, the trees of this land have to assimilate it slowly and sparingly into their fabric of growth. And during the long winters the struggle for survival takes another form, for then the dry and wind-driven snow is a harsh abrasive to buds and twigs.

So the trees that do manage to grow here are usually stunted and contorted. They may attain near-normal growth in sheltered, well-soiled spots, but mostly they are dwarfed by harsh growing conditions, and deformed by wind and the cutting snow that the wind carries for much of each year. A spruce or tamarack here may be only a few feet high after fifty years of struggling growth. And across vast expanses, trees two hundred years old and gnarled with age are no more than ten feet high.

Since each tree represents a hard-won victory over an uncompromising climate and soil, they stand apart and alone, so that it isn't dense forest even where the trees do grow. This is a boon for the ground lichens, which grow best in sun-dried clearings among spruce and tamarack trees, though not directly beneath them. No lichens grow on the treeless bogs that cover most of this land, but on the drained sites where the stunted trees stand, the lichen is thick and rich among them. So as caribou range, it is spotty, but where it occurs, it is good range—much better than in the shaded, closed-canopy forest of the Pre-Cambrian country farther south.

There is footing on the spruce islands, and a man can walk upon them dry shod. But he cannot walk far, for they are only a sparse and twisting lacework in a mire of sphagnum bog and ponds. This land, therefore, is impassable in summer except by canoe on its rivers. But in winter, when the bogs are frozen, the land is suddenly flung open and both man and caribou travel it with ease.

This, then, is the Hudson Bay Lowland, a land that has different names to different people. In the idiom of the Canadian north it is "muskeg." To the forest-geographer, it is "forest tundra," meaning that it is neither forest nor arctic tundra, but the zone of transition between. And to the *Atihk-anishini*, it is "the land of little sticks."

It is a land that Jacob Atook has never seen, a strange and feared land, where unknown spirits dwell.

⫷⫷⫷⫷⫷ Chapter 5 ⫷⫷⫷⫷⫷

JACOB TRAVELED EASTWARD up the shallow, twisting valley of the Ninkik for all of that first day. He stayed on the river ice, because the shore was a dark, snow-clogged tangle of spruce and balsam fir, but the ice with its packed snow was smooth and unbroken. Even the rapids, where the water moved too quickly to freeze in a normal winter, were frozen tightly now.

There were no animal trails, no signs of life above the ice and snow.

The day had been drab and leaden, but late in the afternoon the sun came out, gilding the snow world around him with a yellow glare, and he stopped to camp beside a big rock that would protect him from the wind and throw back the heat of his fire. Using a snowshoe for a shovel, he dug his snow hole beside the rock, raised a framework of poles over it, and strung up the canvas to form a sloping shelter with its open front facing the rock where the fire would be. Shoulder-height at the front, sloping to the ground behind, the lean-to had just enough space beneath for a one-man bed. He closed in the ends with the toboggan, boughs, and mounds of snow, so that it would trap and hold at least briefly some of the heat from the fire.

Now he brushed snow from the rock face and pulled off several handfuls of the rock-tripe lichen that clung in black and brittle flakes to the boulder's surface. Unlike the white, upright caribou lichen that is never a man food, this flaky one is a last-resort starvation food for all the northern peoples.

He cut wood, lit a fire, melted snow, and started the rock tripe boiling. While he waited, he cut balsam boughs and laid them under the lean-to for his bed. The lichen cooked into a gelatinous mush. His stomach tossed rebelliously at the first mouthfuls, for it was bitter, and gritty with sand particles, but he forced himself to eat all that he had prepared. The unaccustomed weight of food in his stomach brought on a slight nausea.

He had not come far since leaving Niska that morning, probably less than twenty miles, for the start had been late, but he was tired now, and although the sun was still up he began laying his bed. The boughs provided good insulation against the cold of the ground, so he would use only the *atihk* skin beneath him. For covering he spread the rabbit-skin robe and the thick flour-bag tick filled with the balsam tips. He removed only his snow-caked moccasins and trousers and crawled into the bed wearing everything else —the tuque on his head, the heavy parka, even the mittens. He took the moccasins and trousers into the bed with him to dry them overnight with his body heat.

The valley of the Ninkik along which he had come stretched back westward, and he had a good view of the sinking sun through the space between the rock and the edge of the shelter. Now he lay, raised on an elbow, feeding the fire and studying the coppery disk on the ice-blue horizon as the cold of the northern night sharpened.

"You'll bring a fine day tomorrow, won't you?" he said to the sunset. "And more fine days after that until I reach the *atihk* country. Then wind, Sun; you'll bring wind then, because the hunt is always better when the wind blows."

Like most men who spend much of their lives alone, Jacob Atook habitually talked to himself, usually without being aware that he was doing it. He talked to himself for company, and he talked to himself to aid and give substance to his thoughts, for within the limited intellectual confines that his background imposed, Jacob Atook was a thoughtful man.

"*Atihk*, I'm not a good hunter, but I'm going to kill you this time. If the *Manito* who sees even the sparrow fall tells me not to shoot you, *atihk*, I'll put moss in my ears so that I don't hear. It's hard to kill, but I will, *atihk*, I will, because there must be meat to put the milk in Niska's breasts when the little one comes. I don't know why it has to be this way. I only know that's the way it is."

He was a man with a curious and restless thrust of mind. He was a man who could gaze with dreaming wonder at the burnished fire of the sunset, and ponder the unknowables of life and living which seemed at that moment to be making his life a part of the sunset and the sunset a part of him.

In another society he might have been a poet or a priest, but here he had to be a hunter, because in these Ojibwa forest and muskeg lands that reach northward to the muddy tideflats of the great Hudson Bay, there is nothing else a man can be. There is only one living here—the living that the forest grudgingly yields. Here a man's worth has only one measure—the measure of the beaver he can trap and the moose and *atihk* he can kill. And it was Jacob Atook's curse to be a hunter with a mind that sometimes brooded sorely on the hunter's need to kill.

Isolated in a land that only aircraft can reach, the *Atihk-anishini* are a people whose culture is a nondescript composite of old and new. They trap mink and beaver and exchange the pelts of their traplines for goods at the Hudson's Bay Company posts, and in this way some of the white man's culture—some of his foods and some of his wares—has become a part of their culture, too. But it is only a veneer. Under it, they are a primitive hunting people still, who leave the trading posts and disperse through their forest land each fall and winter, where for some eight months of each year they have to depend mainly on the foods their hunting skills can wrest from the land around them.

There had been another early white-man influence in the making of Jacob Atook. The government had occasionally sent a teacher to conduct school for the *Atihk-anishini* children when they gathered for the summer in the village of tents and cabins that clustered around the post at Wapanishee Lake. Jacob had attended the classes during several of his childhood summers and he applied himself diligently because he was curious and wanted to learn of the white man's strange ways. He had learned to speak English moderately well, much better than any of the other children with the exception of Niska, but there had been time during the brief summer classes for the teachers to pass on little more.

Childhood passed, and Jacob had to learn the skills by

which he would live. He traveled with his father and learned the sprawling waterways that were the travel routes of his land. He learned how to handle a canoe in turbulent white water, how to make snowshoes, how to trap and hunt. He learned where to set the nets in the lakes and rivers for the most fish, and how to imitate the honking of geese to lure them within shooting range of the bough blinds on the shore. And at times in the wintering camp deep back in the bush, he learned of the hunger that came when the hunting failed.

A sharp awareness formed, however, that he was not a good hunter, and there were hazy, fleeting times of insight when he felt that he was on the verge of understanding why. In those moments of searching reflection the thought would come, vague and shrouded, that he and the forest animals were not just contestants in a contest of death, but at the same time partners in a partnership of living. He killed, usually without any conscious awareness of regret, for it was the only life he knew. Yet sometimes he killed with wonder, asking why it had to be this way.

So Jacob Atook was not a good hunter, because no skill is honed to its full potential when its motivations elude and confuse. But his mind didn't probe the thought pathways that far. It could only play about the fringes of the problem, enough to trouble and bewilder, but not resolve and explain.

And it was into this confusion that Father Webber came with the strange and haunting message of the sparrow hymn.

↑ ↑ ↑ ↑

Long before that, however, Jacob's brooding perplexity had begun to manifest itself to others around him. In a

society as small and self-contained as the *Atihk-anishini,* it
was inevitable that his fellows would soon learn that Jacob's
attitude toward hunting was a bizarre one. It wasn't a thing
that a hunter could hide.

It finally came out during an *atihk* hunt at Amihk Lake
with Taka Cheechoo when Jacob was seventeen. Taka was
two years younger, but already as big and strong as Jacob,
and as a hunter he had far outstripped Jacob and all the
other youths then learning the hunting skills of their people.
Even by that time Taka had killed a moose and *atihk* on
hunts by himself and was already being eyed as a desirable
son-in-law by several fathers of Wapanishee Lake's mar-
riageable girls, including Joe Nimawassa, the father of
Niska, the pretty one.

They had gone by canoe down the Wapanishee River to
Amihk, picking blueberries to dry for winter, and there, on
the second day, Taka's restless, searching eyes detected the
rounded prints in the wet sand of the lake edge where the
animal had been down early that morning to drink. Taka
Cheechoo's hunting instincts were suddenly unleashed like
the recoil of one of their childhood bows when its drawn
bowstring slips from the finger.

"*Atihk!* A big buck!"

The blueberries were forgotten then, as Taka led Jacob
off on a frenzied chase that lasted all that day and into the
afternoon of the next. Jacob marveled at the skill with which
his younger companion stayed on the animal's trail. It was
too early for snow, and the *atihk*'s tracks disappeared every
few yards in the soft moss beds or on the bare rock ridges.
But Taka would dash on, brown eyes probing the shadows,
circling, seeking, always picking up the trail again, because

he knew, as surely as the *atihk* itself knew, what it would do next and where it would go.

Taka's only miscalculation was the timing of the sighting the next afternoon. They overtook the *atihk* browsing at a bog edge a little earlier than he had anticipated, with the result that it was Jacob who happened to be carrying their only gun at the time. Taka had warned that the *atihk* was near and had led Jacob on a wide circle to approach upwind. When they saw almost simultaneously the flash of the great buff-white neck through a screening curtain of spruce boughs, the *atihk* had not yet seen or scented them. Taka was several paces ahead; Jacob would have to make the kill.

The gun snapped automatically to his shoulder, and the sights steadied on the aiming point of the shoulder just behind the white ruff of neck. Then Jacob began to tremble as a ponderous censuring filled his mind and restrained the finger on the gun's trigger.

The weather was warm. The meat would soon spoil. The hide would be of little value at this time of year, for the hair would still be slipping. They could carry little of the meat back to Wapanishee, twenty-five miles away. Fish were plentiful, and the geese flocks would soon be coming south.

It would be a senseless killing.

Jacob could see Taka up ahead, crouched, rock still, staring fixedly at the buck. Jacob knew he was waiting for the crack of the rifle and the stumbling pitch of their prey. But the stillness held; the air was brittle with a massive, compressing silence. Taka's hand, almost hidden in the ground growth beside him, began making small hurrying motions, but his eyes were still frozen on the *atihk* ahead.

Now he raised the hand, risking discovery, chopping the air in an urgent signal. But when still no shot sounded, his brown face turned slowly, creased first with wonder, then with disgust and dismay as he saw Jacob leaning motionlessly against a shoulder-high rock, the gun lowered to his side.

Suddenly Taka was up and running back to take the rifle from Jacob. And then the *atihk* heard. The white neck and great head tossed upward, the animal bolted across the few paces of sphagnum bog into the surrounding wall of spruces. For a few seconds there was a rattle of snapping branches, and then the silence again. The *atihk* was gone.

Taka snatched the rifle, pulling it from Jacob's grasp. "Why? Why didn't you shoot?"

"We don't need the meat."

"I track him a day and a half," Taka shouted. "I give you a good shot. And you let him go. He'll run now for miles before he stops again."

"It would only spoil, we don't need the meat," Jacob repeated.

Taka's face became a flushed mask of contempt. He raised the rifle and brought it down butt-first in a jabbing blow at Jacob's head. Jacob ducked, and the rifle struck the rock behind him with a sharp crack of splintering wood. Taka examined the gun, then his eyes snapped up, black with fury.

"You've broken my rifle!"

"You did it yourself."

"But it was your fault!"

A splinter an inch or so wide and five inches long had split off the rifle's stock where the lower butt-plate screw entered the wood, and the metal strip of the butt plate was bent and twisted sideways around the stock's broken bottom corner.

"It's nothing," Jacob told him. "You can still use it. And don't blame me."

Taka picked up the splinter from the ground, studied it, then threw it angrily away.

It took them two days to get back to Wapanishee—two days in which neither spoke. As soon as they reached the post, Taka told the story of the *atihk* that Jacob had permitted to get away. At first the old ones smiled, for it was a familiar kind of story for young hunters to tell, to excuse their hunting failures. But he had the splintered rifle stock to prove that part of the story, and they all knew that Taka Cheechoo was a good hunter who didn't have to lie, and soon they believed. They began to avoid Jacob, to smile and whisper when he walked by.

And it was only the beginning of Jacob Atook's disgrace.

⸗ ⸗ ⸗ ⸗

Next autumn the white hunters first began coming to Wapanishee Lake for the goose shooting, and Jacob faced another time of testing.

Their three red and silver float-planes roared one by one over the wooded shore, glided out to the lake's center with muted engines, and then settled to the water with floats rumbling and billowy tails of white spray spiraling behind them. The engines roared again as the planes turned and taxied in toward the beach in front of the village, and the spruce walls swelled the din with their echoes.

The *Atihk-anishini* ran down and gathered in curious

silence to watch the arrival. As the plane pontoons grated on the gravel and the engine roar died, the hunters clambered noisily from the cabins. They carried shiny luggage instead of packsacks, wore high-cut boots with the glister of newness still on them, and red caps, and hunting jackets that were mostly red, too, and cluttered with crests, buttons, leather flaps, and shell pockets. They carried expensive guns; Jacob knew they were expensive because they had things like pump action, ventilated ribs, and choke controls, which he knew about and could recognize but had rarely seen on any of the guns that the Indians got for their beaver pelts at the Hudson's Bay Company store.

He stared and marveled and began to wonder whether the coming of these loud and alien hunters was going to be good or bad for the *Atihk-anishini.*

It quickly appeared that it was going to be good. They came to hunt the geese, the white men said, and they wanted to hire Indian men as guides and helpers. They would pay ten dollars a day, and when the *Atihk-anishini* men learned this, they sought the jobs eagerly, because ten dollars was often as much as a man earned in a week on his winter trapline.

The strangers talked to Mr. Fennel, the Hudson's Bay Company trader, and they learned from him that Jacob Atook spoke English better than any of the other *Atihk-anishini.* They spoke to Jacob then, and Jacob spoke back to them in their language, making his words slowly and carefully, because the English required strange voice sounds and accents that his own tongue didn't use. And he was the first that the hunters hired from the curious, staring circle of Indian youths and men around them. The Indian men chuckled and nudged each other and they knew then that the white hunters were as stupid as they looked; maybe they could fly airplanes and own expensive guns, but they were not smart enough to know what every *Atihk-anishini* knew—that Jacob Atook, this first man they hired to guide their hunting trips, was the poorest hunter in the Wapanishee Ojibwa band. And later, when they learned that Jacob was chosen because he could act as an interpreter as well as a guide, they continued to regard it as an amusing joke.

"These white hunters," said Joe Nimawassa, the father of Niska, "do they think the *Atihk-anishini* have to call down the geese in English?"

The big tents went up along the shore below the Indian village. Jacob and the other Indian men who had been hired as guides cut firewood and made bannock and baked whitefish and then washed dishes when they and the hunters had eaten. The white men talked steadily and loudly and few of the *Atihk-anishini* men except Jacob could follow what they talked about. But there were some words they used repeatedly and monotonously that Jacob didn't understand.

Mostly they talked about the *Atihk-anishini* girls they had seen in the group that met their planes earlier in the day, and in this context, too, there were unfamiliar words that kept recurring again and again, always with laughs or smiles or leers. They asked Jacob about the girls, what their names were, which ones were not married. They told him they would pay a dollar to any of the girls who would come down and visit them in their tents that night, and Jacob understood then what the unfamiliar words were. He promised to tell the girls, because he was afraid that if he refused, the white hunters would not continue hiring him as one of their guides. But he had no intention of telling the girls of the white hunters' offers.

One hunter with a pebbly face and a bristling mole on his chin asked about the one specifically.

"You know the one I mean, Jacob. The one with the big round eyes and the cute little nose that turns up at the end. The one that's prettier than all the others. You tell her I'll pay her *five* dollars, Jacob."

And Jacob promised again. But his insides twisted like fraying rope and the anger in him was sour and cold, because the one the hunter meant was Niska.

The Indian men went back to their tents and cabins with instructions to return to the white hunters' camp an hour before dawn to begin the goose hunt. That night in the canvas and moosehide hut where Jacob lived with his parents, he lay awake a long time listening to the loud carousing down in the hunters' tents. He was thinking with eager pleasure of the ten dollars he was going to earn tomorrow, but with twinges of uneasiness over how he was going to earn it.

They set out before sunrise in a flotilla of big freighter canoes with outboard motors, an Indian guide and two or three white hunters in each canoe. There were not enough outboards to go around, because many of the *Atihk-anishini* were too poor to own motors, so some of the canoes were towed by others. They went to the narrows four miles down Wapanishee Lake where there were broad stretches of mudflat and cattail marsh on which the goose flocks often rested and fed.

The canoes dropped off their hunters at intervals along a

mile or more of shore. There was much shouting and guffaw-
ing in the predawn twilight as the groups parted, and some
already were taking long draughts from the flattened shiny
flasks that each hunter had in his hunting jacket pocket.
Jacob went ashore with two hunters, and one of them, by
no accident, was the pebbly-faced man who had asked about
Niska the night before.

"The cute one . . ." he said to Jacob as soon as the roar
of the outboard stilled, "did you tell her I got five dollars
for her if she'll come down tonight and keep my sleeping
bag warm? One dollar for any of that other scruffy lot, but
for her five."

"I didn't have time last night to find her and tell her."

"You'll have time today, Jacob? We'll get back early to
make sure you have time, eh?"

Silently, trembling with smothered anger, Jacob began
cutting spruce and balsam boughs and jabbing the butts in
the mud to make a shooting blind. He worked slowly and
made the blind thicker and higher than it had to be, because he was beginning to feel a distaste for it all. Shots
were already booming down the shore from the blinds of
the other hunters, and Jacob's two hunters were muttering
impatiently and urging him to hurry. He couldn't delay it
any longer. "Okay," he pronounced. The three of them
crouched behind the barrier of green boughs and waited.

He could hear the distant gabbling of the geese out on the
open lake where they had spent the night and were forming
up now to begin moving in to the mudflats and marsh
shallows for the morning feeding. Their V's and lines, looking like strands of black beads against the yellowing sheen
of the sky, began moving along the shore. Shots kept boom-

ing intermittently up and down the lake, but for some time none flew within range of Jacob's blind. The white hunters hunched beside him, fingering their guns, drinking from the shiny flasks, eying with mounting impatience the passing flocks, and muttering the unfamiliar words.

Then a flight of twelve, far out at first, wheeled abruptly and headed in on a course that would bring them over the shore not far out of gun range to the north.

"Okay, Jacob, call the bastards in," the pebbly-faced one whispered.

Jacob cupped his hands around his mouth.

"*Ka-ronk.*" His lips and throat molded the double-syllabled plaint into a perfect imitation of the call of a lone goose, a sound not loud, but resonant and carrying. The big dark birds seemed to hesitate in their flight, their heads turning curiously toward the blind.

"*Ka-ronk! Ka-ronk!*" It was louder this time, more insistent, carrying with it the practiced and cumulative skill of generations of *Atihk-anishini* hunters who had been calling the big geese this way since their history as a muskeg people began in the lost, long centuries ago. Like all *Atihk-anishini* hunters, Jacob had practiced the goose calling since boyhood. It was one of the essential skills that enabled the muskeg people to survive in their austere land, for it gave them the goose flesh which, when smoked and dried, was a major food in the winter trapping camps.

"*Ka-ronk, ka-ronk, unk-unk-unk!*" Jacob injected a sharp edge of coaxing urgency into it this time. Now the line of geese turned and with slackening wingbeats they slanted down toward the mudflat, far out still, but directly in front of the blind.

The hunters raised their guns.

"Not yet!" Jacob ordered sharply, for a shot at this range would only cripple and not kill.

But the guns thundered. The flock turned away, wings pumping violently, and then two of the geese began to drop, each with a wing dragging grotesquely. The flock was well out now, far beyond killing range, but the guns boomed again. A third goose fell away.

The pebbly-faced one slapped his companion on a shoulder. He turned a ruddy, beaming face to Jacob.

"Sharp shooting! That's what I call that!"

Jacob watched as the three injured geese slanted and zigzagged down, to splash into the water far out from shore. It was bad shooting, Jacob thought, with a choking of pain and anger—bungling and impatient shooting that couldn't possibly have killed. But he didn't comment as he jumped to his feet.

"We get them if we can before they swim away," Jacob said.

Pebble-face grabbed Jacob's arm and pulled him back down.

"Leave 'em be," he said. "We'll shoot lots of others. If we go pushing out there in the boat, we'll scare the other flocks away."

"They'll only swim away and die," Jacob said. "You shoot too soon. You can't get geese that way."

"Never mind the lecture stuff, boy. Call us up some more geese. We come for the shooting. If it was geese we wanted we could have stayed home and bought them in a butcher shop."

The vague and indefinable morosity that had been building in Jacob since the hunters first came now broke with a
bitter anger. There were no butcher or grocery shops in
the *Atihk-anishini* lands to hide from men their ultimate
dependence on the fruits and the flesh that the earth gave
them. He was a part of this land, and the three dying geese
out there, which these alien hunters were not even going to
attempt to retrieve, were part of his own pulse and life-
blood. Perhaps there was honor in killing when it was done
as part of the life pattern by which men lived, when it was
done with respect and humility for the spirits of the killed,
but this debasing of the ancient skills of his race, so that
others might kill for fun, suddenly loomed as a betrayal of
self.

The hunt went on until into the afternoon with only
brief strolls outside the blind to stretch the cramps out
of their legs. But no more geese came near their blind.
And the two hunters were incapable of detecting that the
geese stayed out of gunshot because Jacob was deliber-
ately putting a false note into the calling that turned the
flocks away.

The hunters reassembled and all but Jacob's hunters had
geese they had shot. The *Atihk-anishini* guides smiled
knowingly when they saw his empty boat, for they knew all
about Jacob Atook, the dreaming one, and now maybe the
white men who had hired him ahead of all the others would
know it, too.

Jacob didn't turn up at the white hunters' camp for the
goose hunt the following morning.

They stayed a week. And in subsequent autumns they
came again. Each year the *Atihk-anishini* men were eager

to guide them and call down the geese, for they needed the ten dollars a day that the hunters paid. Jacob Atook needed it, too, but he never hired himself out to guide them again.

Chapter 6 ⪻⪻⪻⪻

LATE ON THE SECOND DAY after leaving Niska, Jacob reached the headwaters of the Ninkik, where the river shrank to a stream no wider than the length of his toboggan and finally petered out in a snow-smothered labyrinth of beaver ponds and sphagnum bogs. This was the outer fringe of the *Atihk-anishini* lands, almost two hundred miles by twisting water route from the summering village on Wapanishee Lake, and of all the families, only the Cheechoos and Jacob and Niska had wintering territories as distant as this from the post. Jacob had never been this far before, but he knew that the Cheechoo portage to Mahkwa Lake began somewhere here.

It was dusk, and he had been slogging up a chain of beaver ponds for an hour, when he finally saw the white gash of a clearing in the dark border of forest ahead. A tripod of tent poles had been left standing above the snow, and he knew that this would be the portage landing. When he reached it and pulled the toboggan up the little bank onto the clearing, he saw the black tunnel of the portage trail itself piercing like an animal burrow the dense and darkening barrier of forest.

The portage, he knew, was four miles long, but he could tell from the low skyline ahead that it would be a smooth and easy trail with no big hills to drag over. He had walked perhaps fifty miles in two days with only the bitter and fibrous stews of rock tripe and the *oseepan* barks for food, and he had not even stopped for a meal of that since morning. But he was neither tired nor hungry, for his sinewy body had been steeled since boyhood to this kind of rigorous life. It had adjusted quickly to the demands of the trail, there was no fatigue now as there had been the night before, and he had passed the point of knowing any real intensity of hunger. His stomach was inured to emptiness, and it was only *after* one of the meager lichen and bark meals which teased without appeasing that the hunger pains came, as though his stomach was then reminded of what it wasn't receiving.

His body had made its adjustment to the cold, too, as it always did after the first night out. The cold was sharp and harsh still, pinching the moist nostril linings with a sting at each breath before the breathing passages could warm the air, and frosting the eyebrows and the scraggly beard hairs with a rime of white from the moist air that the lungs exhaled. But except for these small manifestations, the cold now was unfelt, unnoticed, for it wasn't cold by itself that bothered one, it was the sudden change between a warm tent or cabin and the outdoors. Once a hunter was outdoors permanently, the body could soon acclimatize and forget the cold was there.

Jacob knew the portage went directly to Mahkwa Lake, and he knew that the Cheechoo camp was somewhere on the lake's shore. It wouldn't be hidden as the camp on the Little Ninkik was. It couldn't be more than ten miles farther. And if he reached it tonight, Nellie Cheechoo could be on her way to Niska with the dawn.

So he pressed on, entering the portage trail, but as the forest closed darkly around him, a heavy fear and reluctance began dragging at his feet. It was the Cheechoo camp on the Mahkwa, not the hidden tent on the Little Ninkik, where Niska should be. And under the marrying customs of the *Atihk-anishini,* Taka Cheechoo, not Jacob, should be her husband. It was a paining thing, this going to the Cheechoos to admit his failure and beg for food, but the Cheechoos were the only ones near.

He hoped that this famine time, with its bonding of common peril, would erase at least in Nellie the family enmities, but he wasn't as confident about it as he had appeared on that last day with Niska. Yet surely Nellie, with the love and understanding that the old ones have, would overlook the animosity and take the food that Niska needed until he was back with the *atihk* from the little sticks. He could only hope that Taka and his parents would be out on a hunt. For the thing he was doing was a thing that must be done.

He tried to coax pleasanter thoughts. He pictured the Cheechoo camp ahead. It would be a tight, snug cabin of logs, not a tent camp like his and Niska's; it would be warm; there would be food, real food, *atihk* meat and bannock, not rock tripe and barks, because there were two hunters there, and a team could always hunt more successfully than one. And the Cheechoos had not gone that past summer to Father Webber's tent, so the *Manito* would not have spoken to them and told them to let the *atihk* go.

The night came quickly, but no stars came with it, and a sprinkling of new snow began dusting through the trees, flicking his cheeks. He began to feel some fatigue now, because here in the shelter of the trees, the snow was deep and soft; his snowshoes sank into it, the toboggan dragged heavily. With a pricking of fear, he began to wonder why there were no snowshoe tracks packing the trail and making the walking easier.

He emerged onto Mahkwa Lake. It was a narrow lake with low shorelines limned dimly against the night sky through the thinly falling snow. He paused, his nostrils testing the air for a hint of woodsmoke, his eyes studying the shores for a light. But there was no sign. There was only one way to go, for the portage emerged at the lake's southern tip, and he started northward down the lake's center. The lake snow was hard and wind-crusted, making the walking easier than it had been in the forest. Both shores were near and he was sure he couldn't pass the camp without seeing it. There was small likelihood of there being a light because the cabin would probably have no windows, but there would be a clearing that would show white against the dark forest behind, possibly a tang of smoke on the air, and maybe sparks from a chimney.

He was about a mile down the lake when he first detected the white notch of the clearing on the eastern shore ahead. Dark blotches appeared against the snow—a small square one that would be the cabin, two conical ones that would be a woodpile and probably a smoke lodge. But there were no chimney sparks yet, nor any taint of smoke on the night air.

He was still perhaps a quarter mile away when the absence of signs—no tracks on the portage and down the lake, no sparks or smoke, no howling dogs—coalesced suddenly in his mind and communicated its obvious meaning.

He trudged on, suddenly very tired now, and icy ripples of fear began clasping his waist. He didn't call when he reached the shore in front of the cabin. The door was snowed in deeply and he had to remove a snowshoe and dig for several minutes before the door was cleared and would open enough to let him squeeze through.

It was black dark inside. He struck a match, found a stub of candle, and lighted it, and the cabin's interior emerged in the feeble, shivering glow. There was little there—an oil drum converted into a stove with stovepipe rising through the roof, a food box, firewood, some blackened cooking utensils, and some dry heaps of balsam boughs on the earthen floor that had served as beds. The *Atihk-anishini* carried few comforts with them on the long treks to their winter camps.

Jacob went immediately to the food box and jerked up the lid. There were only a few dented tins inside. Quickly he tested the weight of each one. They were all light, empty. Now he held the candle high and his eyes darted around, but there were no fat flour or sugar sacks, no large pails of lard. Panic gripped him, parching his throat, racing his heart. He ran outside, hastily strapped on the snowshoes, and went behind the cabin looking for the outdoor food cache. It would be an elevated platform on which their fish, goose carcasses, and *atihk* meat would be hung to keep frozen and beyond the reach of scavenging animals. He found it immediately, etched starkly against the sky, a bare and empty rack of poles.

His shoulders sagged as the brutal weight of defeat and fear plunged down upon him. The Cheechoos, too, had had difficulty finding food in this winter of famine. They were gone, perhaps back to the post on Wapanishee Lake, or perhaps all of them—Nellie and the children, too—had moved out to the little sticks to be nearer the *atihk*. It didn't matter where, because it had been long ago, their trail long since had been hidden by new falls of snow, and Jacob now would never find Nellie.

He unlashed the packsack from the toboggan. The snow had thickened and he could feel it pelting his cheeks heavily now; if this kept up, there would be a new fall of perhaps a foot by morning.

Back inside, he lit a fire in the stove, then made another search for food, even rummaging through the mattresses of balsam boughs for a bone or scrap of frozen meat that one of the Cheechoo children might have dropped and lost. There was nothing. He took off his moccasins, parka, and trousers; he spread the *atihk* skin and rabbitskin robe close to the stove, lay down, and bundled them around him.

His body tightened. Then it shook with a brief sob.

Chapter 7

THEY WERE A SMALL BAND. There were fewer than thirty children around Jacob's age among the families that straggled in out of the forest every May and June to spend the summers in the tents and nondescript shacks that clustered around the Hudson's Bay Company post on the Wapanishee shore. So Jacob had always known Niska Nimawassa.

Normally they would not have spent much time together during childhood because boys and girls played in separate groups—the boys at hunting, the girls at homemaking, preparing even then for the adult roles they would later assume. During those childhood years, however, Jacob and Niska were thrown together more than would normally have occurred, because of the little tent school that the government teachers conducted for varying periods during the Wapanishee summers. Most of the *Atihk-anishini* children quickly lost interest and attended the school sporadically, but Jacob and Niska had outreaching minds that the lessons stimulated, and they came regularly whenever the school was there. In fact there were times when they were its only pupils.

It was sometime during the early teens when Jacob made the discovery that Niska was different, not just in her interest in the school lessons, but in a new and suddenly exciting fashion—she was pretty in a way that the other girls with their vacant, round faces and eye-pinching cheeks were not. After that, during the long harsh winters back in the bush with his family, Jacob looked forward with a new eagerness to each coming summer at the Wapanishee post, not because of the school, the chocolate bars, the chewing gum, and the store food, but because Niska Nimawassa would be there.

But the summers were short, Jacob and Niska were often separated when they had to accompany their families on fishing or berrypicking trips away from the village, and Jacob had a shyness that was slow to break down.

He was eighteen, Niska was a year younger, but with the emergent womanhood already filling out her slender body, before he asked her dry-mouthed and hesitantly one day after the school lesson if she would walk with him that evening on the beach. He thought she nodded, but it was so slight he wasn't sure, and he was afraid to ask again. But he waited that evening down at the shore amid the beached canoes, and when the dusk had thickened and he had given up hope and the beach was almost hidden in the night, she came. They walked on the soft warm sand, while wavelets murmured and an amber moon reached out to them with its linking arrow of silver across the water. They talked about the world of the big towns and cities far away that the schoolteacher had been describing to them that afternoon. They practiced their English words. And when they reached the big rocks at the end of the beach a mile down the shore, they sat close together, and their hands touched many times, but that was all, because the shyness was a smothering mantle still that masked the emotions Jacob Atook was beginning to feel.

But they were a stoic people, made that way by the hardships of the life they led, and it had given them a capacity for intuitive communication. Thus, by that autumn—the autumn the white goose hunters first came to Wapanishee —it was understood between them without words or pledges that Niska Nimawassa, the pretty one, was Jacob's girl.

Two more years passed. Long and lonely winters when he traveled with Isaac, his father, on the traplines and on the *atihk* hunts out of their winter base camp, and the picture of Niska with the gentle mouth teasing, the nose upturned, and the eye whites flashing in their ebon frames was always before him—in every cloud, in the shadowed etchings of every sunlit glade. Brief bittersweet summers when they met often in the shrouding dark of evening at some spot where Joe, her father, could not observe; and the forging fire of their love expressed itself only in modest touches and holding hands, yet even in this restraint there was new fuel for the fire, new depths, in every secret meeting. Then the autumns, and quickly after, the departures for each family's ancestral winter hunting grounds, and the choking pain of parting until another spring.

In the autumn when Niska reached twenty and Jacob twenty-one, Taka Cheechoo brought the *atihk* antlers with their symbolic message to Niska's tent. She told Jacob about it on the beach that night. The antlers were huge, she said, bearing many points, obviously the rack of a big prime buck—a strong and wise one that would severely test a hunter's skill.

Her voice low and husky, Niska repeated the exact words that Taka had used.

"I shot it two days ago down the Amihk," Taka had told her. "I shot it alone, without another hunter to make the hunting easier. It's the kind of *atihk* I'll shoot for you when you move to the Cheechoo tent and become my wife. Jacob Atook can only snare rabbits like a woman and talk in the English words and describe the dreams he sees, but *I'll* bring you *atihk,* the biggest *atihk* in the *Atihk-anishini* land."

"What did you say?" Jacob asked her quickly.

"What could I?" she answered, standing close to him, her eyes pinched with tight little scorings of pain. "I said: 'Yes, Taka, you're a good hunter. But it's not for me to say whose wife I'll be.' "

The pain in Jacob's heart could not have been greater if the sharp points of Taka Cheechoo's *atihk* antlers were piercing and twisting there.

A desolate and haunting fear traveled with Jacob Atook on the snowshoe trails that winter. Even without Taka's antler gift to Niska, the fear would have been there. Because Niska now had the body of a woman, and by *Atihk-anishini* custom it was time for that body to fulfill its woman's role. And in the *Atihk-anishini* tradition, marriage was too serious, too subject to adversity and to the evil *manitokay* of offended spirits, for a boy and girl to be allowed to decide their own.

There were problems and pitfalls in marriage that only the old and wise could understand. In the case of daughters especially, it was a father's responsibility to ensure that a girl married wisely, above all else to a good hunter. And only the old ones could unravel the intricate and far-reaching kinships—the distant cousins and the entwining of in-laws, with their strict taboos about whom a boy or girl could marry without bringing the ire of the forest spirits upon their households. Only the old ones could understand the need to keep the *Atihk-anishini* partition of family hunting territories evenly distributed by marriages that placed the newly created families into territories that could support them. For a marriage was not just a new mixing of family bloodlines, it was a family bargaining too that often entailed a readjustment of hunting lands.

There had been no indication yet that Joe Nimawassa was arranging a marriage for Niska, but it was inevitable that he would be soon. And Joe was one of Jacob's most outspoken deriders. It was no secret that he didn't intend to have Jacob Atook, the poor hunter, the dreamy one too lazy to guide the white men, as a son-in-law.

Another apprehension loomed in that twenty-first of Jacob Atook's winters. The Atook hunting land had shrunk. For two generations there had been more daughters than sons, and several of the daughters were homely, and to get marriages they had had to marry into families with adjoining territories and take parcels of Atook hunting land with them as part of the marriage bargains. Isaac Atook took his paternal responsibility too seriously to tell even Jacob, his eldest son, what he was planning for him, but on the lonely trapping trails that winter the elder Atook had hinted a number of times that Jacob might be marrying a Pishkip girl—one of a family near them, who could bring some of the lost and needed land back into the Atook domain.

So the following May when the ice breakup came and the lakes and rivers opened, Jacob joined his family for the long canoe trip back to the trading post, dreading what another Wapanishee summer might bring.

✦ ✦ ✦ ✦

They met without prearrangement on the beach that first night the Atooks were back, for the Nimawassas were already there ahead of them. She came to him, running, the silhouette of her hair tossing. He grasped her hands and drew her close until their bodies almost touched, and his love, his joy at seeing her again, was a choking in his throat that held back the words he wanted to say. She stepped back and in the darkness he saw now the pinched eyes and the twisted mouth corners. She told him then, with her first words, in a frail and faraway voice:

"Joe talks tonight with the old one of the Cheechoos. I heard them making the arrangements."

He drew her toward him again, silently, not daring to let himself speak. So it had come. Taka Cheechoo was a youth whom Joe Nimawassa or any of the other fathers would be proud to have as a son-in-law.

The emotion rising in Jacob was a despairing amalgam of anger and fear. He had never known an *Atihk-anishini* boy and girl to begin living together against the wishes of their fathers, or without the wedding feast and public proclamation that was the marrying way of their people. Under the autocratic paternalism of their society, it would be hard to do, and if it was done it would bring oppressive problems.

The biggest problem would concern the winter camp

and hunting territory. The defiant couple would be barred
from joining either of their families, they would have to
winter by themselves in some unclaimed area, and the only
such areas were the ones that were poor hunting and trapping lands. With this kind of inauspicious beginning, there
would be cautious limitations too on the credit that Mr.
Fennel at the Hudson's Bay Company store would extend
for wintering food and gear.

The winter life was hard and hazardous, and the *Atihk-
anishini* guarded against the hazards by always wintering in
family groups that put two or more brothers, or a father
and grown-up sons, in a hunting band together. Despite the
casual acceptance of the dangers of their land, it was re-
garded as foolhardy and stupid for a man, or a man and
wife, to winter alone. Even at the best hunting times it was
harder for a single hunter to set up killing opportunities.
When one was alone, the hunts were always longer, the
chances of failure higher. And a man by himself was much
more vulnerable to the blunders and accidents that will
come at times to the wisest and most experienced. Snow
blindness, a frostbitten hand, a fall through ice, a broken
ax handle, a slashed foot from a deflected ax blade, the
shattering of a snow-plugged gun barrel—they were
usually minor mishaps when a man had a partner with him.
But for a hunter alone, one such accident could weight the
odds, tip the survival balance, and bring death not only to
him, but also to the wife and children dependent on him.

And there was still the other, the most frightening hazard
of them all. The spirit beings would surely disapprove and
send their evil upon a marriage that was done without the
old ones' approval. And again, a lone hunter was the most

defenseless, for the spirit ones usually shunned hunters in groups that could outnumber them. There were many instances in the tribal lore, for example, in which *muchiyachak,* the evil one, had brought a tree crashing down on a hunter alone, but never on two.

These were Jacob Atook's thoughts that night in the dark of the Wapanishee beach as love's physical hunger struggled against the restraints of shyness, and Niska finally moved so near that his face was almost touching her hair. But he knew, despite all the problems and dangers, that he would ask Niska to be his wife when the time for it came.

The next night the fears were confirmed, the time had already come.

"Joe said today I'll be the wife of Taka Cheechoo," Niska told Jacob as soon as they met. "He's holding back his five best beaver skins for the marriage gift to Taka Cheechoo's father."

"When?" Jacob asked, his voice struggling.

"When the summer fishing lets up so he can go out and kill a moose for the wedding feast," she said. "It'll be before the autumn. Joe says it'll be a good marriage, so he must have moose nose and lips to serve at the feast to Taka's father."

"You won't do it, Niska? We'll go away first and set up our own winter camp?"

"No one has ever done it before."

"*We* will!"

In the darkness he saw her head drop until the dim oval of her face was hidden. He held her hands, and he could hear her breath quivering. She waited what seemed an interminable time until her breathing was normal again, then she spoke softly.

"Maybe, Jacob . . . maybe we will."

She moved closer. He could feel the soft press of her breasts rising and falling against his chest.

"Jacob, love me the way that Mr. and Mrs. Fennel and the white men do. Touch my lips."

He extracted a hand from hers. He could see her lips in the gloom, pursed like a rosebud on the verge of bursting into bloom. He touched them with a finger.

"No, with *your* lips."

Now he knew what she meant, for the *Atihk-anishini* had seen the Fennels do it, and they knew the white man's way of kissing. But it was a thing for snickering, another of the white man's strange behaviors, and Jacob held back because he was afraid.

She pressed harder. Her breasts were tight against him, and her face was raised and very near his own. It took only an imperceptible movement to bring their lips together. He felt the hot flush flow between them, and a dizzy whirling filled his head, but the fear was still there and he jerked his lips away.

"Jacob, do it again."

Now the fear was suddenly gone. He threw an arm around her shoulders and crushed her so tightly she gasped. A billow of hair fell across her face and he raised a hand and pushed it impatiently away, and then their lips came together, hot now, pulsing, and they kissed again—a much longer kiss than the white couple's ever were.

ᐊᐊᐊᐊᐊᐊᐊ Chapter 8 ᐊᐊᐊᐊᐊᐊᐊ

TWO DAYS LATER the event occurred that partially diverted their attention for several weeks and brought a new excitement into the lives of Jacob Atook and Niska Nimawassa.

A big Canso flying boat, freighting in supplies for the Hudson's Bay Company store, taxied ponderously in to the dock, its two engines straining thunderously and its great belly pushing a billow of white water before it. The fuselage door opened and the first man to hunch through and step up onto the dock was like no other white man that Jacob had ever seen before. The *Atihk-anishini* who had gathered on the shore knew at once that he was some special kind of emissary, not just a hunter or fisherman as most white visitors were. He wore a black gown to his ankles. Instead of a gun or fishing rod, his hands held an enormous black book. He was short, almost frail, but there was a self-assured strength and resoluteness immediately recognizable in his small, thin face.

He lost no time in explaining his mission. After a few quick strides down the dock, he stopped, drew himself erect, and began to address the assembled *Atihk-anishini,* unaware yet that few of them could understand the English he spoke.

"I have come to live among you," he told them. "I come as a brother and teacher and friend, to bring you word of my God. I am not a trader. I do not want your furs. I want only your friendship and attention. I have come to tell you that the gods and spirits you fear and worship are false and imaginary. My God is the only true God. He is not just the God of the white men, he is the God of all men on earth everywhere. We know this because long ago he sent us his Word. I have it here. It is his Holy Bible. It tells us the way to everlasting life, for in God there is no death, there is everlasting life for all who will accept him and live by his commandments. . . ."

Thus Father Webber of the Canadian Arctic Evangelical Mission arrived at Wapanishee to bring the Christian message to the *Atihk-anishini* heathen.

Jacob listened with a tingling excitement. He knew that the spirits of the white man's world were different from those of the *Atihk-anishini* because there had been school-teachers during some of the childhood summers who had told them a little about the white man's religion. And Jacob knew that long ago, before his time, there had been other black-robes like this one who had lived among them. According to the stories Jacob had heard from the older ones, the last black-robe had been here in the years just before Jacob was born and had left because the white people were fighting a war and had no money to pay for missions to the *Atihk-anishini.* The black-robe said he would be back, but he never returned, and the people of Wapanishee Lake had soon slipped back to their pagan beliefs. Now, more than twenty years after the last black-robe had left them, the only relic that remained from that and the previous, sporadic Christian missions was a sprinkling of Anglicized and Biblical names that had crept at those earlier times into their culture.

So Jacob at least knew there was a white man's religion that was different from their own, and now he realized with a warming thrill that he was to have the opportunity of learning everything about it. He had always recognized that for white men to have so many wonderful things, like the little box radios and airplanes that could take them through the sky, their religion with its one big boss god must be much more powerful than the religion and all the little spirit people of the *Atihk-anishini.*

While the missionary was talking, Jacob glanced a few times at the women who, in the custom of his people, had gathered farther away in their own group apart from the men. And he had noticed Niska there, listening intently, as excited and eager as he. But most of the others, men and women, were shuffling self-consciously, their faces vacant, obviously understanding little. And now the missionary stopped, a bewilderment creeping across his features. Mr. Fennel stepped up to him, spoke briefly, and Jacob overheard.

"They don't understand English, you know. Surely you knew that?"

The missionary stared at Mr. Fennel, slowly shaking his head. Jacob heard him answer: "The mission office just told me to come. They didn't tell me what to expect."

Now the missionary glanced back quickly at the gathering of Indians, embarrassment drawing out his thin face. Then he turned and without saying anything more began fussily overseeing the removal of his equipment from the plane.

The Indians dispersed. Jacob waited. Then he noticed, off to the side, that Niska was waiting, too.

"We'll help you, Father," Jacob told him. Jacob could remember having heard that the black-robes were always addressed as Father. And he was pleased to be able to use his English again, because there had been only Niska and the Fennels with whom to use it before.

The missionary turned sharply, with first a surprised look, then a delighted smile.

"Some of you speak English then?" he asked.

"Yes, some, a few, the younger ones," Jacob replied.

Jacob and Niska helped him carry his tent and boxes of supplies to the high ground above the lakeshore. Now some of the other Indian men came back and began assisting. They went into the bush and cut tent poles and raised the missionary's tent. It was a big tent, the biggest Jacob had ever seen, and the missionary explained it would have to be a church and classroom until he could build one of logs. The men lost interest and drifted away again, but Jacob and Niska stayed. Jacob watched curiously as the little man bustled around unpacking and arranging. There was a small table that he put at the back of the tent and covered with a white and gold cloth. He produced a shining metal cross and stood it on the top of the table and then carefully he placed the big black book beside it.

"I could get you a bear skull," Jacob offered, "to put with

the god's book. There's much spirit power in a bear skull."

And the missionary spun around and stared, his eyes wide and glaring.

"You must not believe that witchcraft any longer! It is pagan! You will have the true religion, the church of Jesus Christ, to believe in now."

The black-robe continued to glower at Jacob. Niska was frowning at him, too.

The missionary resumed his unpacking. Jacob's eyes kept straying back with a kindling fascination to the big black book that lay beside the shining cross on the white and gold table cover. The Indian spirits had no book that they wrote in. They talked to the *Atihk-anishini* in dreams, and only the old people who had had many years of dreaming knew the spirits' wishes well. The white man was fortunate his god talked in a book. This was more proof that the white man's god was more powerful than the *Atihk-anishini* spirits. Jacob eyed the book again. He felt a surging desire to learn all that it had to say.

Later, when the unpacking was finished, the missionary thanked them. "Bring all the children in the morning," he said. "You'll interpret so that I can talk to them?"

Jacob and Niska nodded eagerly.

"I'll concentrate on the children until I learn your language," he said. "Then when I can speak to them myself, I'll begin taking the Word to the grown-up ones. I'd like you to teach me your language. You'll do that, too?"

Again they nodded eagerly. He asked them their names, and they told him.

"Kneel with me and pray," he said.

He knelt. They watched and did the same.

"Father, help me in your mission of salvation to these, your pagan children. Help me speak to them in words and parables that their simple minds will comprehend. I thank you, Father, for putting at my side so promptly, as guides and helpers, your daughter Niska, your son Jacob. I pray —for them, Father, I pray—that you will open their minds to the glorious truth and ancient wisdom of your Holy Word. . . ."

↑ ↑ ↑ ↑

Father Webber had no need to worry about the opening of Niska's and Jacob's minds. In the Bible stories—the story of the ten commandments, the story of Jesus and his preaching—they found the same fascination of intellectual adventure and discovery that the summer-school English lessons had opened in earlier years.

They attended the gatherings in Father Webber's tent regularly, almost daily, taking groups of the Indian children with them, interpreting his words for the children who had limited knowledge of English. And when each gathering ended, Jacob and Niska often stayed behind to ask Father Webber more questions about God and Jesus, and to teach him their own *Atihk-anishini* tongue. Father Webber was making good progress with the children, but he was not communicating much with the adults. It was harder to reach them through the interpreting of Jacob and Niska, and the old ones would have to wait until Father Webber could speak to them himself. Among the adults, however, there was no opposition to his mission, for there was general recognition that the white man's dominant position in the world was clear and unequivocal testimony that his religion was more powerful than theirs.

Jacob and Niska learned to think of Father Webber's god as the *Manito*. It was not an *Atihk-anishini* word, there was no need in their religious vocabulary for a word to designate a single, all-powerful spirit. But Father Webber gave them the word, explaining that it was the one other Indian people used for the white man's god, and encouraged them to use it. And *Manito* did have linguistic roots reaching into their own *Atihk-anishini* tongue, because their own term for the supernatural power of the forest spirits was *manitokay*.

Father Webber varied the Bible readings and storytelling by teaching them hymns, because the children loved to sing, even when they didn't understand the words. And they loved to hear Father Webber play his mouth organ with which he taught them the tunes and accompanied their singing. It was during these hymn sessions that he taught them "God sees the little sparrow fall," and one day Jacob stayed to talk to Father Webber about it, when the children left.

"Does God also see the moose and *atihk* fall when the *Atihk-anishini* hunters shoot them?" Jacob asked.

"I'm sure he does," Father Webber answered.

"Then God doesn't love the moose and *atihk* as much as he loves the sparrow," Jacob said.

Father Webber's eyes narrowed searchingly.

"Why do you say that?"

"If God loves the moose and *atihk* as much as he loves

the sparrow, why did he put them here in a land where the
Atihk-anishini have to kill them or starve?"

"The animals were put here for man's use," the missionary said. "God gave man dominion over all things of
the land and sea."

Jacob was staring thoughtfully at the trampled grass that
formed the floor of the big tent. He wondered if what he
was thinking were wrong and sinful thoughts.

"If God made the earth and everything on it," he resumed
slowly, "and if God loves them all the same, why did he
give stomachs that have to have meat to the *Atihk-anishini*,
to the wolf and fox and weasel, and to all the other meat-
eating ones? The moose and *atihk* are big and strong yet
their bodies don't need meat, they eat the lichen, and
leaves and twigs of the trees, they have stomachs that keep
them strong without need for meat. God could have given
stomachs like that to all things—to the *Atihk-anishini*, too—
and then there would be no need for killing."

Now it was Father Webber's eyes that were turned down
pensively to the tent floor.

"God loves them all," he repeated hesitantly, "and he
has promised that a time will come when there will be no
killing. He has told us the wolf shall dwell with the lamb,
the leopard shall lie down with the kid, the cow and the
bear shall feed side by side, and the lion shall eat straw
like the ox. I am sure that eventually God wants it that
way, that someday that is the way it will be."

"And the *Atihk-anishini*," Jacob asked, "we'll eat moss
like the *atihk*, and not have to kill them for their meat?"

Father Webber didn't answer, there was a troubled confusion on his face, but his head nodded gravely. Jacob left the tent, but the bewilderment haunted his mind more than ever.

⁊ ⁊ ⁊ ⁊

Jacob saw Taka frequently during these weeks, but always at a distance, never near enough that they had to speak. Taka didn't seek a showdown with Jacob, nor did he have to do any courting of Niska; the marriage was decreed, the pressure of tribal tradition demanding it, and the courting could wait until afterward, which was often the *Atihk-anishini* way.

Absorbed with Father Webber's enthralling new religion, Jacob and Niska made only brief and inconclusive references to the marriage that Joe Nimawassa was planning. The fear and misery of it still bore heavily and constantly on Jacob's mind. Niska had still not said she would be his wife, but he was afraid to press the issue until the time of crisis came and it could be postponed no longer.

The late-summer decline in fishing came. One morning Jacob saw Joe Nimawassa bringing his net ashore. Jacob's stomach knotted. The time of crisis was near. That afternoon, during the gathering in Father Webber's tent, Niska leaned close and whispered: "Joe's quit fishing. He's leaving today to hunt a moose for the wedding feast. Taka's going with him."

Jacob stiffened, trembled. The familiar tent scene— children squatted on the ground, Father Webber at the front playing his wheezy mouth organ—grayed and receded until only Niska's taut and hauntingly beautiful face remained. But still, he feared and waited. And the fear was not that Joe and Taka would quickly get their moose, it was a fear of what Niska would say when he had to ask her.

Several nights later they met on the beach in their usual place, and Niska spoke the news that had to come.

"They're back. Joe says Taka shot the moose for him. It's down on the Amihk and it'll take them three or four days to bring the meat in. Joe's telling everyone the wedding feast will be in six days."

Jacob drew her close.

"I want to learn more about the wishes of the *Manito* from Father Webber," he began slowly, "but there's no more time." Then a strength and resolve came into him, and he talked rapidly now, but his voice was thick and shaking still. "We'll have to go and stay for the winter. When we come back in the spring, they'll have to accept us then as man and wife. We'll have to winter alone, somewhere where Joe and Taka will never find us. On the Little Ninkik, Niska. No one hunts there now, or claims it as their own. It's too far— ten days, maybe fifteen, I'm not sure. Almost to the little sticks. They'll never think we would go that far. It's farther than any of the *Atihk-anishini* families go, except the Chee-choos, who go to the Mahkwa, and that's two days to the east of the Little Ninkik. It's not good hunting land, I know, because I've heard the Cheechoos have tried to hunt there. But there'll only be two of us, and there'll be game enough for two."

They began walking silently along the beach. When many long and dragging moments passed without a response from her, he put the question bluntly: "Niska? We'll be man and wife?"

But the silence settled again. Jacob began to tremble.

"I love you, Niska. The old ones say that you get married and then the love comes. That only the married ones can love. But it's not that way with us. We feel it now. We do . . . don't we? Don't you, Niska?"

She spoke now, but with a husky quaver that made the voice seem far away.

"I feel the love, Jacob. But it's hard to go against what the old ones say is right. Against the *Atihk-anishini* way."

"Do you want to be the wife of Taka Cheechoo?"

"No."

"I'll show this winter that I can be a good hunter. We'll bring in many furs in the spring. Your father will accept me then as his son-in-law."

She murmured: "Yes, Jacob, the Little Ninkik . . . we'll go there." But then the hesitancy returned. "Father Webber . . ." she said slowly, "he says it's a sin against the *Manito*'s laws for a man and woman to live together who have not been married in the sacred way of the *Manito*'s church. And maybe Father Webber won't want to marry us, if our fathers don't tell him to."

"We'll go right now and ask him," Jacob declared.

Father Webber stared moodily at the brown, dead grass of his tent floor, and he talked quietly, haltingly, more to himself than to Jacob and Niska. Some of it was a mumble that Jacob could barely understand.

"God's Word . . . clearly . . . fathers and mothers are to be honored . . . respected," Jacob heard the Father saying. There was more, under his breath and unintelligible, then the frail voice sharpened: "But only pagans dictate the marriages of their children!" The voice dropped again,

stammered. "I must get through to them . . . the old ones
. . . win their respect. . . . God yearns for their souls.
But if I defy the old ones this way . . . will it be harder
then?"

He looked up, his eyes drawn and his face lined. "They
didn't tell me there would be problems like this," he mum-
bled. "They didn't tell me what to do."

But then his voice hardened.

"It is Taka Cheechoo?"

Jacob and Niska nodded.

"The one who never comes to our church?"

They nodded again. And now Father Webber looked at
Niska with his brow lowered, pinching his eyes.

"And if you marry him, you won't be able to come to the
church either?"

Niska murmured: "No."

They saw his mouth tighten into a thin straight line before he turned his back and faced the gold cross on the
table. He started to pray.

"Father, guide me in this decision. Is it right that I should
defy their marriage customs before I have had time to teach
them the church's way? Father . . . one of the souls that
I have delivered unto you is to be snatched back into the
pagan pit of wickedness. . . ."

He stopped it there, and the small body stiffened suddenly under its black gown. He spun around.

"It must not happen!" he declared abruptly. "I'm sure it's
a sin and sacrilege in the eyes of God. You are of age.
The law says I can marry you without the consent of your
parents. Secretly, if necessary! And the laws of my govern-

ment are the laws of the *Atihk-anishini,* too. A soul given
to God must not go back! I'll show them there will be none
of these pagan interferences in the work of God I have been
sent to perform!"

So Niska Nimawassa and Jacob Atook were married
three days later in front of the little altar with its splendid
white and gold cloth, its shining cross and Bible. No one
else knew except Mr. and Mrs. Fennel, whom Father
Webber had asked to attend and sign the papers that would
make Jacob and Niska man and wife. Jacob didn't know
whether it was God or the big bosses in Father Webber's
government who required the signatures to make the
wedding right. But he was glad that Mr. Fennel came, because after putting his name down on the wedding papers
Mr. Fennel could not refuse the credit that Jacob now required to obtain the canoe, tent, traps, and food that he
and Niska needed for the winter in the bush. Even then,
Mr. Fennel allowed Jacob only the barest minimum.

They assembled their outfit secretly in the darkness of
two evenings. On the third night, the night before Niska
and Taka Cheechoo's wedding feast was to have been held,
Jacob and Niska met again on the beach as soon as the
long midsummer twilight had faded. They pushed off
silently in their heavily laden canoe, and for all of that
night they paddled hard, without rest, their arms and
shoulders aching, until they reached the river that led into
the maze of waterways beyond. It was there, just before
dawn, that the hum of the outboard motor for which they
had been listening all night first reached them, like the drone
of an insect far away.

There was beach here which would reveal footprints and

keel marks in its sand, and Jacob dug hard with his paddle
to reach a rocky shore that would show no marks of a
landing. He brought the canoe in hastily, but carefully, so
that it would leave no paint streaks on the rocks, and then
hurriedly they carried the packsacks into the screen of
alders that lined the river shore. The noise of the outboard
was a roar now, but the approaching boat was still hidden in
the predawn darkness. They carried the canoe up last, and
had it hidden in the trees only moments before the outboard revved down to a murmur and the gray blur of the
boat appeared, cruising up the river below them.

They crouched in the leafy bank growth, Niska's hand
trembling in Jacob's, and watched the boat come slowly
upstream. There were two men in it. The craft passed within
a dozen paces of their hiding spot, and in the glimmer of
starlight they recognized the faces of Joe and Taka scanning the shore as their boat went by.

"They might come back, paddling, not using the outboard, hoping to surprise us," Jacob whispered.

They carried their packsacks and canoe back deeper to
where the spruces were thick and hugged the ground, so
that the hiding place would bear a daylight scrutiny and
still not be revealed. Then they waited, listening, not talking, as the dawn came.

An hour later the muffled burble of a paddle stroke
signaled Joe and Taka's return, the motor silent now, the
boat ghosting through the water. They watched through the
trees as it entered the lake and turned along the shore. And
it was over for now, but not ended, because Jacob knew that
Taka Cheechoo would go on searching in the months ahead
for the one whom tribal custom had decreed was his.

They would have to hide during the day and travel at night, staying off the main water routes, so they spread their bedding skins on the needly duff of the forest floor, not pitching the tent. There, in the red light of early morning, Jacob gently drew the brown and lissom body against his own. There was no shyness now, nor fear, and that which the *Manito* had joined in spirit three days before now joined in the first fierce, enraptured fusion of youth's demanding flesh.

◄◄◄◄◄◄ Chapter 9 ◄◄◄◄◄◄

IN THE DESERTED CHEECHOO CABIN on the Mahkwa, Jacob lay on the floor beside the oil-drum stove, sleepless, the weight of defeat heavy on him.

The Cheechoo camp was an empty shell. It was giving him warmth, because there was firewood here, but that was all. He could feel a cold glimmer of relief that there was now no danger of Taka finding Niska, but the relief was annulled by its correlated knowledge that Nellie Cheechoo would not be going to her either, with the food that Niska needed.

Another tight, strangling sob filled his throat.

"Niska, the old ones know . . . they are wise . . . Joe was right. Love is not enough. Love doesn't put food in the belly, it puts the little *keekishkawasso* there, and the need for more food. You should have married Taka, as your father wanted. Taka wouldn't have listened when the *Manito* talked."

He rolled restlessly. He got up and put more wood in the stove. He went to the door, opened it, looked out. It was still snowing heavily. He stepped outdoors and turned the toboggan up on its side so that it wouldn't be buried in the morning.

Then he went back and lay down again, his mind reconstructing the chronology of its guilt and despair.

◊ ◊ ◊ ◊

Joe and Taka had not appeared again after that first morning of the flight from Wapanishee.

The night travel was slow and difficult, Jacob and Niska were carrying several hundred pounds of food and gear, and to escape detection they traveled on secondary, little-used routes where the portages were frequent, overgrown, and often long. So the birch and poplar leaves were already beginning to fall in a golden rain when they came at last to the Little Ninkik.

They chopped out a clearing on the shore, leaving a screen of spruces in front of it so that it wouldn't be visible to anyone passing on the lake. They pitched the tent and began the preparations for the winter.

The first cold came, shrinking the days as cold water shrank the cheapest socks that the trading post sold. The net was left permanently in the lake now and Jacob lifted it every day for the whitefish, pike, and lake trout it always contained. He built a smoke lodge of boughs and bark for smoking the fish they didn't immediately need for food. From a birch selected for its straight grain, he split two planks and with the ax and crooked knife trimmed them down until they were a quarter of an inch thick, then he steamed them and bent them back at one end to form his winter toboggan. He worked on it carefully for several days, making it as long as he was tall, lashing poles on each side to reinforce it and take the ropes that would secure the loads it would have to carry. From the same birch he split strips and made snowshoe frames that Niska laced with thongs from an old *atihk* hide, because Jacob had not gone out yet on an *atihk* hunt and there were no new thongs from a fresh hide with which to do a sturdier job.

Jacob was not a knowing and observant husband, and in the busy preparations for the winter he didn't notice that Niska had ceased gathering and drying the soft sphagnum moss for her menses. The first light snow was on the ground, and she had been pregnant two months before she finally told him.

Jacob's initial reaction was one of startled fear. His mouth dropped open, and his lips twitched as his mind wrestled with the calculation that the news had posed. Niska read the concern on his face and smiled.

"Don't worry. The birth time will be spring. We can be on our way to the post by then, and stop off with one of the families where there'll be women to help. But not the Cheechoos!"

Then, in the tides of emotion surging through him, he saw the fuller meaning that a baby of the seed of Jacob Atook could bring.

⁊ ⁊ ⁊ ⁊

They had left Wapanishee as convinced Christians, but now, back in the traditional forest environment of their people, living again the primitive life in close communion with the wilderness, away from Father Webber, away from the white influences of the trading post, the spirit world of the *Atihk-anishini* began to assert itself again. It had been easy to deny the existence of the forest beings and concentrate on Father Webber's *Manito* while they were back at Wapanishee, but it was harder here in the lonely forest hunting grounds where the spirit ones had always dwelled and exerted their power. Once again Jacob became aware of the presence of *pinayssi*, the thunder spirit; *wapahkwa*, the white-bear one; *mishipishoo*, the great lynx that lived in the river rapids, and *weentiko*, the giant and feared one with the heart of ice who ate people but could survive by eating its own fingers when the hunting was bad.

The *Atihk-anishini* religion was largely one of fear, of how to fend off the spirits that lurked in the forests, and protect against the evil they could bring. It concentrated on behavior and relations here. But Father Webber's religion had a different emphasis. Its stress was on the other life that would be in heaven, and on the things the *Manito* demanded before he would grant it. It was an explanation of origins and purpose, it revealed why and how they were here, and this, for Jacob, had been its big fascination, because Jacob had wondered about such things even in the days before Father Webber came.

Jacob and Niska frequently talked about it all during those autumn weeks. No firm decisions formed in their minds, but the feeling grew that since the two religions had different spheres of emphasis, they complemented each other rather than conflicted. Slowly, unobtrusively, the religion of Father Webber began to assume the form of an addition to rather than a replacement of the old *Atihk-anishini* beliefs.

Jacob summed it up finally, a little fearfully because he thought that Niska might still disagree.

"We know the spirit beings are here," he said. "I've heard them talking when I'm alone in the forest, Niska. They have visited me and talked to me in the dreams. Father Webber doesn't know it, but I'm sure the forest spirits are his *Manito*'s helpers. Probably soon the *Manito* will write this in his book and then Father Webber will know it, too."

Niska nodded slowly. She didn't disagree.

So the faith in the *Manito* remained firm, but the old faith, the old fears, the mystic legacy of their race, came back to take a place beside it.

And so, when wolves killed the *atihk*, Jacob obeyed when the spirits told him to hang the bones high on the poles to appease the bone spirits of the dead one. And then, when he found an *atihk* trail in the first thin snow, he listened and dutifully obeyed when this time the *Manito* spoke and told him not to hunt it. For Jacob Atook then, there was no conflict, no incongruity, in these two actions.

✦ ✦ ✦ ✦

It came upon them slowly, covertly, with animal-like cunning. There were dim foreshadowings and an older, more experienced hunter might have seen it coming, and made the preparations, and taken the precautions that could have softened the harshness of its impact. But Jacob didn't recognize the warnings. The full dimensions of the crisis were upon him before he saw it for what it was.

The snows whispered down, sifting through the trees, shrouding the forest floor. The deep cold came, and it remained far below zero week after week without release. One dense snowfall lasted for a night and a day and a night without easing, adding two feet to the ground before its leaden clouds dissipated and blue sky returned.

But there were plenty of fish, and Jacob waited without worry, confident that the *Manito* would speak again and tell him he could hunt when the need came. And while he waited, perhaps they used the flour and the store food faster than they otherwise would, for fish alone was a monotonous diet, and the temptation to vary it with other foods was strong.

He saw one of the warnings eventually. It was the humpy build-up of ice from spray around the midstream rocks and along the edges of the rapids at the inlet to Little Ninkik Lake. It was a narrow stream but its rapids were fast and loud and turbulent, and Jacob knew that in a normal winter they would not freeze completely over. But now the ice bridge began creeping outward from the shores and from each midstream rock, a little each day, and Jacob watched with the first faint prickings of fear.

He didn't know that fish require well-oxygenated water to breathe and remain active, and that a lake's oxygen supply is cut off when winter ice covers it, removing its contact with air. Nor did he know that the tumbling waters of a rapids pick up much oxygen and carry it under the ice into any lake they feed. Jacob had only the knowledge of a hunting race who lived by knowing intimately but unscientifically the lifeways of their land. And it was this knowledge that told him that the fishing would remain good as long as the rapids remained open, that the fish would sleep and stay out of the nets if the rapids froze.

He put on snowshoes and walked down to the rapids almost every day. The below-zero cold persisted and the ice continued to creep outward from the snow-sculptured shore, taming foot by foot the wild white waters. Then one morning when he awoke, there was a naked, numbing silence outside the tent. The distant voice of the rushing waters was stilled.

In a week or two the catches of fish in the nets began dropping off, and by the third week there were no fish at all coming up in the linen meshes. They began using the fish they had smoked and dried earlier in the winter. And they prayed. They prayed that the *Manito* would send an *atihk* to the Little Ninkik and tell Jacob he could kill it. They prayed that the *Manito* would put the hares back in their forest runways, or fish back in the nets. And their faith was firm, so still they ate the store food with no attempts to ration it and make it last.

It dwindled rapidly. It dwindled because the *Atihk-anishini* can neither afford nor carry enough trading-post supplies to serve as the mainstay of their winter diet; it can never be more than a supplement to the game of the hunt. Item by item, the dried fish, flour, rolled oats, rice, and beans disappeared until only tea remained. Jacob began gathering the barks and lichens, but it didn't appease and the pain of hunger now was always in their stomachs.

He ruled out going back to Wapanishee post. It was far and Niska was weak from the *keekishkawasso* sickness, as well as from the hunger. The *Atihk-anishini* are accustomed to periods of winter famine, and hunger is one of the hardships they stoically accept. But most of all, he ruled it out because he feared the taunting he would receive from the others when they returned in the spring and learned that

Jacob had had to come back like an old and senile one and beg for the white man's aid.

The deep cold stayed. The hunger time went on and on. Their bodies wasted and weakened, the bones began ridging the skin, the dizzy spells began. *Pipoon,* the time of late winter, came, and with it at last came the grim awareness that the hunger was no longer just hunger, it had become starvation.

Only then did Jacob Atook, the reluctant hunter who had found in the sparrow hymn a release from the obligation to kill, realize that the *Manito* was not going to hear their prayers and speak again. Only then did the fear begin to form that this was the wrath and punishment of the forest spirits for the marriage that was done without the parents' permission. But more and more, during the long periods of inner searching, the burden of blame came back to himself, until he saw with pained and racking self-denunciation that he had failed and bungled as only the poorest hunter could. He had bungled by using up the store food faster than was necessary, and by delaying the hunt until the game was gone.

And now there was only the *atihk* that would be far out in the land of little sticks where the snow was always hard and thin.

‹‹‹‹‹‹‹‹ Chapter 10 ‹‹‹‹‹‹‹‹

THE CANDLE FLAME BURNED LOW and then stuttered out,
but the fire in the stove continued to spill yellow splashes
onto the floor through the draft holes in its door. Despite
his fatigue, Jacob lay awake a long time, because his mind
that night was too disordered and knotted for sleep. Its
decision, so slowly and painfully made, was back, unmade,
demanding to be made again.

He was tortured by the thought of her, lying back there
in the tent on the Little Ninkik, the *keekishkawasso* stirring
within her, while she waited for Nellie, who would never
come. The love burned in him, filling him with a demand to
be back with her, where whatever came would come to
them together.

She had food for ten days; two of those days were already
gone, and every day he traveled farther would mean another
day returning. The *atihk* might be far away, and the hunt
might be long. Too long? Should he go back, and should
they try even now, at this late time, to reach the Wapanishee post where he could beg for the food that would be
there? Was that what the Cheechoos had already done? The

Cheechoos were good hunters, they would have store credit, they would not have to beg as Jacob would have to do. But it wasn't pride now that held him back, nor fear of the ridicule that a retreat to the post would bring; it was fear of the trip itself and what its rigors might do to Niska and to the *keekishkawasso* that still moved in the hard round nest of Niska's belly. He might do it alone and return with food for Niska, but the two-way trip would take at least twenty days, and surely Niska didn't have that much time. Yet should he try? Had it become the safer choice now, with the Cheechoos gone?

"*Manito,* I don't know. Tell me, *Manito,* tell me."

And he listened, and there was only the soughing murmur of the fire. The *Manito* did not speak.

Then the soughing was of a wind in spruce trees, and he was far away where he had never been before, because the trees were gnarled and little sticks of a kind he had never seen in the *Atihk-anishini* forests. A spirit one was there before him, and Jacob had not walked to this distant place because there was no snow encrusted on his snowshoes, and there were no tracks leading to where he stood, so the spirit one must have brought him, as only the spirit ones can. He knew it was a spirit *atihk,* not a real one, because it was not afraid, and its eyes didn't move when it looked at him, and then he saw that they were not eyes, but shining stones. And only a spirit could see with stones where the eyes should be. It moved now, beckoning Jacob to follow with a toss of its great antlers. And when it moved, it still left no tracks in the snow.

Jacob followed. There was a mighty strength in him, because he moved at a speed so great that the wind of it put a chill on his cheeks and set his parka snapping. Yet he moved at this speed of a swallow's flight without breathlessness or fatigue. It was open country where the trees were small and few and offered no impediment to travel. The spirit *atihk* stopped far ahead of him, and Jacob came up to it and stopped, too. Jacob looked where the stone eyes were turned downward and he saw a great hole in the form of an *atihk*'s body that was melted in the snow. It was a perfect outline—legs, head, antlers, ears, even the stub of tail. And there were tracks leading up to it and tracks leading away, proving that the one that had left this melted form in the snow was a real *atihk,* not a spirit one.

Now the soughing was the fire in the Cheechoo cabin again, but Jacob knew much time had passed while he was on the journey, because the soughing was faint and the fire in the stove was low. He trembled, for he knew it had not been just an ordinary dream, but a dream journey with a spirit helper. This was the way the *Atihk-anishini* spirits spoke, not through a book like the *Manito*'s, and there was always deep meaning in what the dream spirits revealed. And this one was a familiar type of dream journey—this visit to a place where an animal form was melted in the snow. When it came to a hunter, it meant the hunt would have success, because a spirit one was aiding.

But he continued to tremble, remembering Father Webber's stern admonishments that the forest spirits were false and only the *Manito* was real. Yet the spirit *atihk was* real; he had seen it too vividly for it to be just a creature of the sleeping mind. And then he knew again, as he had known for a long time now, as Father Webber did not yet know, that these spirit ones of the forest were the *Manito*'s helpers.

"*Manito,* it was you who sent it. It was your message the spirit *atihk* carried. Tell me, *Manito;* tell me this is so."

And Jacob listened, and still there was only the murmur of the fire.

But the twitching came suddenly then to the finger that belonged to the trigger when the gun was in a hunter's hands. This, too, was a familiar *Atihk-anishini* sign. It meant the hunter would shoot game. The twitching moved up his arm, even into his shoulder. Now an excitement filled him, because this meant the meat of the hunt would be heavy, and even the big muscles of the shoulders would have to strain under its weight.

Jacob was satisfied now. His trembling ceased. The *Manito* had spoken. If the forest spirits were his helpers, then of course the *Manito* could speak in their ways, too.

He rose and put new wood on the fire. Then he lay again beside it, his mind at rest. The *Manito* had sent a spirit helper to tell him the hunt would produce food for Niska much sooner than a long trek back to Wapanishee post. The decision was made. He would not go back to tell her that Nellie Cheechoo was gone, because it would waste three or four more days and accomplish nothing. He would go for the *atihk,* directly, from here. It was new and strange country, and he wasn't sure of its travel routes, but he had come east from the Little Ninkik to find the Cheechoo camp, so now if he turned north down the Mahkwa it should lead him out into the land of little sticks. But he didn't know how far it would be.

He would go with the first dawn light.

Now sleep came, and the spirit *atihk* with the eyes of stone didn't come back, but another dream visitor did.

The vision was hazy, ephemeral, as dreams always are, but the noise that came with it was so life-like that that part of it hardly seemed to belong to the dream. It was a strident creaking of the cabin door, nerve-grating even in sleep. Jacob saw the door slowly opening, saw the gray rectangle of light, and the hunched figure vaguely silhouetted against it. Its head was covered with a big parka hood, the features shadowed and hidden. The dream vision lasted only an instant, and then was gone.

But for a few moments afterward it brought him fully awake. He rose onto an elbow and forced heavy, languid eyes to focus on the door. It was closed. There was nothing there. He listened but could hear only the murmur of wind outside. Then, almost instantly, he was asleep again, and this time no more dreams came.

↗ ↗ ↗ ↗

The cabin was dark when he awakened, but there were pale fingers of light between some of the logs where the moss chinking had dropped out, so he knew the day was arriving. He rose and built up the fire. He put on his trousers and moccasins, took the cooking pot from the packsack, and stepped outside the door.

It had stopped snowing. A smooth white blanket, clean and new, lay over yesterday's old snow, hiding the tracks of his arrival, whitening the webs of the snowshoes he had left standing outside. In the dim light he saw the snow piled in a humpy drift on the windward side of the toboggan that he had turned on its side the night before, and there was a hollow in the toboggan's lee where the snow had not reached.

He scooped up a pot of snow, took it back inside, and put it on the stove. When it had melted, he dropped in a couple of handfuls of the flaky rock-tripe lichen that he had gathered the previous day, and as it boiled he thought again of the dream figure at the cabin door, wondering if it, too, could be a spirit message. But he knew it couldn't be. The doorway vision had been too shadowy and fleeting, not sharp and lasting as the journey with the spirit *atihk* had been, as the spirit visits always were. It was simply an ordinary sleep dream with no meaning to convey.

The rock tripe cooked. His stomach churned and he couldn't eat it all, but he drank the blackened water in which it had boiled and got some of its nourishment that way.

He carried the pack and bedding roll outside. There was no sun, but it was full daylight now, and he studied the sky-line for clues to the lay of the land around him. First he looked back south and west, and a scalding racked his heart and a yearning filled his mind, because that was the Niska way. Then he turned and faced the north. Mahkwa was a long and narrow lake that ran roughly north and south, and there was a notch in the hills far down at its northern end which indicated that the river emptying it was there. And that would be the way of the little sticks. The way the spirit *atihk* had taken him during the night.

He strode determinedly to the toboggan, not looking back the Niska way again. He put down the pack and bedding roll and stooped to turn the toboggan over for loading. And then, in the hollow beside the toboggan where the new snow hadn't reached, he saw the hole piercing the old crust. It was an oblong hole, three hand widths deep, familiar, instantly recognizable—the print of a gunstock that had been jabbed there to stand a rifle upright in the snow.

He stared at it, his heart thumping as the gun print pressed its message on a mind that didn't want to believe. He stooped, trembling, feeling the hole in the snow with his hand. It was real, not a vision that a spirit one might imprint on the eyes. So the figure at the door had not been a dream, nor a spirit visitor either.

Jacob scanned the lakeshore again, searching, squinting his eyes against the whiteness of the fresh new snow. His eyes came back to it, fearing, but irresistibly lured. They studied it again. And now he saw that it was not the usual print that a rifle stock leaves in snow. It was jagged at one end, and shorter than it should have been.

Somewhere in his mind an obscure strand of memory was struggling to weave a pattern, signaling that this gun-butt print had a vague familiarity that he should recognize. For a tantalizing minute or more it eluded him, then the sought-for picture came. Suddenly he was remembering another *atihk* hunt—the one at Amihk Lake four years before, and the gunstock that was aimed at his own head, and missed its mark, and splintered against the rock behind him.

There was only one rifle in the *Atihk-anishini* band with a broken stock that could leave a hole of that shape in the snow.

≪≪≪≪≪≪≪ Chapter 11 ≪≪≪≪≪≪≪

SOMETIMES IT IS A CRUEL LAND, for its emphasis is on life's renewal, and no sympathy is wasted on the dying.

That September in the land of the *Atihk-anishini* the annual period of life renewal among the caribou had begun to manifest itself in the age-old ways. They had fed well in the rich growing time of the summer, and now the fat was thick on their backs and rumps. The paler, heavier winter fur was coming in, and the necks were swelling with shaggy ruffs—gray and modest in the females, but a resplendent white that formed tossing beards beneath the throats of the males. The antlers on the mature bucks were broad, sweeping, and many-pointed, full-grown for another winter—and beginning to itch now, because the blood supply that fed them through the encasing velvet was choking off, and the velvet was dying. Underneath, the antlers were hardening into rigid bone. To relieve the itching, the bucks were rubbing them on trees and bushes, tearing the velvet away in bloody strips, and since antlers are products of the sexual cycle and zones of erotic sensation, the rubbing off of the velvet was a stimulant to the burgeoning reproductive drive.

At the same time, the hormone flows were changing and sharpening, as glands dormant for a year were triggered into new activity by the waning light of autumn's shortened days.

Now caribou that had been solitary all summer felt a goading urge to join others of their kind.

↑ ↑ ↑ ↑

On the height of land between the Ninkik and the Mahkwa, a band of seven came together that autumn as the first hard frosts were turning the bearberry leaves to crimson. The dominant one, the overlord, around which the others gathered, was a four-year-old buck in the prime of life, with massive neck and shoulders, a heavy white mane, and an antler span as great as his shoulder height.

There was one other buck, an old lean one with the gloss of virility no longer on his coat, and the leg joints stiffening with advancing years. His antlers were puny and slender against the great spreading rack of the four-year-old, because antlers are shed and regrown each year and become progressively smaller with the physical decline of age.

With them were two calves of the past spring's fawning, awkward and gangling still, and three does. Two of the does were antlerless like the calves, but the third carried a heavy rack, for it is a peculiarity of caribou that sometimes the females, too, can be antlered ones. The antlered doe was in her third year and just arriving at the prime of adulthood. She was large for a female, nearly as powerful and sinewy as the younger buck and only slightly smaller.

The time of rut came. It filled the two bucks with a new, strongly possessive attraction toward the females and a belligerent jealousy toward each other, but it was the younger, heavier buck who repeatedly carried the challenge of battle to the other. Whenever the old one approached or showed any interest in one of the does, the four-year-old would lunge at him, head and neck outstretched, ears laid back, great antlers menacing. At first the old one held his ground in the face of these charges, and rattling sparrings of antlers would occur. There would be much feinting and pushing while sharp hoofs tore up the earth, and necks and eyes bulged with the strain. These clashes were tests of strength and endurance, however, not deadly duels, and only an occasional bruise or surface wound resulted. And before long the greater weight and antler size of the four-year-old were accepted by the older one, and he would retreat at the first sign of challenge, the fighting spirit in him quelled. But the retreats were short, he didn't leave the herd, and it satisfied the victor if the old buck simply kept a discreet distance from the does.

When his supremacy was established and the harem of three cows indisputably his, the lead one began diverting attention to his does, lunging at them with the same outstretched neck and lowered antlers with which he had previously been challenging the male rival. But now there was something else—a stiff-legged, mincing stride that was the courtship invitation. In the does, however, the physical conditioning for mating had not yet fully developed, and they interpreted the buck's charges as attacks and fled from him, as the old buck had before. It was thus for two more weeks, but as their sexual cycle ripened and ovulation neared, the escape dashes of the does became slower, less spirited.

The antlered doe, the healthiest and most vigorous of

the three females, reached her receptive time a full two weeks before the others. It was a morning when a sheen of frost sparkled on the ground lichens in the spruce clearings. The male came as he had countless times before, testing, urging, the throat beard swinging, and this time the doe's fear was gone. She had never mated before, but the compulsions of instinct were now controlling her, and her hind legs stiffened and spread, lowering the haunches. The male circled once around her, tossing the great head, displaying the mane and antlers. Then the lunge, the rearing, and the sudden mounting.

As in all of the hoofed ones, it was fast and brief—a single swift, driving thrust, and impregnation was accomplished. Another of life's renewals had begun.

⁊ ⁊ ⁊ ⁊

In a few more weeks the inner flames burned out, freeing energy again for the physical girding against the coming winter cold. Fat layers thickened. The fur grew denser and longer until even the muzzles were covered. It was a superbly insulating two-layered coat—the underlayer thick, soft, woolly, the outer a mat of long stiff guard hairs, each one hollow and filled with air. Because much of the air that the fur entrapped was held within the hairs instead of among them, it was an insulation that little cold could penetrate.

At the same time the hoofs were changing, the horny portions growing longer to give them more grip and supporting surface on the snow, and to provide the stiff, sharp shovels they would soon require for digging down to lichens. They were hoofs eminently adapted for supporting them in deep snow, because each was split up its middle, and the two halves spread like a gaping, inverted Y when the hoof sank into snow cover—the deeper it sank, the greater the supporting area became.

Winter's procession of storm-breeding low-pressure areas began moving down out of the arctic and across Hudson Bay, one following swiftly after another. The bay waters were still open and would remain so for much of the winter, so the air masses that moved across them picked up heavy burdens of water vapor which coalesced and froze into dense, gray clouds of snow. But on their southward, overland sweep across the boggy plain of the Hudson Bay Lowland, the air masses clung tenaciously to their snow load because here the land was as flat and low as the sea over which they had come. It was not until the winds were slowed and deflected upward by the forests and rocky elevations of the Canadian Shield, two hundred miles inland, that their supporting capacity weakened and the snow could begin to drop out.

Thus, by mid-November the snow already lay a foot deep in the forests of the Shield, while the Hudson Bay Lowland to the north was still bare. Snow would come soon to the Lowland, too, but the tendency for snow clouds to jump the coastal flatlands would continue, and throughout the winter the snowfalls in the land of little sticks would be lighter than in the forests farther south.

The snow cover of the two regions would also contrast sharply in texture. In the forests the snow would lie where it fell, packing down slowly, each new fall retaining its pillowy softness for a long period. But out on the bald reaches of the Hudson Bay Lowland, the wind would blow unhindered for much of the time, lifting and driving the snow before it. It would sweep the snow cover thin in the open stretches where the wind blew hardest, and it would drop its snow load to form great tapering drifts along the rim of every valley and hollow, and in the lee of every boulder or clump of trees—anything that would slow the wind or produce an eddy, reducing its snow-carrying power. This constant working of the snow, the tumbling and grinding of crystals against one another, would break off the microscopic points and barbs, reducing the star-like flakes to a fine dust of shattered particles that would pack tightly together. Thus the snow of the land of little sticks would quickly become a dense, crusted snow on which wolf and caribou could walk with little breaking through, although man, with less supporting surface, would still need snowshoes to travel it with any ease.

For the caribou herd on the high forested land between the Ninkik and the Mahkwa, life changed dramatically with the coming of the snow. Now the lichen graze was covered and feeding was no longer the casual and unhindered activity it had been before. The lichen mats no longer gleamed white in the blowdowns and clearings; now they had to be found by scent, with noses snuffing the porous snow. And when found, the lichen had to be uncovered by digging feeding craters in the snow with rapid, scooping movements of a foreleg and hoof that flung white clouds behind them. But all this was routine winter behavior for caribou; the hoofs were sharp and the snow was thin, and although feeding required more effort than in the balmy days of autumn, it was still relatively easy feeding.

It would remain easy as long as the snow got no deeper

than about thirty inches. But beyond this threshold, difficulties compounded rapidly, and the energy consumed in digging for food became greater than that which the food could replace. In a normal winter the snow would rarely exceed this depth, and when it did, it would be local and the caribou could move out and find snow beneath the critical depth-threshold not many miles away. And periodically there would be a brief thaw that would melt and pack it, reducing the depth, letting the snow build-up start again.

But this was not a normal winter.

The forest snow deepened, remaining soft and fluffy, because no thaws came to moisten and consolidate it. It built up gradually until the last days of December, and then for a night and a day and a night without interruption the air was a white opaqueness of falling snow, and two feet came down in that single, concentrated fall. Suddenly it was far above the caribou's critical depth.

They lay that second night in their bedding hollows and let the snow sift deeply over them. The storm passed a few hours before dawn, and at daylight when the gnawing of the morning hunger wakened them, the animals raised themselves stiffly, shaking the snow from their backs and manes, and a vastly altered, all-white world confronted them. Even their broad and spreading hoofs let them sink to their bellies, and they could move only with galloping, exhausting bounds. Now the scenting of lichen had suddenly become inaccurate and difficult, because the deep snow blunted and diffused the ground smells filtering through it.

They began digging. Powdery snow fell back into the feeding craters almost as fast as their hoofs could fling it out. Craters dug in a few seconds the day before now required minutes, and when ground level was finally reached, a crater a yard across at the top would be no more than six inches at the bottom. Even then, there would often be no lichens there, because the scent distortions of the snow frequently misled them into digging where no lichens lay below. And soon their own trampling was adding to the difficulties, packing the snow, putting an impervious cover on the scents, and making the digging harder.

Goaded by hunger, they occasionally snatched at the willow and alder twigs protruding through the snow, but these were not caribou food. Unlike deer and moose, caribou do not possess a digestive system that can properly break down and assimilate this woody browse. They can use it in small quantities, but it is lichen their bellies need.

So they fed meagerly for many hours until the wan halo of sun coming through a translucent cloud layer had climbed high among the spruces. But the hunger pangs stayed in their bellies. And now the deep snow became a stimulus, unlocking within the complex intertwining of instinct and intuition a response as old as their species. There was no reasoning in it, no drawing on the wells of experience, because among the seven caribou in the herd above the Mahkwa that morning there was not one, not even the old and senile buck, that had ever experienced snow of this depth before. It was a decision, but with no process of deciding having gone into it. It was a restless inner prompting, instinctive and automatic.

It said: Move.

The young buck led them, because his legs were longer, and it was he who could travel easiest and break a first track in the untrodden snow. The others followed, usually in single file to take advantage of the trail of those ahead. The antlered female took her place behind the lead buck, because in the order of social dominance within the herd the second rank was hers. The other does followed her, then the calves, and finally the old male who was still staying as far as possible from his younger, more powerful rival.

The leader had no sharply defined plan or strategy, yet the leading did have a consistency and pattern that even he himself barely recognized. For whenever possible, in those first hours of the trek, he led them *down*. He led them down from the ridge along which they had been feeding, and when they reached the bottomland below, he turned and followed its contours downward. And when they came to a small and snaking stream, again the way he chose was down. Yet it wasn't choice, it was the hidden guidance of an instinct that was a part of the subconscious survival lore that had kept his species alive for millennia in this snowy land. He didn't know that by always seeking a lower level, he would come eventually to a lake or broad river where the snow would be wind-packed and the traveling easier.

In most spots they could travel only in leaping bounds— even the old one at the rear who had the broken trail to follow. Sometimes they came to thicker areas of forest where the canopy overhead caught more snow than elsewhere, making the ground snow thinner. They would walk easier here, spreading out, straying from the leader's trail, their noses testing the snow eagerly for lichen scents. But no lichens grew in these areas of thicker forest, because the denser canopy that caught the snow also blocked sunlight in summer.

The hunger tightened. The fatigue grew. The buck breaking trail finally tired and dropped back and the antlered female moved forward into the lead.

They reached Mahkwa Lake in the gray twilight of a colorless sunset many hours later. The doe led them out onto it, yet the travel became only slightly easier, for although the lower snow layers were packed, the wind had not yet had time to work and knead the soft new fall on top.

On the broad, flat expanse of the lake, there was no longer a downward way to lure them, but now another prompting took over. It was a part of the life-preserving store of instinct among the forest-dwelling caribou herds that when the forest snows lay deep, the way to survival was north—away from the long slant of the noontime sun. They didn't know why, for it is the nature of instinct to guide without explaining. And nature had a simple process for preserving such survival knowledge, because whenever a deep-snow winter came, those caribou born without an instinctive knowledge of what to do for survival would starve, and the faulty genes of ignorance would be erased with them.

In the antlered female the inheritance of her race's survival experience was full and sound. She turned them north now, down the long reach of the Mahkwa, toward the land of little sticks they had never seen and didn't know was there.

Far back in the forest a wolf pack howled. In all of the caribou except the aged buck at the rear, this tocsin cry of the archenemy produced only a momentary turning of their heads, a momentary pricking of ears, and then a stoic ignoring. It wasn't a reasoned thing; it wasn't the knowledge that a prime and healthy caribou could outrun a wolf pack in winter snow; it was just that the wolves were always around them, and there was nothing in a routine and distant wolf howl to spring the gates of fear.

The fear would come, terrifying and desperate, the moment the wolves gave indication that they were on a serious hunt.

But it was different with the old one struggling at the herd's rear. In him the wolf howl brought instantaneous fear that lifted the neck hair and sent the blood pounding through him. He didn't know why. For the wolf fear had never been in him before.

The wolves howled only once, but though ignored, they were not forgotten. Later that night, still many hours before dawn, the caribou reached the end of the lake where the dark shores closed in, narrowing to a river. They stopped here, shunning the river, and they bedded down in the lake snow far out on the ice, where the wolves, if they came, would have to come openly and not attack from the screening cover of a nearby shore.

But no wolves came.

The caribou were up and moving with the first light. Testing the breeze and finding no taint of wolf scent on it, they entered the big river that flowed northward from the Mahkwa.

Downstream, two or three hours later, they began to detect a thinning of the snow. They went on with a new anticipation strengthening them, and the layer of new snow that had lain two feet deep back where they had started now dwindled to six inches within a few more miles.

The lead buck took them from the river, through the

alder fringe, and up to the ridge top where the lichens would be. The lichen scents came pungently to their nostrils. They began to dig, and there was little of the fresh and powdery snow here to slide back into the feeding craters. The lichen cushions were thick and spreading, and they ate rapidly until their bellies were filled. Then they went back to the river ice and lay there, resting and chewing cuds, while strength built in them again. The urge to move was sated. They would wait here now until another snowfall raised the snow level over critical depth, triggering the moving urge again.

↟ ↟ ↟ ↟

The respite was brief. New snow came every few days, and it was only a week before the herd had to move again.

It was a pattern that persisted as the winter advanced. The critical depth was constantly overtaking them, like an invisible corralling fence relentlessly creeping up behind and driving them before it.

It became a winter of erratic snowfalls, and after the first shifts northward, subsequent moves in that direction didn't always take them into areas of thinner snow. So the instinctive urge to move north was dulled by the overriding discipline of experience, and the moving became just a drifting, a seeking, a testing—down the lake and river chains whenever their courses suited, or through the muskeg forest when an overland route seemed the better way. And sometimes the prime buck with the massive antlers led them, and sometimes it was the antlered female, the one with the new life growing in her.

If movement took them into areas where snow was deepening, they would veer and move in another direction, and another, until the snow showed signs of lightening. And when they found the direction in which thinner or hardened older snow lay, they would hold to that route until they came once more into a snow region that would let them feed again. It was like water on a mudflat that keeps sending out probing fingers of flow to find the lowest levels.

Yet the wandering did have an invisible pattern. For each snowfall started lighter on the flat plain of the Hudson Bay Lowland, and grew heavier as its air mass rose into the higher forested land of the Canadian Shield. And though movement northward was not always the way to shallower snow, it was the way more often than not. So, by an erratic route with many temporary reversals and interruptions, the drifting of the caribou was slowly bringing them nearer to the land of little sticks.

Chapter 12

THE CARIBOU HAD BEEN MOVING down a broad river for most of a day, and now once more they were emerging from the region where new snow had fallen the night before. They left the river ice, struggled through the dense willow and alder thicket of the springtime flood plain and into the spruce forest of the higher ground beyond. It was dense, as it always was in the protection of the river valleys, but this time there was a change from the uniform forest snow profile they had always known before. As they climbed the valley slope and neared its top, the snow deepened suddenly as though a great avalanche of it had poured into the valley from above. It hung over the valley's rim in a massive lip that buried trees halfway to their tops, and the buck in the lead floundered into it until he sank to his shoulders and had to struggle back out again. He led them now along the base of the snow wall, seeking a route of shallower snow that would let them climb above it.

The buck tired, for it was deep snow even here below the main mass of the drift, and the antlered female took the lead. It was almost an hour later before they came to an area where the slope flattened slightly, and the snow thinned a little, and the doe veered upward to make another attempt to climb from the valley. Two lunging bounds put her into snow over her depth. It was up to her haunches and shoulders, and her legs thrashed in it—like swimming, with the difference that the snow failed to buoy her up as water would. The big hoofs flailed, dug; one of them found momentary purchase on a rock or log deep beneath, which drove her forward a body length before she sank again.

A minute passed before her struggling packed down the snow and the hind hoofs once more found a tenuous footing. The powerful legs recoiled, and this time she hurtled forward in a great arcing leap that carried her a full ten feet upward before the momentum of it was spent. The snow was harder here, for it was exposed to the wind lash of the valley crest. She plunged on, her chest plowing snow before it. And now her scrabbling legs found solid ground. She made another vaulting leap. Suddenly she was up on the thinner and harder snow of the flatland above, and there she waited, legs trembling from the effort, the breath snorting in white jets from her nostrils.

The younger buck came close behind her, then the two does, but they waited a long time for the two calves and the old one. The calves stopped frequently to rest, bleating querulously to the others waiting above, sometimes with little but their muzzles above the snow. The old buck came last, stiff limbs striking out weakly and eyes glazing with fatigue. Though the snow was churned and trodden now, it took him as long as all the others combined to struggle to the top.

From the river level below, there had been no sign that

the forest here was any different from what they had always known, though the great drift of snow had been a warning to expect something unusual. Now from the crest, as the antlered doe waited for the others to reach her, she saw that the spruce trees were thinning, spacing out, becoming smaller; and the wind, unfelt below, was suddenly steady, deliberate, purposeful, like the wind of a big lake where it can blow great distances without obstruction. It swept a ground-hugging spume of fine, gritty snow before it, and she could feel the cut of the snow particles even through the dense and wiry hair that covered her legs.

There was another puzzling change. Under the trees ahead, a soft and diffused line of light was showing, and it wasn't the light of a small clearing, wind blowdown, or beaver meadow, for it extended on both sides as far as she could see.

When the other caribou were up beside her, she led them forward at a fast trot, because light meant an opening in the forest, and an opening could mean lichen. Even here among the trees, the snow had a hard wind-slab on it, and they moved easily. And then, with a startling abruptness, they came to the light's source—a vast reach of open country where the forest ended.

There was a slight elevation here, and they stopped at the edge of the trees to stare distrustfully at a terrain they had never seen before. Theirs was not the sharp, farseeing vision of animals accustomed to living in open places, for they depended more on sound and smell, but they could see, through eyes blurred by unaccustomed distance, that they had suddenly emerged into a land of strange and frightening space. Their myopic eyes strained to encompass it all. Slowly it emerged—a flat white plain that ran on and on without hill or obstruction to an equally featureless horizon that was hazy now with the ground drift of blowing snow. They stared for a long time, because they had never seen a horizon before.

It was not totally empty; there were trees here, scattered thinly in loose, island-like clusters or in twisting ribbons which formed a tangled tracery of black and stood out starkly against the vast white areas between. Yet they weren't really trees—just ragged shrubs, stunted and bent before the wind.

The caribou moved out into the open, hoofs sinking shallowly, for only on the largest lakes had they known snow this firm before. But it was not the barren and scentless snow of lake ice, it had faint mossy smells when they pressed their muzzles into it, and the caribou knew that it was not lake but sphagnum bog below. There was no trace here of the lichen smells they sought, and they moved on toward the nearest cluster of spruces a quarter mile away.

It was a peat hummock about a hundred yards across, rising only slightly above the surrounding bog, and the trees grew on it sparsely with broad spaces between them. The caribou approached it hesitantly, unsure of this strange and open land. They came to it from downwind at first, testing the air for wolf scent, and then they circled cautiously, making a half circuit, before they moved in. So it was the northern, windward side they entered, and as soon as they were among the trees they sank into soft deep snow that had dropped and piled up here because of the sudden blockage of the wind. They struggled through it toward the lee side where the snow became shallower, and the lichen scents began to reach them. They commenced digging. The lichen was abundant, in luxuriant round cushions packed tightly together with no spaces between. And one feeding crater here produced as much graze as three back in the forests they had known.

⁊ ⁊ ⁊ ⁊

For the next few weeks life was easy. The lichen was scattered, but readily found, for it grew wherever there were trees, and in this land the small thickets and ribbons of woodland stood out like black islands in a white sea.

Outside the clusters of trees the wind blew constantly, usually from the north. There was always a scudding sheet of snow whipping along the surface, rasping the caribou's legs, filling the hollows, and piling up great humped drifts within each spruce clump. The drifts were deep—too deep to dig through—along the northern, upwind side where the wind would suddenly slacken and drop its snow load. But in all except the smallest spruce islands, the drifts didn't extend completely to the downwind edge, and here the snow was thin and the lichen digging easy. It was often hard snow, even among the trees, but not too hard for their sharp hoofs, and the hardness let it lift away in chunks, making easier digging than in the powdery forest snow.

The caribou would feed in the early morning for a few hours, then move out into an adjacent open stretch of bog to lie down and rest during the middle of the day, backs to the wind, bodies forming bowl-shaped hollows in the snow. And always their ears were alert, twisting, listening even in sleep for any sounds that could override the crying of the wind. They would return for another feeding in the afternoon, then bed down again in the open for the long night, choosing a spot with good visibility all around and the nearest trees upwind, so wolves couldn't approach undetected.

They heard and scented wolves frequently. A few times they saw them, as wolves came out into the open, circling and sizing up the herd. But running was easy on the hardened snow, the caribou were fleet and well fed, and there was no difficulty in gauging their movements to the movements of the wolves so that the gray silhouettes were never given an opportunity to get into an attacking position. At each encounter the wolves moved on quickly in search of easier prey.

As long as the caribou remained well fed, the wolves would get only a rare, obviously sick or crippled one, or the carrion of a dead one, and the wolf feeding would be slim. But that winter the land of little sticks was moving to a crisis that would have an urgent role for its predators. The day of the wolf was coming.

✦ ✦ ✦ ✦

It was a winter in which the air masses coming down from the north were unusually heavy with snow. Much of the snow still passed over the lowlands to fall on the higher ground inland where the forests grew, but there were frequent and heavy falls, too, here in the land of little sticks. The drifts that began at the upwind side of each woodland clump crept farther and farther, burying more and more of the lichen beds under snow too deep for the caribou's digging.

When they had first arrived, a typical lichen bed pro-

vided three or four feedings before it became pocked and
churned with craters and the caribou had to move on to
another. But now the areas of lichen available to them
dwindled until there was rarely more than one feeding before they had to go on. They were constantly on the move,
with little or no midday rest periods, and the moving with
its lengthened exposure to wind chill increased their energy
requirements. Thus, a cruel perversity of the animal-food
relationship—that as food supply wanes, the energy required
to find it goes up—made their food needs greater than before.
The hunger came again, and the snow was deep now everywhere, so this time the hunger stayed.

They began encountering areas where other caribou had
been ahead of them, eating and trampling the most readily
reached lichens, for all along the forest margins the caribou
of the taiga were drifting out of their snow-choked ranges
into the land of little sticks.

The seven caribou that had come from the highland between the Ninkik and the Mahkwa were driven to digging
in deeper and deeper snow. Now, when they ate, their
muzzles and forefeet were deep down in the feeding craters,
their hind feet high on the surrounding snow rims, white
rumps tilted upward at the sky. Their hoofs became cracked
and worn down, making the digging slower. The fat disappeared from their backs and rumps as each caribou body
in its search for the raw materials of energy turned inward
to feed upon itself. And when the fat layers were gone and
the bodies gaunt, starvation began.

They began searching and feeding even at night, and
the instinctive alertness blunted, because the need for food
was now a coercive thing that filled the senses and left

room for little more. And another behavior pattern blunted. There had been a herd deference before, a sociality linking them, at times a pooling of strength and resources, but now, driven by the tyrannizing need for food, each animal lived for itself alone. When they found a lichen bed where the snow was not too deep, each one dug frantically, shouldering its neighbors, to get all it could while lichen remained. But with seven bellies to fill, no one caribou—not even the young buck or the antlered doe—obtained enough food to satisfy its needs before the lichen was gone and the herd had to move on. So they declined together, the weakness spreading through each, but with the old buck and two calves faring poorest in each feeding scramble. The difference, though, was not enough to weigh significantly the tilting balance of survival, and the entire herd was slipping inexorably down a communal way that could only end in starvation for all. Where seven now were starving, a smaller herd might survive.

The herding, which in a normal winter had protective value and social purpose, had now become a threat to survival. But there was no instinctive prompting to tell them to separate and make more effective use of the land's restricted food supply. There was no such prompting, because the ecological interweaving of lifeways in the subarctic has a more efficient method of food rationing.

It was a night with a thin overcast that was letting some moonlight through, and the caribou were bedded down on an exposed bogland. Hunger and fatigue had dulled some of their innate caution, and they had dropped down to rest only a hundred yards or so from the screen of trees in which they had just found a meager feeding of lichen.

The antlered doe was the first to pick up the musky scent of wolf. At the first faint whiff she came to her feet and turned upwind toward the trees, her nostrils wide, ears inclined and funneled. Suddenly one hind leg reached out sideways and stiffened awkwardly in the alarm stance, and when the others saw it, three leaped to their feet and turned to stare searchingly in the direction the doe was looking. The remaining three—the old buck and the two calves—raised their heads and stared, too, but remained lying in the snow.

A wolf appeared along the edge of spruces, barely visible against the dark backdrop of the trees. Three more appeared a few seconds later. They moved past the trees, out into the open where their silhouettes sharpened against the background of snow, but the silhouettes remained side-view, and the caribou watched, tense but not alarmed. In the old one and the calves, the enervating fatigue was still a stronger motivation than the menace of the wolves; their hind legs were drawn in tightly beneath them, ready to spring, but they were still lying on the snow.

The four wolves circled, moving at a slow trot, continuing to show unaltered, lateral silhouettes. The caribou turned with them, following the wolves with extended muzzles, eyes peering in the dim light, nostrils snuffing harder and faster as the wolves moved out of the upwind quarter and their scent weakened and disappeared.

They had made about a quarter circle when the silhouettes abruptly foreshortened, constricting into ovals of shadow that now began to bob up and down against the snow as they broke into a leisurely lope. It was still not an attack, just the routine feeling out, the testing that they had practiced on the caribou many times before that winter without turning it into a determined chase.

This was the point in the ritual when the flight response was suddenly unlocked in the watching caribou. Hind hoofs digging for traction, they executed a half turn in mid-air and mid-stride, and were instantly away at a full gallop. The ones on the snow were also immediately up and in full stride, the rising and getting away losing them only one bound on the caribou that had been already standing. But it was enough to leave them a good two lengths behind.

Always, in the past, this was the point at which the wolves would nonchalantly turn away to seek easier prey. But this time the easy loping strides suddenly quickened and lengthened, and the wolves were skimming across the wind-packed snow in full chase.

The way of the wolf is hard, for he is not the facile and effortless killer that folklore makes him out to be. He has little chance of overtaking and bringing down a healthy caribou; he doesn't try. His hunting technique is to test, to probe, checking each herd for the limp or the hesitant breakaway of an old, sick, or crippled one. And he doesn't launch the pursuit until some such label of weakness in the prey springs to full vent his hunting drive.

It had happened that night with the herd of seven caribou. The wolves knew this herd; they had approached it many times before, but the caribou had always broken away with a fleetness which the wolves knew they could not match. But this time there had been a subtle change in the caribou flight. Despite the feeble light, the pack leader had detected that at least three of them had shown a momentary hesitation, and in one, a buck with the reduced antlers of old age, there had been a trace of dragging stiffness in the hind legs as he bolted away. It was infinitesimal, but enough, and the keenly honed hunting instinct of the wolves was instantaneously cut free.

After a few galloping bounds to gain full momentum, the caribou swung into the rolling trot that normally no wolves could equal. But the calves and the old one, who had lost a second or two in the breakaway, were now dropping farther behind. Instead of presenting a tightly bunched group, the herd was stringing out, and the old buck was the hindmost. And this, an obvious straggler, provided the final stimulus the wolves needed to unleash the maximum effort their gaunt bodies could muster.

The wolves were driving themselves at a pace they couldn't maintain for more than a minute or so. They ran silently, as there was neither breath nor energy for needless howling. They closed the gap rapidly and were soon near enough that the unprotected skin of their muzzles was stinging from the snow kicked up by the old buck's heels. The pack leader was larger and faster than the others, and slowly he pulled ahead. With a final lunge of speed, he caught one of the old buck's flashing legs a few inches above the hock and brought the caribou down in a sudden flurry of exploding snow and flailing hoofs.

This closing-in at top speed with an animal four times its weight has almost as much danger for the attacker as for the attacked. The wolf lost the leg hold in the caribou's fall and went somersaulting past, taking a pummeling first from the buck's hoofs and then from the cutting crust on the snow beyond. In that instant he picked up bruises that would be weeks in healing. But without hesitating he rolled to his feet and was back while the caribou still struggled to rise. He hurled himself in; the jaws missed the tossing neck but struck a shoulder instead, which sent the buck toppling again onto his side in the snow. The wolf lunged once more, dodging the raking hoofs and antlers. And now the teeth sank deep into the old buck's throat, the thrashing legs stiffened, and the warm blood was already sending up a cloud of steam from the snow when the other wolves arrived.

The remaining caribou disappeared in the night. The wolves fed avidly, tearing at the still-warm carcass, for it had been two weeks since they made their last kill. By dawn their bellies were gorged, and they moved into the nearest trees to sleep.

The next day three ravens came to feed hungrily on what the wolves had left. For two more nights the wolves returned, feeding ravenously again, until only the largest bones and torn strips of hide remained on the blooded snow.

The wolves didn't forget that there had been other caribou in the herd who had also shown that slight hesitation in the escape response to the wolves' testing. They sought the herd now with methodical single-mindedness, circling to pick up a fresh trail, checking each lichen woodland for recent caribou scents. Six nights after the first kill they found where the caribou had fed only hours before, and they set out on the new trail, noses skimming the hoof-pocked snow.

A few hours later they killed one of the calves.

Three more nights passed. They picked up the caribou trail again. That night they killed the second calf.

↑ ↑ ↑ ↑

Now that there were only four caribou left, the feeding improved. The drifts kept reaching downwind, covering more of the lichen, but enough remained under thinner snow to keep four alive where seven would have starved. The hunger persisted, but it was no longer the irreversible starvation that could kill. Now some measure of litheness and vigor came back to their limbs. The wolves returned from time to time, but the bolting getaway of the caribou was fleet and sure, and finally the wolves didn't chase again.

The same grim sacrifice was being enacted throughout the land of little sticks that winter. Wolf packs were moving from herd to herd, culling the old, the weak, the sick, the young—the expendable ones; for the old and sick no longer had anything to contribute to population survival; and in the case of the young, the biological investment was still small and quickly replaceable. Only the strong and prime would make an immediate contribution to the species' revival when the winter famine ended, and it was to these that the wolf-culling was apportioning the available food.

⁊ ⁊ ⁊ ⁊

It is a cruel land, for the biological codes that mold its lives are harshly practical ones with no leaven of sympathy in their application. They are codes that have evolved to perpetuate the group, the herd, the flock. The individual is nothing; only the broad and impersonal population units have purpose and meaning. Population survival, not individual survival, is the aim, the determinant, the all.

⁊ ⁊ ⁊ ⁊

The days lengthened and the sun arc swung higher in the southern sky. But even by late March, winter was not releasing its grip on the land of little sticks. On days when the sun was bright in an empty sky, temperatures still climbed only slightly above zero, and during the nights receded far below. Less snow fell now but the gales still blew, and the snowdrifts formed and re-formed in ever-changing patterns.

All three of the caribou does were pregnant, and their udders were swelling and bodies rounding with the fetal growths within them. The young buck was entering another phase of his annual cycle and the pedicels on the skull which anchored the great rack of antlers were hardening, loosening their hold, preparing to shed the antlers, so the buck could begin growing a new rack for the next autumn's breeding time. During one of the feedings a curving prong hooked a tree limb and one antler broke off, leaving only the red, scabbed knob of its pedicel behind. For two days he carried the other antler, the grand head now a grotesque, lopsided deformity, and then it dropped free. Now, except for his greater size and thicker mane, he looked no different from the two antlerless does.

The three does chewed compulsively on the buck's shed antlers, not knowing that the antlers were rich storehouses of phosphorus and calcium which their growing fetuses needed, knowing only a craving for the tart mineral taste that lured them back repeatedly until the antlers were gnawed to their hardest central cores.

In the antlered doe the shedding cycle was later than that of the buck. The fetus within her was demanding all the calcium her body could acquire, leaving none for hardening the antler bases. She would continue to carry her antlers until after the calf was born.

She was younger and more robust than the other females, with the rapid and vigorous metabolism of adulthood's prime. The same high level of biochemical functioning that had given her the antlers was now hastening the fetus development, bringing her more rapidly to the calving time.

It was her first breeding, so there was no memory to explain the faint stirrings she now began to feel within her. They were weak and uncertain at first, but as the days passed they strengthened and became more frequent, filling her with a vague and fretting anxiety, a sense of looming urgency, though not a fear. She knew only that it was a time of vital purpose; her senses could comprehend no more.

Gradually the anxiety assumed a different form. The impulse that had driven her to seek others of her kind and to join a herd during the autumn before now waned. She began feeling an irritable intolerance for the other caribou. Sometimes now, when feeding crowded them close together, she would lunge in a peevish outburst of hostility at whichever one happened to be nearest. And finally the intolerance became a demand—a restless, driving desire to be alone.

She left them as casually as she had come, six months before. It was midday, and they had spent the morning stripping a lichen bed. As they started across a swath of snowy bog toward the next cluster of dwarfed woodland a mile away, she simply turned and headed for a cluster of trees that lay another way.

≪≪≪≪≪≪ **Chapter 13** ≪≪≪≪≪≪

JACOB ATOOK'S GAZE lifted slowly from the rifle-butt hole in the lee of the toboggan where the new snow hadn't reached. He scanned the forest around him, feeling a quiver of fear, wondering if hidden eyes were watching. Then he caught himself and immediately resumed preparations for the day's journey, because there were always advantages in a hunted one's not letting on that he knew he was being hunted.

He turned the toboggan over and began lashing the pack-sack and balsam-filled tick to it. As his hands worked, his mind was working, too.

Taka had traveled late into the night to reach the cabin. This meant it had probably been a long trip, because one was always impatient after a long journey and wanted it ended. And probably he was alone, because if children or his parents were with him, they would have camped; only a young hunter could snowshoe all day, and then late into the night, too. Furthermore, if anyone else had been with him, there would have been voices, and Jacob would have awakened and heard.

Taka had seen Jacob's snowshoes and toboggan at the cabin door, and would have known that someone was inside, but he wouldn't have known who. He might have suspected that it was Jacob, and perhaps think that Niska was also there. So he had looked in briefly, stealthily, and confirmed in the faint light of the stove that it was Jacob, alone.

But why had he left without confronting Jacob? Taka was armed; Jacob was asleep. Was it all imagination? The vision at the door? The butt print, too? But the mark of the rifle stock in the snow was real, unmistakable.

Jacob studied it once more. Then he put a moccasin track directly over it, so that if Taka came back he wouldn't see the butt print and suspect that Jacob had seen it, too.

He put on the snowshoes, slung his own rifle onto his back, took up the toboggan rope, and headed toward the lake. There were no other tracks in the new snow, no sign of the way that Taka had gone. Jacob turned northward down the lake's center, feeling eyes on his back like the sting of mosquitoes in the spring. The urge to turn and search the shoreline behind was a nagging, almost overpowering demand, but he walked on steadily, not once looking back, so that Taka, if he watched or followed, wouldn't guess that Jacob knew.

Two hours later the shores constricted to a river, and Jacob went on, following it, because there was only the one notch in the hills; this had to be the way. The snow softened here, for there was not the wind of the open lake to pack and crust it. His snowshoes and toboggan sank into it, making the hauling harder.

He watched for signs of old tracks that would tell whether *atihk* or the Cheechoos had come this way, looking far ahead where the long angle of vision might still show the shallow depressions of a filled-in trail. But the snow had nothing to tell.

The river was straight, as though it knew where it wanted to go. It was a fast river, dropping rapidly, because there were hummocky mounds in its mantle of snow that indicated rapids beneath, and there were frequent small falls encased in ice which forced Jacob ashore to get around them.

The torment stayed in his mind. He kept wondering where Taka had come from, where the other Cheechoos were. Ahead in the little sticks?

Near midday he came to a spot where the river swept down through a narrow gorge with steep rock walls on each side. Here a large spruce had fallen, barring the way so thoroughly he would have to chop an opening through it to get the toboggan past. Snow was drifted deeply around the lower branches. He brushed last night's new snow from the horizontal trunk and found an old layer, thick and crusted, underneath. He estimated that it had been at least a month since the spruce had fallen.

The tree's upper branches which now lay prone on the snow were heavily festooned with gray, beard-like tassels of tree lichens. They usually grew on conifer branches high in the air, so they were not a normal *atihk* food, but whenever a tree fell, bringing them down where *atihk* could reach them, they were eaten hungrily. There were no broken twigs, no lichen-stripped branches, no indications of *atihk* browsing. *Atihk* would have passed here on their way to the land of little sticks, for they would follow the river routes, too, and they would not have left this lichen uneaten, had it been here when they went past.

The tree's other message was obvious: there were no ax cuts through it.

Jacob chopped out several branches and pushed the toboggan underneath. Then he went on, no longer looking for signs of a Cheechoo or *atihk* trail on the river before him.

If Taka had not come this way, the Cheechoos were not on an *atihk* hunt out in the little sticks ahead of him. There was no hunting anywhere else, so they must have gone back to Wapanishee post. Taka would have made the trip with them, because there were several children and no other man, and his father would have needed his help hauling a toboggan on the long ten- or fifteen-day snowshoe trek.

Then why would Taka come back to the cabin on the Mahkwa alone? To go to the little sticks? To prove he could bag an *atihk* even in a winter when hunting famine was sending the others back to the white man's post? But Taka's reputation as a hunter was well established; he didn't have to enhance it with foolhardy dramatics of that kind.

The shadows were long from the west, and his mind was still pondering when he stopped and dug his snow hole and raised the tarp on the dugout's upwind side to make the lean-to camp. He cut balsam boughs for his bed while *oseepan* boiled on the fire. He trimmed a willow stick with his knife and cut three notches through the green bark to the white wood beneath—one for each day he had been on the trail. And he remembered the fallen spruce tree, and he left the calendar stick long with room for many more notches, because if no *atihk* had passed this way for many weeks, as the spruce tree told, they now were far away.

The *oseepan* was easier to eat than the gritty rock tripe, but when he had eaten, the feeling of fullness that lay in his stomach was not a comforting fullness; the hunger was still there. He lay on the balsam boughs, fully clothed except for the snowy trousers and moccasins, and he drew the bedding around him, but the light of dusk was still in the sky and he waited, holding his eyes open, because he didn't yet want to sleep. He watched each breath smoke white in the frigid air above his face, until the sky out the open front of the lean-to had darkened and the stars began pricking through. He had wondered often, in the times before Father Webber came, what held the stars up there, but now he knew that it must be the *Manito* doing it. Therefore on clear nights like this when the stars came close, the *Manito* must be closer, too. It was hard in the bright, harsh light of day to feel the presence of the *Manito* up there in a vivid and distant sky, but it was easy when the night sky brought the stars and the *Manito* down until they almost touched the trees. So now was the time he awaited. And Jacob Atook closed his eyes and pressed his palms together under the *atihk* robe and prayed.

"*Manito,* it's good weather for the hunt because the wind is strong. Keep the wind blowing, *Manito.* And lead me quickly to the land of little sticks where the *atihk* are."

He spoke it aloud. Then a stronger gust of wind whined in the spruce trees on the valley rim above, muffling his voice, and now Jacob shouted, because he wanted the *Manito* to be sure to hear.

"Take me to the *atihk* quickly, *Manito,* because Niska and the *keekishkawasso* can't wait for a long hunt. The lichen and *oseepan* only fill the belly without feeding the body, and the fish you sent won't feed Niska long. Take me to the *atihk* that left the form in the snow that your spirit helper showed me. Do it quickly, *Manito,* for there isn't much time. . . ."

Suddenly he stopped, threw off the bedding, and sat up so quickly that the dizziness made his head whirl. He reached for the packsack and snatched out the calendar stick he had cut to keep track of the hunt's days.

"*Manito,* it was wrong! The tree on the river . . . it didn't speak the truth. The *atihk* won't be far away!"

And he cut the stick short with a swift slice of the knife, because now he was sure he would not be putting many notches there.

One other prayer remained to be made before he could let himself sleep.

"*Manito,* I thank you for the snow last night that covered my trail before Taka could follow it back to the Little Ninkik. And now you will bring another snow, to hide my trail again."

For Jacob knew now why Taka had come. Taka was still looking for Niska. He had guessed that Jacob and Niska would travel far to find a winter hiding spot; he had known that these outer fringes of the *Atihk-anishini* lands would be the place to search for them.

Probably Taka had considered an open confrontation last night in which he would demand to know where Niska was, but its obvious risks would have quickly ruled it out. He would know that Jacob would hold out stubbornly, refusing to tell, confident that Taka couldn't carry out the ultimate threat and kill him, because to kill Jacob before he learned where Niska was would be killing Niska, too. And there was a better way.

The new snow that was covering Jacob's trail back to Niska was hiding Taka's trail, too. By morning there should have been no sign that Taka had been there. So all he had to do was stay on Jacob's trail, and Jacob, unknowing, would sooner or later lead him to Niska.

But Jacob did know.

"You will bring another snow soon, *Manito*, before I find an *atihk* trail, so that Taka will lose me but I won't lose the *atihk*. This I pray, *Manito*. This is the prayer of Jacob Atook."

⸗ ⸗ ⸗ ⸗

The next day the hills flattened and disappeared. The river's straight course became one with many loops and bends, which Jacob knew to be a sign of flat country with sluggish drainage. The valley was deep, and from the river ice he could see nothing of the surrounding country. But what he could see of the valley slopes was no different from the forest land he had always known—the trees were large, the forest dense. It was not yet the land of little sticks.

The twisting of the river accentuated. It kept looping back upon itself, taking him east, west, and even south more frequently than in the direction he had to go. Finally, when one of the great bends turned him southward again, Jacob stopped and gazed ahead along the river route that stretched back southward now as far as he could see.

"River, you play tricks! You lead me away from the land of little sticks and the *atihk* that are there. I am going to leave you, stupid one, because you are lost and no longer know the way."

He turned back and faced the north. The bank was steep and drifted with a deep overhang of snow, and he had to dig his moccasins through the toe holes in the snowshoes to anchor himself while he yanked the toboggan up behind him. He entered the forest, and the valley slope was steep, too, and the climb was hard. Near the top the wind rose to a keening moan, and he could see a ground drift of wind-borne snow cascading over the valley rim. The snow had piled up here with a vertical, cliff-like front that was twice Jacob's height, and he stopped and stared at it with the fear building in him, because he had never seen so much snow before. He made his way along its base, and it was some time before he came to a small tributary valley cutting down from above that reduced the snow wall and opened a route to the level ground on top. He struggled over the valley rim, and then the wind struck him and the snow needles stung his face, for suddenly the trees were sparse and stunted, and a few toboggan lengths farther on they petered out. The land beyond was a flat, bald land with no forest to tame the wind.

Jacob knew at once he had reached the land of little sticks and, furthermore, that he had been traveling through it perhaps most of that day. Down in the river valley, where there was protection from the wind, and slopes to drain the soil, the forest was dense and heavy, with nothing to suggest that the land of little sticks began just over the valley's top where he couldn't see.

He hunched forward into the wind and moved out to the edge of the trees. But they were not trees here, only scraggly bushes, many of them leaning as though too weak to stand upright, and all of them so low that Jacob, raised as he was by the snow, could almost reach their tops. Now a bewildering vista opened before him. Suddenly the land had acquired a new dimension of distance that forest country never had. It reached out before him, as flat as the ice of a great lake that had no end, and the immensity of it filled him with fear because surely in a land so strange there would be strange spirits he had never known before.

It was a white land, hazy with blowing snow. From the twigs and brown fuzzy leaves of the tea bush piercing the snow near him, he knew it was bogland underneath, because the tea bush grew only on the miry edges of bogs. But it wasn't solid bog, because now, through the snow haze, he could make out dark, widely separated ribbons and ragged patches of stunted trees twisting across it. Jacob stared, his eyes blinking against the driving snow, his body taut and trembling. He was accustomed to bogs and clearings, but they had always been islands in a sea of forest before; here the shreds of shrunken forest were the islands in a sea of endless bog.

Yet despite its strangeness, the feeling came that he had been here before. And then he remembered: this was the land to which the spirit *atihk* had brought him.

The day was late. The pale, yellow-gray smear of sun behind the overcast was near the horizon. So he turned and retraced his route back down into the valley forest to make his camp where the wind didn't blow. And the fear left him, for this was forest again, the environment he knew. He ate *oseepan*, his only meal since morning; then as dusk darkened the forest he walked down to the river edge and looked back the way he had come, searching for the yellow fleck of another fire.

Even without the bend of the river, which gave him only a limited view of the back trail, he knew no fire would be there. No matter how confident Taka was that he had been undiscovered, he would never take such an obvious risk as that.

Slowly and wearily Jacob trudged back to the lean-to, his mind sifting, still trying to fit new pieces into the analysis it was making. Taka would know that only a desperate crisis would force Jacob to go to the Cheechoo cabin—that Jacob and probably Niska, too, were starving. And Taka obviously was not. The lack of a food cache at the cabin indicated that Taka had no intention of picking up supplies there. If he had been back to the post with his family, he would be hauling food with him now, probably enough for the rest of the winter, as he wouldn't return to the Mahkwa country expecting to live off the land. And the fact that he had traveled late into the night to reach the cabin proved that he was still well fed and strong.

Jacob crawled into the lean-to bed. Darkness fell, bringing the *Manito* nearer, and Jacob thanked him for guiding him quickly to the land of little sticks when the river became an evil one and tried to lead him away.

Then he remembered the calendar stick, and took it from the pack, and cut another notch in it. He counted. Four. The white grooves taunted cruelly, wrenching a shudder through him. This was the day that Niska would be expecting Nellie. Would she guess that something was wrong, and begin rationing what was left of her food?

"Tell her, *Manito*. Tell her."

≪≪≪≪≪≪ Chapter 14 ≪≪≪≪≪≪

AS HE STARTED OUT onto the land of little sticks the next morning and the forest suddenly dropped away from around him, he felt like a naked and helpless one taken too soon from the mother.

It was the way of his people to personify everything, and he had always known the forest as a female one—mother, creator, nourisher—but with the variant mood of the seductress who yields all her favors one time and jealously guards them another. That winter, the forest mother had yielded little, the seductress had become a teaser and torturer, yet Jacob left her now with a clutching in the heart that was like the hunger squeeze in the belly. And as he went he talked; he talked to stem the fear that was mounting in him as the embracing forest, the cradle of his race, fell behind; and he talked so that any new and unknown spirit ones would understand that he hadn't come to stay, because this was not *Atihk-anishini* land, and the feeling was strong in him that he had come to a place where he shouldn't be.

"I am Jacob Atook. I am *Atihk-anishini*. I come to the

land of little sticks because Niska and the *keekishkawasso*
need *atihk* meat and the *atihk* are here." He paused as a
sullen moodiness assailed him, and he lowered his voice,
because he wanted to explain but he didn't want the *Manito*
to hear. "I come because the *Manito* forgot to send the
atihk back again, and he didn't hear the praying, not even
Niska's praying, and Niska prays better than I do. But I
will return tomorrow, Mother One, because the *Manito* is
helping now. He sent a spirit *atihk* to help me. The hunt
will be short."

The hard, dry snow supported his snowshoes so that
they left only a shallow trail, and the toboggan skimmed
across it. But the wind that hardened the snow and made
the travel easy had another price, for the bitter cold of it
slashed his cheeks like a thornbush, pressed the clothing
tightly to his body, and drove its chill even through the
atihk-skin parka. Jacob pulled the drawstrings of the parka
hood around his face until only a small oval of eyes, nose,
and mouth was exposed, but the wind was still a stinging
pain on the skin that remained uncovered. He raised the
mittened hand not needed for the toboggan drawrope, covering his mouth with it, raising the thumb so that it extended
up between his eyes, because there, where the sharp line
of the nose bridge cut the wind, was the coldest spot of all.

But he wanted the wind, and maybe the *Manito* didn't
know why. So he removed the hand from his mouth, and
he shouted to make his voice carry above the wind's wail.

"You will keep the wind blowing, *Manito*. A hunter needs
a wind that will blow his scent behind him, and howl in the
trees with much noise so the hunted one can't hear the
hunter coming."

The wind kept a fine spume of snow racing like smoke across its surface, but it stayed low, little of it reached eye level, and the visibility above it was good. Jacob was crossing a broad open stretch toward a black line of trees a mile or so away. As he came nearer he studied them curiously, eyes squinting in the wind. The trees were small and spaced out. Many of them were bare-branched, for they were tamaracks—the needled one of the bogs that dropped its needles every fall as the leafed ones dropped their leaves. But most were spruces—black spruce, the bog-growing one, not white spruce, the forest kind—and they grew in dense clumps, so there was still cover here where an *atihk* could be hidden.

Jacob unslung the rifle and held it ready before him. He approached slowly, cautiously, scrutinizing the snow ahead for the shadowed depressions of *atihk* tracks, and for the melted form in the snow that the spirit *atihk* had shown him, because he realized now that he had seen these trees before —yes, this was the spot to which the stone-eyed one had brought him on the dream journey from the Cheechoo cabin.

Despite the leveling mantle of snow, he could see that the trees grew on a ridge slightly elevated above the surrounding bog. He entered its wind shadow where the wind abruptly slackened and the snow softened. With no wind buffeting his eyes, he could see more clearly now, and he stopped and searched, but the snow ahead was smooth. He moved forward again, putting his weight down carefully at each stride to reduce the crunch of snow beneath the snowshoes. He entered the trees, and they were just high enough to hide him, slightly too tall for him to see over their tops. But before they swallowed him, screening his back trail from view, he looked back, and it wasn't for Taka—it was a quick, paining glance at the black line of forest that still showed above the valley rim far behind. Then he turned and went on with the cold squeeze in his heart again, the heart hunger for familiar things.

The snow was thinner here along the downwind edge of the spruce island, but it deepened sharply and was carved like sand dunes as he approached the northern side. In less than a minute he had passed through and was out in the wind lash again. He turned back and made a full circuit of the island, a bewilderment gnawing him. For there was no melted *atihk* form in the snow. And there were no feeding craters, no *atihk* signs of any kind. He was mistaken—this wasn't the place to which the spirit *atihk* had taken him.

He slung the rifle onto his back again, leaned into the wind, and went on toward the next black thicket of trees.

They grew in ragged patches with tentacles reaching out like spiders' legs into the surrounding bog; they grew in round islands with open centers, and they grew in snaking ribbons that occasionally meandered on for miles. And always the trees were small, gnarled, bent before the wind, with a shaggy look of age upon them. Where the islands were separated by only a few hundred yards, the wind stayed puny like a forest wind; but where the next patch of trees was a hazy smudge a mile or two away, the wind would be a raging, squalling blast that tore the breath away and put a numbing frostbite on the bridge of Jacob's nose if he removed his hand for more than a few snowshoe strides.

↟ ↟ ↟ ↟

All that day Jacob moved from one island to the next, his eyes constantly scanning, searching, as a hunter's eyes must—and not just ahead, but to the trail behind, too, for he was both hunter and hunted now. But no figure appeared behind, and no sign of *atihk* broke the snow ahead—not even in the wind shadows where there was little snow movement and some evidence of tracks would remain for a long time.

Late in the afternoon he dug a snow hole in the lee of one of the islands and raised the lean-to. Now the longing for the forest, for the Mother One, became acute, for now he could see with a new and vivid sharpness that this land of little sticks was not a place for an *Atihk-anishini* to be. None of the helping ones a hunter needed grew here. There were only the useless ones—tamarack, and the hard and brittle bog spruce. There was no balsam fir with the springy boughs that would make a soft bed and insulate a sleeping hunter from the frigid ground beneath him, and no poplar or birch to yield the bark *oseepan* for a hungry belly. Nor were there rocks on which the other starvation food, the rock-tripe lichen, could grow. He could have brought a supply of *oseepan* with him from the river valley forest, but he hadn't known that it would not be growing here. And it was too late to go back for it, because Taka Cheechoo might be there, and anyway, the *atihk* would come tomorrow; he would not be staying long.

He had to use spruce boughs for his bed. He cut firewood, but the only dead wood above the snow were a few brittle white snags, twisted like rope, the largest no thicker than his arm, and the spruce island was crisscrossed with snowshoe tracks before he had found enough wood to last the night.

The work tired him, because there was a sapping weakness in his body, and now the dizziness never totally left his head, but the pain of hunger was gone. Pausing frequently to rest, he dug with a snowshoe along the edge of trees where the tea bush grew, and he stripped the small dried leaves and boiled them into a brown tea. The warmth of it was pleasant, but for only a brief time, because it woke the stomach from its slumber and brought back the hunger pain.

He cut the largest green tree he could find, chopped the slender trunk into arm-length pieces, and stood them up to form a reflector behind the fire that would throw heat under the lean-to. He melted more snow in the blackened aluminum pot, changed his socks, and soaked the ones he had been wearing in warm water. Then he hung them over the ridgepole of the lean-to until they were frozen, and beat the ice out of them with a stick, which left them almost dry. They would finish drying in the bed with him overnight. The balsam twigs that filled the flour-bag tick had packed and bunched up, and he shook it to loosen the filling, making it softer and increasing its insulation against the cold.

One task remained. Two of the white man's products had become such vital essentials of survival that even the *Atihkanishini* could no longer exist without them, and Jacob now gave them the close inspection that had long ago become a nightly routine.

The matches first. He looked in the packsack to make sure that the baking powder tin in which he carried them was there, and not mislaid somewhere in the snow. He removed the lid and checked to see that no snow had got in to melt near the fire and dampen them. Then he carefully replaced the wadding of sphagnum moss which kept the matches from jiggling and breaking, and made sure that the lid was put back tightly again.

Next he inspected his rifle. It was a 1917 British Army Lee-Enfield .303 that he had inherited from his father. The foreshortened stock was dented and scratched, worn shiny at the handgrip and cheek piece, and flecks of rust stippled the barrel. Its original ten-round magazine, which had once projected beneath the stock, had been replaced by a five-cartridge clip that fitted flush for easier underarm carrying.

He slid out the clip, raised the bolt handle, snapped up its headlock, and withdrew the bolt so that he could sight down the barrel and see that it was not clogged with snow. He checked the bolt carefully, then the chamber and magazine, to ensure there were no twigs or needles snagged in any of the action. Then he returned the bolt, worked it and the safety catch and trigger several times to free the oil on them, and reinserted the loaded clip. He stood the rifle in the snow while he spread the bedding. When the bed was laid, he placed the gun carefully under the flour-bag tick where it would be near him and get some body heat to prevent the oil from congealing in the bitter nighttime cold.

He lay down. The spruce needles of his mattress were stiff and sharp, not soft like the balsam, and they pierced the worn rabbitskin robe beneath him. The brittle boughs soon broke and packed down, letting the cold of the ground seep through.

There was no sunset that night, and no stars. The sky remained a black, faraway emptiness, so Jacob prayed to the spirit *atihk* first, while he waited to see if the *Manito* in his heaven would drop down any nearer.

"*Atihk* One, this is Jacob Atook, the hunter you took on the dream journey from the Cheechoo cabin. I've come to the place you showed me, but I haven't yet found the melted form in the snow where the *atihk* lay. You'll take me there tomorrow. And you'll not warn the *atihk* that I'm hunting for it."

He spoke softly, not raising his voice, because the spirit *atihk* would be near among the spruces, not far away where the *Manito* was. And now he waited to see if the stars would appear and bring the heaven nearer. The cold penetrated. He had never felt night coldness like this before, yet there had been colder nights, many, and he knew it was the thinness of the bough mattress and the lack of even *oseepan* in his belly to feed the body fire that were bringing the cold into the bed with him tonight. He built up the fire frequently, because the wood was small and it burned quickly. But still he shivered with the cold.

And still no stars appeared. He would shout the prayer loudly and maybe the *Manito* would hear.

"*Manito*, this is Jacob Atook. . . ." He was shivering so much it was hard to keep his palms together under the *atihk* skin. He made it a long prayer. He asked for warmth to fill his body so that he could sleep. He asked for strength to take him tomorrow to where the *atihk* was. He asked for snow that would fall behind him and hide his trail from Taka, because the blowing snow was only dimming his tracks without obliterating them, but he asked that there be no snow ahead to fill the melted *atihk* form before he found it. He asked the *Manito* to care for Niska and the *keekishka-*

wasso. He prayed so long that his voice grew hoarse with the shouting. And he ended it: *"Manito,* a hunter needs a son to hunt for him when the old age comes."

As these last words went out into the darkness, they startled him, for he had never thought of his growing old before. From the exalted eminence of youth's vigor and narcissism, the view of life ahead had always seemed a path that reached unchanging as far as he could see, but now the weakness in him was like a foretaste of the enfeeblement of age, and suddenly he glimpsed another Jacob Atook there, stooped and withered, a hunter no more.

"Manito, this one kicks in Niska's belly; it will be a son." Then the voice dropped to a suppliant plea: "And *Manito,* there must be a son of the seed of Jacob Atook so Taka and Joe Nimawassa and all our people will have to accept the marriage that Father Webber made."

Through it all, the wind had been a moaning lament in the stunted spruces a few feet over his head, and Jacob wondered if the *Manito* had heard. Now, in addition to the cold, there was the ache of missing Niska, the longing for the sweet enchantment of her body, for the ecstasy of the *keekishkawasso* place that even the long hunger had not dulled. After a while a warmth did begin to permeate him, so maybe the *Manito* had heard. It was not a snug and ample warmth that a mattress of balsam boughs and many *atihk* skins and Niska's body tight against him would give. But it was enough, and Jacob Atook slept.

Chapter 15

HE FOUND THE SIGNS NEXT DAY. They were only shallow heavings in the snow, so indistinct he almost passed them by, and he was still uncertain when he stood looking directly down at them, for they could be just snow humped over bushes underneath. But he knelt and jerked off a mitten and began running his bare hand slowly back and forth, furrowing the snow surface. He plunged his hand in deep and brought up handfuls of snow, squeezing it in his palm and feeling its texture between his thumb and fingers.

Beneath the humps there was old, hard, disturbed snow, the hardness varying for there were crusty chunks scattered through it. The shallow depressions between were hard snow, too, but not quite as hard; the snow there had a finer, uniform texture as far down as he could reach, indicating that they had once been holes that had filled in later. He jerked off a snowshoe and dug down through the hip-deep snow to ground level. And then he was sure. For there—trampled, shredded, pulled up, and scattered—were the white wiry strands of caribou lichen. The *atihk* had been here. But long ago.

He went on, always northward, deeper into the land of little sticks, struggling into the fangs of the wind. And the snowshoes grew heavy, and his head grew light, for the brew of the tea-bush leaves was not a food, not even a bad food as the rock lichen was. The hunger was no longer a thing of the stomach, it was a torpor of flesh and spirit extending through him everywhere.

Atihk signs appeared several times that day, always in the form of shallow pockings on the snow's surface along the downwind edges of the spruce islands where the snow was thinnest. There were no hoof tracks, for hoofs left only small prints that soon filled with snow. But the big feeding craters and the mounds of snow around them left such hummocks that weeks of blowing snow could not completely hide them; faint hollows and undulations always remained to denote the old disturbances beneath.

Several times Jacob dug down into the snowed-in craters. Often the softer, newer snow of the craters ended before they penetrated all the way to the ground, and there would be a layer of older, granular, undisturbed snow still lying over ungrazed lichens beneath, indicating that the snow had been too deep or the lower layers too hard for the *atihk* to get through. Sometimes, where the digging had uncovered bushes, the twig ends were bitten off, and they were not the clean, sharp cuts of rabbit browsing, but frayed and ragged as *atihk* teeth leave. And from this Jacob knew the *atihk* were starving, even here in the little sticks, for only starving *atihk* will eat woody browse. It was a bad sign. It told that the *atihk* were constantly on the move and ranging far in their hunt for lichen; they would be hard for a hunter to find.

Fatigue spread in him, taking the substance from his muscles like maggots burrowing deeper and deeper in bad meat. The snow was hard and his snowshoes didn't sink more than a few inches in most places, but now even this was enough to clutch and hold them. Walking was no longer an automatic, involuntary act that came without thought. It had to be willed; he had to remember to lift the snowshoes each time to keep from tripping in the snow.

"Soon, *Manito,* soon, it must be soon now."

But it couldn't come soon, because all the sign was old, the *atihk* were far away.

It was afternoon when he heard the guttural croak of the *kahkaki.* It came above the puling of the wind; it came, muted and hesitant, through the woolen tuque and the muffling fur of the parka hood. He stopped and held a hand over his eyes to shield them against the wind, and first he searched the slate-gray sky, and the raven wasn't there, and then he searched the ground and found it, a gray speck far ahead, blurred and indistinct through the ground drift of blowing snow. It was the first living thing he had seen in many weeks, except the fish on the last day with Niska, and Taka Cheechoo at the cabin door.

He dropped the toboggan drawrope, unslung the rifle, worked the bolt to lift a cartridge into the chamber, and slipped the safety catch. A breathless trembling seized him as he moved forward toward the raven. *Kahkaki* was not normally a food flesh, but any flesh would be food now.

"*Manito,* you will hold the black one's wings so that it

can't fly until I'm near enough for my bullet to reach it. You'll do that, *Manito*. You will!"

There were no trees near for stalking cover. He could only move up slowly in the open, fully exposed. He left the toboggan behind him, so there would be less movement for the *kahkaki* to see against the snow. He bent far forward with the gun arm downward and the other held out horizontally before him, because in this way the arms resembled *atihk* antlers, and his silhouette would be similar to that of a feeding *atihk*. Sometimes it was possible to get near to *atihk* in this manner; maybe it could fool a *kahkaki,* too.

The ground-hugging snow spume cleared a little. The raven emerged sharply now, black, no longer gray. Its head was turned, watching him. He could make out the big bill and the shaggy feathers of the throat, but it was still beyond accurate range. Jacob got no nearer. The black wings lifted. The big bird rose effortlessly with slow and lazy wingbeats and croaked once more, a raucous, taunting laugh; then it turned and flew away close to the snow's surface until a spruce island hid it.

Jacob shouldered the gun as the wind whipped tears in damp trails back across his cheekbones. He returned to the toboggan. And suddenly the hunger pain was back, an agony again in his stomach, and he pulled his belly muscles tight to try to squeeze the pain out, but the pain stayed.

Suddenly he stiffened as a new thought came. *Kahkaki* was the arctic's carrion bird; did it have a reason for being down on the snow? He went forward eagerly, keeping his eyes fixed on the spot where the raven had been. And while still far back he saw the dark prong of the antler protruding above the snow. Abruptly a new strength was coursing through him. He ran. He came up to it breathlessly, the cold air searing his lungs from the running. Only a fragment of antler showed above the snow. He yanked it upward, it gave, and a portion of *atihk* skull came with it. There were shreds of frozen brain tissue still within the skull cavity. It was a wolf kill, or a starved one maybe, and it was very old, for the snow was smooth above it. He tried to dig with a snowshoe, but the snow was too hard, because it had been trampled by wolves that had been coming back throughout most of the winter to search for the remnants of flesh and bone that might remain.

Jacob loosened the snow with the ax. He lifted the chunks out, breaking them, powdering them with his bare hands so as not to miss any fragments of bone or carrion frozen within. He worked feverishly but carefully for half an hour, until he had sifted through all the snow of an area at least a dozen feet wide and deeper than his knees, and when he was finished, his fingers were bleeding from the sharp snow edges. He found three hoofs with gnawed shank bones and small tatters of meat still attached. There were frozen shreds of entrails, and then several ribs, and one of the ribs had a fist-sized chunk of meat on it. One thigh bone was almost intact, and he cut it with the ax and examined its marrow; it was brown with frozen blood, not white and fatty, which indicated the animal was starving when it died—or when wolves killed it because it was dying. He saved everything, even the little strips of hide, and a double handful of thumb-sized splinters of bone, piling it all carefully on the toboggan. When he reached the lowest level where the snow was saturated with frozen blood, he cut it out in chunks and saved that, too.

And he sucked his own blood from his abraded fingers, so that that, too, would not be lost.

When there was nothing more, he pulled the toboggan into the nearest trees, his mouth already tasting the broth and *atihk* meat. But after the first few ax blows to cut firewood, he stopped. The hunger was a pleading pain in his stomach, and he didn't want to wait, but he stared back to the open snow where the *atihk* bones had lain. He had left nothing there as a dwelling place for the dead one's spirit. It would be angry and warn the other *atihk* that Jacob Atook was hunting them. Slowly he made his way back to the toboggan and stared down at the bones, wondering what he could spare as a dwelling place for the spirit one.

The proper dwelling place, of course, was the remainder of the skull. He wouldn't miss it, for it was just a shell with no rich marrow. So he cut three of the largest trees he could find, trimmed the branches from them, tied their tips with some of the rope lashing from the toboggan, and suspended the skull piece there. He raised the tripod so that the skull swayed in the wind as high as he could put it. And it wasn't very high, because the trees were small, but it was high enough that wolves couldn't reach it, and ravens wouldn't perch on a skull that was swinging on a rope.

He stepped back, glad of what he had done, for now he knew he had not done it for the *atihk* spirit alone. In this strange land there would be other spirits he didn't know, and they would be pleased at this respect for them that Jacob was showing.

Now he raised his head and shouted to the sky: "*Man-ito,* it is necessary, this thing that I do!"

↗ ↗ ↗ ↗

He resumed cutting firewood. The dead snags were a little larger, the wood supply a little better, than in that first camp of the land of little sticks the night before. He melted chunks of blooded snow for cooking water, so that the good of the blood would be in the broth, and dropped in the hunk of rib meat and several bones, breaking them first with the ax so that the marrow could boil out. Then he added a couple of handfuls of green spruce needles, because he could use them now that there would be a meat broth to kill their bitter, resinous taste. The three hoofs and shanks and many of the smaller bones he saved for tomorrow.

When the shelter was raised and the spruce bed laid, Jacob hunched over the fire, inhaling the savory steam that was rising from the simmering pot. While he waited he took one of the hoofs and chewed on the shreds of frozen meat attached to it; the ice crystals in it crunched between his teeth, but even frozen, the rich meaty taste was there—a taste he had almost forgotten. When he could wait no longer, he scooped up a mugful of the hot broth, dipping shallowly so that he would get plenty of the beaded fat on its surface. It burned his throat as he swallowed it, but he couldn't pause, and he gulped another scalding mouthful. Then he forced himself to wait while the zero air quickly cooled the rest of it, before he drained the mug. He drank several more mugfuls with a relish that was close to delirium, then he ate the meat and sucked on the bones to get their marrow.

He was warm in bed that night. There was a placid contentment in his stomach, and already he could feel a strength returning to his body. The *Manito* seemed very near, for the stars were brilliant—so brilliant he could see the tripod and *atihk* skull etched against the sky, and he wondered with a twinge of guilt if the *Manito* was seeing it, too. But it was a small guilt that was quickly displaced by the sudden surge of a new and different remorse that came when he remembered the calendar stick and thought of Niska. There were not even *atihk* bones for Niska tonight—only *oseepan*, and rock tripe, and maybe the last small piece of fish. His feeling of contentment, the relishing of the first good meal in months, suddenly turned to shame, and the lingering meat taste in his mouth became a puckering bitterness.

"It was only carrion, Niska. Only an old wolf kill. It wasn't all that good."

He started the prayer, then stopped it abruptly. You could talk to the forest spirits lying in bed, but now he was remembering that the *Manito* demanded a special way of prayer. Throwing back the *atihk* skin and tick, he got to his knees and bowed his head, closing his eyes, pressing his hands together. And he didn't shout, because now he realized that a prayer was not a prayer unless you said it on your knees, and now he was sure that the *Manito* would listen and would hear despite the wind.

≪≪≪≪≪≪ Chapter 16 ≪≪≪≪≪≪

HE SAW THE DARK GASH of shadow on the snow as soon as he rose from the bed in the yellowing gray of dawn. It was out in the open bog, crosswind where his scent hadn't reached during the night, and he knew at once what it was. He strapped the snowshoes on, coolly and without haste, for he was not surprised. After the knee praying of the night before, he was sure the *Manito* would bring an *atihk* near before the morning. He would have been surprised if the fresh *atihk* sign had *not* been there.

He walked out to it. It was a semicircular, bowl-shaped hollow melted in the snow where an *atihk* had rested several hours during the night, unaware that Jacob's camp was near because it had come by after his fire had burned out. It was not a perfect outline showing head, legs, and tail as the one in the dream journey had been, but it *was* the form that the spirit *atihk* had shown him; it had this imperfect shape now because it was real, no longer in the dream journey where the spirit ones could change it.

Jacob studied it. There were a few round pellets of excreta. He removed a mitt and picked one up, rolling it between his thumb and fingers. It was hard and frozen. He pinched it, and it crushed easily, and now the excitement made his head whirl, because the freezing was only a thin shell on the surface, and the center of it was still moist. The cold of the air was intense, there had been no warming during the night, and these small pellets of excreta would freeze solid in minutes.

His head jerked up. He scanned the snow for the trail the *atihk* had left when it moved away. There was still not full daylight, and the hoofs had only shallowly marked the hard snow, but he could see the big round hoofprints leading off toward another spruce island less than half a mile away. Each hind print was almost on top of a front print, the strides were short, the dewclaw marks behind each track were at an angle to the direction of travel, not across it. So the *atihk* had walked away slowly. It had not trotted or galloped, showing alarm; it had gone without scenting Jacob, without knowing he was near. He squinted into the wind and scanned the low thicket of spruces to which the tracks led. Jacob knew it was there, only minutes away, because its belly would be empty after the night, and it would stop to dig for lichens at the first opportunity.

He ran back and grabbed up the rifle from its place in the bed where he had carefully laid it after the ritualistic check the night before. He had been out of the bed long enough now for the cold to begin to penetrate it, so he kept his mitts on to prevent the moist skin of his hands from freezing to the icy steel of the barrel. There was a separate trigger finger in the right-hand mitt, and he was calm, deliberate, as he worked the trigger and safety catch a few times to free the oil that might have thickened from the extreme cold of the night.

He went through his own spruce island to the side that faced the other island where the *atihk* was, and he kept himself concealed in the trees while he surveyed the territory ahead. The *atihk* wasn't in sight, but he knew where it would be, because he could make out a line of spruces taller and thicker than normal along the far side of the other island. On the near side, in the lee of those bigger trees, the snow would be thin and soft, and the *atihk* would be digging for lichens there. Off to his left, unnoticed before, he saw a slender finger of spruces that snaked across the open bog, joining his island with the other. And a taut smile sprang to his face, and there was a whispered "Thank you, *Manito*" on his lips as he moved along quickly toward the linking finger of spruces. It would give him stalking cover and make it possible for him to reach the *atihk* without exposing himself outside the trees.

Everything was working for him. The *atihk* was alone, and thus much easier to stalk, because when there was more than one there were always sentries watching while the others fed. At this time of early morning it would be preoccupied with the feeding, especially since, as Jacob now knew, the *atihk* even here in the little sticks were starving. It would have its head down in the feeding holes much of the time, where its vision would be blocked. And the wind was strong, its noise a raucous howl; he wouldn't even have to use care to approach quietly.

Yet still, Jacob felt a disconcerting apprehension. It was too perfect, too easy, and he had a hunter's distrust of hunting situations in which everything favored the hunter, because it wasn't the way a hunt should be. He didn't despise the *atihk* or feel that it was an inferior one, as Taka Chee-choo and all the good *Atihk-anishini* hunters would do. To Jacob the *atihk* was a brother and partner, who was striving, as he was, to get the stuff of survival from the forest Mother One who had turned against them all and put a hunger on the land. It was a noble one. Jacob could even feel a love for it, not the kind of love he felt for Niska, but still a love.

So the hunt should not be easy. There should be struggle. There was no time for reverence, no esteem for the hunted one, in an easy hunt. It cheapened. There was an unclean-ness in it, a dishonor.

"But I'm going to kill you, *atihk*. Because Niska waits, and there must be a son of the seed of Jacob Atook, and there's no time left for a long hunt."

He edged slowly along the linking finger of trees, reached the other island, and then made his way toward the bigger spruces where he knew the *atihk* would be. Everywhere else the trees were small, with broad openings between them. Wherever a tree gave him cover, he stopped to search the region ahead before stepping out into the open and ad-vancing quickly to the next clump of trees. The wind was on his left cheek, no scent would be traveling ahead of him.

He moved down to the edge of trees where the spruce and tamarack clumps grew more thickly along the bog margin. The wind died for a few moments, then gusted with a new vigor, shifting erratically, hitting him full in the face for several seconds before it moved back to his left cheek again.

"Keep the wind blowing, *Manito*. Don't change it now."

Far ahead he saw the tracks where the soft snow in the

island's wind shadow had let the *atihk* sink deeply for a few strides before it entered the trees.

He snapped off the safety catch on the gun and resumed the slow progress forward. The wind was gusting and dying at intervals. He stood still when it softened, and went on when its noise would cover the swish and crunch of his snowshoes on the snow.

Then he saw it, right where he expected to see it—in the wind shadow of the bigger spruces. He saw the white rump first, indistinct against the snow, and it was several seconds before the rest of it—the legs and the dark outline of the haunches—disentangled themselves from the branches and shadows, and it all emerged.

He raised the gun, his finger on the trigger. But he couldn't shoot yet, for only the oval of rump was showing, and there was no need for haste, because the wind was carrying his scent to the side and the *atihk* was not alarmed. Its rump was tilted high, the hind legs up on the snow, the head and most of the front quarters obscured in a feeding crater. And Jacob was well hidden; even if the *atihk* lifted its head and looked toward him, it would not see him in this gray light if he didn't move.

He waited, studying it down the gun barrel, hoping it would rise and turn, giving him a high lung shot, because that was best. The spot he wanted was halfway up the chest, just behind the shoulder, where the large veins and arteries were. A deflected bullet there might even sever the spinal cord. Death would be quick. And he wanted it that way. For a hunt should be long and hard, but the killing, when it came, should be fast and sure.

The head jerked up, and turned a little. Jacob's breath

hissed out of him. The gun barrel wavered. For he saw all of the head now, and it had large spreading antlers, like a buck's. But by this time of late winter the bucks would have shed their antlers, and the barren does without calf would have shed theirs; only a pregnant one with the *keekishkawasso* still in the belly could have the antlers now.

He thought of Niska and the other *keekishkawasso,* and a choking was in his throat and a scalding in his heart.

The *atihk* turned a little more; he saw the furrows of the ribs, the signs of starving, but under the leanness, under the bone ridges, there was a rounding and a fullness—like Niska, who was also starving with the stomach empty but the belly full.

His mind spoke without his mouth saying the words: "*Atihk,* does the little one kick in you, too? I don't want to kill you, *atihk,* but I must . . . I will."

He waited for it to turn farther, to give him the high lung shot, the rifle still poised, ready.

And then the *Manito* spoke.

It was strong without being loud, firm without being dictatorial. Jacob heard it clearly, despite the keening of the wind, because it was not outside him, not from the heaven, it came from within.

"Jacob, it's a mother one. You will let her go."

"No! Not this time. To let her go will be letting Niska and the *keekishkawasso* die! Why do you bring the *atihk* to me, and then tell me to let her go?"

The gun began to tremble. The wind died again for many seconds, then he heard the moan of it returning through the trees. But when it reached him, it wasn't a chill on his left cheek, it was a great slap on his back, pressing the parka to his shoulders. Suddenly a frantic fear filled him. There would be no time now to wait for the *atihk* to turn and give him the high lung shot. The *atihk*'s antlered head tossed upward, and she was instantly in full stride, bounding away. The small bobbing rump was a difficult target; his trembling now was violent, and the wind on his back was so strong it was hard to stand steady against it.

He fired. The shot went wild, too high. And the *atihk* was through the spruce screen and gone, with no time for a second shot.

He ran after her, but only a few paces, then his body sagged, a great sob was in his throat. The *atihk* would be far away on the hard snow of the bog beyond before he could reach the edge of the trees.

He started back toward the camp, the snowshoes suddenly leaden again.

Chapter 17

IT IS A BIG LAND, a land with long vistas, this land of the little sticks. It is a much bigger land than the forest lands that Jacob Atook knows, for there are no walls of forest here, crowding in, shrinking the land as forests do. And it is a place for big thoughts, a land where the mind can reach out as the eyes reach out, with no shackling of trees to press in and smother the mind and keep the thoughts small.

✓ ✓ ✓ ✓

The dawn was still only a yellow wash across the overcast eastern sky when Jacob returned to the camp, made the fire, and put on the stew pail with more of the blooded snow and bones.

He gazed at the flames and the little jets of steam that began pulsing from around the stew-pail lid. Periodically the smoke got in his eyes and he had to move from side to side to avoid it, because the wind was still playing tricks, dying at intervals, shifting its direction as it had done to send Jacob's scent to the *atihk*. Jacob trembled at what this erratic wind behavior could be portending.

His stomach growled like distant thunder, the hunger pains were coming back. The steam that hissed from the stew pail was not the fragrant steam that last night's was, for the richest meat and bones had been used then. And as he waited Jacob Atook's mind was reaching into a hazy region of thought where it had never delved before.

It was a blind groping, unwilled, undirected, but out of it a tangled structure of thought was shaping. Jacob was seeing it only faintly, and he knew he wasn't seeing it all. He could sense that it was like a tiny bush, with little showing above the surface for easy scrutiny, but with deep and spreading roots hidden below. He was fumbling gingerly around the thought fringes in tender exploration, for it was all frail and tenuous, as a small bush is, and he was afraid that if he attacked it vigorously and openly, it would break off, as the bush breaks if it is jerked too harshly. Then the deeper roots of thought that he wanted to see would remain lost and hidden forever in the indiscernible soil beneath.

It was hard to lure out and expand them, for he had none of those aids to thought that Father Webber and Mr. Fennel and the schoolteachers had. He didn't have the books to read that the teachers had, or the big book of Father Webber's. And there was the arithmetic. He could add and carry the tens from one column to the next, and he could subtract, if the figures were not too large, but the multiplication was harder because a hunter had no need for that, and he had forgotten most of the tables. And it was the multiplication he needed now.

The windless periods were becoming more frequent. There was a long interval now during which the air was still, and as he listened anxiously for the wind howl to resume, the thoughts were smothered and gone.

Then, far away, a wolf pack howled—brief and tremulous, so faint he never would have heard it if the wind had been blowing. For a moment he felt a fear for the *atihk,* but then he realized that the howl was too distant, and in any case, wolves never howled a warning when they were on a serious hunt. It was the first wolf howling he had heard since he came to the land of little sticks, but that would be because the wind had been muting the howls, not because the wolves were not here. Now the other thing came plunging back to his mind, for suddenly he thought he saw more of it, and the wolves seemed a part of what he saw.

He needed a pencil and paper. It would come to him if he could write the figures down and stare at them while he coaxed the thoughts. But there was no pencil and paper, not even back in the tent on the Little Ninkik. And then he was sorry that the pencil and paper idea had come, because it had made him think again of the tent and Niska, and the memory of Niska brought a sudden surging anger for the thing that the wind had done.

He drank a mug of the bone broth. It was watery, but it still had a meaty taste, and it routed the pains from his stomach. He waited for it to boil some more, and while he waited the gray cloud roof dissolved, and the new-risen sun became a blazing ball hanging alone in an empty sky. It shot daggers of light from the snow, so dazzling that he could no longer detect the flames of the fire. It was the first brilliant sunlight he had had since far back on that first evening after leaving Niska, for although most of the nights had been clear, the days had been overcast, as windy days usually are. The glare from the snow burned his eyes even when he squinted them, for the land around was a great white mirror, not an opaque darkness as forest was, and he knew the snow blindness would strike quickly if he didn't protect his eyes against it. He had no dark glasses like those that Mr. Fennel sold at the Wapanishee post, but his people had lived with this threat of the eye-burning snow glare for long-lost generations before the white man introduced them to the dark glasses.

Taking the *atihk* skin from the bed under the lean-to, he cut a strip from along one edge of it where most of the hair had worn off. He left the center portion wide enough to cover his eyes, but he tapered the ends and rolled them between his palms to form tie strings. He laid it on the toboggan and cut two narrow slits to see through, tried it on, and then cut the slits a little larger to make the spacing of the eye holes fit. Next he took a piece of charcoal from beside the fire and blackened the white edge of hide around the eye holes to eliminate glare from it. He tied it around his head and pulled the parka hood back up, because the cold was stinging his ears. The mask didn't interfere with forward vision but it reduced the light reaching his eyes from the sides, above, and below, where most of the glare was coming from. His eyes were comfortable now without squinting. He could see the flames of the fire again.

There had been one more brief gust moaning in the spruce tops over his head while he worked on the eye mask, but minutes passed now and no more gusts came. The silence was a ponderous thing that seemed to have more weight and substance than the wind howl had had before. The crackle of the fire and the gurgling hum of the stew pail mounted in volume as though trying to fill the nakedness that the dying of the wind had left.

"*Manito* . . . why? It was a mother one, but she's the only one. It might take days to find another. And the wind is gone. You've stopped the wind. The hunt will be much harder now."

Jacob drank more of the broth, and tried to figure out what to do, because he knew now that the *Manito* was not going to tell him.

⟁ ⟁ ⟁ ⟁

The sun moved up the sky until the shadows of the spruces were fat and round on the sparkling snow. Its passage seemed almost that of a bird in flight, for the spruce shadows rapidly lengthened, and it was midafternoon, and still Jacob Atook sat and thought.

Now a new anxiety came. His gaze kept lifting, scanning yesterday's trail. A lattice of branches partly screened his camp from that direction, but there was enough visibility through them that he could keep a close watch on the dark line of the nearest spruce island half a mile or so behind, through which his trail had come.

Taka would be staying well back to avoid overtaking him. He would know that Niska and the wintering camp would not be out here in the land of little sticks. Only a snowstorm, threatening to hide Jacob's trail, would force Taka to speed up and move in closer, and the *Manito* had brought no new snow in answer to Jacob's prayers. Jacob's camps, marking the starting points each morning, would tell Taka the rate at which Jacob was traveling, and Taka would gauge his own speed to stay about one day's travel behind.

But he wouldn't be expecting Jacob to stop for a day. Unless he was searching the trail ahead with guarded care, he might blunder near before discovering that Jacob was here. And if Taka had been staying a day's travel behind, he could be appearing any time now.

Jacob pondered the possibilities. Should he give Taka some warning that he was camped here? Should he play Taka's game, and give him an opportunity to remain hidden and continue believing that Jacob didn't know he was back there? Postpone the showdown that was going to have to come? Or let it come now?

As he pondered it, defeat and desperation built anew within him. The *atihk* was gone, far away now. The *Manito* had turned against him. Was there any use in going on after the *atihk* if the *Manito* was going to shift the wind or warn her in some other way every time Jacob closed in for the kill? Taka would have food—maybe only Taka could save Niska.

The decision formed in a desolation of anguish and surrender. He moved quickly, scooped up snow, and threw it on the fire to put it out, so there would be no more revealing smoke. Then he watched the other spruce island with a fixed stare, and waited for Taka to come.

The tree shadows grew long and slender. Without the fire the cold began to penetrate, and his body shivered

under the parka. The pains of hunger came back. But the
sun sank lower and the shadows grew longer, and Taka still
didn't appear.

Jacob had been staring at the other spruce island so long
now that when he closed his eyes he could still see every
bump and shadow of it engraved on the inside of his
eyelids. Could Taka have seen some evidence that Jacob
was here, and could he be hiding there now, waiting for
Jacob to move on? Taka's eyes were the eyes of a hawk
that sees the mouse in the marsh grass from high in the air.
It was possible that he had seen some small sign of Jacob's
camp before he showed himself outside the distant trees, but
the chance was so small that Jacob could give it little cre-
dence. At that distance the gray canvas of his lean-to would
look like another patch of shadowed snow through the
screening of trees. There had been no smoke or fire for a
long time. And Taka would expect Jacob to be a day's travel
away, he wouldn't be looking ahead carefully.

Jacob's mind clutched eagerly at a new hope. Taka's coming to the cabin and his disappearance afterward were not
proof that he was following Jacob now. There were other
possibilities. Maybe Taka wasn't searching for Niska, and
had simply come back to be on the hunting grounds for the
beaver and muskrat trapping in the spring. Or since he had
discovered that Niska was not with Jacob, could he be
searching somewhere else for her, knowing now that Niska
was alone? The latter thought brought a bristling apprehension but only briefly, because the Little Ninkik was chosen
well, hidden, far off any main travel route. Taka wouldn't
search there.

The hope became conviction. Again he gave the other spruce island a careful scanning. The sun was low, lighting it more sharply with horizontal rays that undercut and pierced the trees, and still there was no sign of another one there. Now Jacob was sure. The belief that Taka was following him was only a delusive fantasy that his fears had made.

He relit the fire, letting the smoke column rise above the trees again. He put the bone broth on to reheat.

Now the wolf howl came once more, quavering—a small pack, for there were only three or four wolf voices in it. The wolves were starving and dying, too. It brought his mind back to the other thing, to the bush with the roots he couldn't see.

He wished he knew the multiplication, for that would make the seeing of it easier. He was drinking the broth, sipping it carefully between pursed lips to keep the bone chips out of his mouth, and when the mug was nearly empty and his head was tilted back to get the last of it, he saw the clusters of small brown cones at the top of the spruce tree overhead. He dropped the mug and jumped to his feet.

"Cones, you'll make the multiplication for me!"

It was a small old tree, with the cones all at its top, an arm's length higher than he could reach. He cut off the tree at snow level with a few quick blows of the ax, making no attempt to muffle them, for he was sure now that there was no one coming up on the back trail to hear. He picked the cones quickly and piled them on the toboggan. They were small and round, about the size of his thumbnail, not long like those of the other spruce that grows in the forest.

When he had picked them all, they made a pile on the toboggan bigger than the cooking pot. He pulled the toboggan out into the open of the bog where the snow was smooth and clear.

He placed two cones beside each other on the snow.

"Cones, you are sparrows, a mother one and a father one. You build the nest, and you lay four eggs in it."

Jacob drew a circle in the snow for the nest and placed four cones within it.

"And the eggs hatch and the little birds fly away and now there are six sparrows. And the mother one and the father one build another nest, and the mother one lays four more eggs."

He drew another circle in the snow and placed four more cones in it. Now there were ten cones.

"And maybe you make a third nest and have a third family, but that I don't know for sure. But you do have two families; that I've seen. So there are ten sparrows, five mother ones and five father ones, for the nesting time of the next spring."

He moved back and forth, shifting cones, adding more from the pile on the toboggan, until soon the cones were spread out across several feet of snow. For a long time he just stood staring down at them, until his eyes swam, and a dizziness came that wasn't the dizziness of hunger.

Questions seethed in him. There were moments when he thought he was on the verge of seeing clearly down the deep dark cavern of mind, but the haziness kept coming back like the morning mists of spring, and the vision kept dimming and disappearing. Yet one thought, one part of it, stayed with him, and he was afraid of it, and tried to push it back into the cavern of darkness with the others. But it wouldn't go. And finally he could keep it smothered within himself no longer.

"*Manito!*" It was only a murmur on his lips, but to Jacob's ears it was like thunder in the still and brittle air. "You *don't* love the sparrow!"

He cut himself short, trembling violently. The *Manito* would be angrier than ever after that. The wind would never come back now. But Jacob gazed at the cones and was angry, too.

Then the anger left him, and a guilt came. There was a sob in his chest, pushing on his throat, but he swallowed and set his teeth and kept the sob inside him. He gathered up the cones, piled them on the toboggan, and took them back to the fire. He was going to put them in the packsack and save them for more of the multiplication later. But suddenly he stiffened, scooped up the cones in his hands, and flung them away, scattering them across the snow. He would not do any of the multiplication again! He was afraid of what it seemed to say about the *Manito*.

Suddenly the silence was broken by a whir of wings and the startled *cruck* of a raven. Jacob's gaze jerked upward. The big bird had apparently come in low over the trees, not knowing that Jacob was there until it was directly over his camp. It must have been a different *kahkaki* from the one that had shown him the *atihk* bones buried in the snow, because now it was rising rapidly on violently flapping wings, *crucking* again with alarm, obviously surprised to find a man here where only wolves and *atihk* should be.

The notes were the hoarse and rattling ones that a *kahkaki* always uses when it comes upon a hunter unexpectedly. Jacob grabbed his rifle. The raven was a wise one, for it had dropped low again out over the bog, putting trees between them. Jacob ran toward the bog edge. He didn't have snowshoes on and every few strides his moccasins broke through the surface crust, clutching his feet, holding him back. When he finally emerged from the trees, the raven was out of range, far out over the bog.

Jacob watched it go with the same crushed dejection that he had felt that morning when the wind changed and sent the *atihk* bounding away. The raven's alarm was gone, it was flying again now with its normal, lazy flight pattern of alternate flapping and soaring. Jacob turned away to return to the fire. But he had taken only a couple of strides when the significance of the raven's flight path hit him. He spun around, ran back, searching the sky to pick it up again. When he found it, the raven was still flying toward the other spruce island half a mile away.

He watched it for nearly a minute, his eyes squinting against the red glow of the sunset to keep it in view as its silhouette diminished. Once it turned and Jacob's throat tightened as it flew briefly in a direction that would miss the other island, but it swung back and headed for the island again. He lost it for many seconds as it approached and disappeared against the distant ribbon of trees. His eyes strained, for if it was going to happen, this would be the time. He didn't really expect it to happen. But it did.

Despite the distance Jacob could recognize the same sudden upward swooping of flight and violent turning away—

the distinctive behavior of a raven that suddenly encounters a hunter where it expects no hunter to be.

He went back to the fire. The red of the sunset waned and darkness came. He searched the other island for the glow of a fire. None showed. But he didn't have to see a fire to know. The *kahkaki* had told.

◀◀◀◀◀◀◀ Chapter 18 ◀◀◀◀◀◀◀

JACOB AWAKENED and slowly shook the muddy stupor from his mind. It was a dawn of vivid sun and cloudless, windless sky, the level rays of sunrise pouring like liquid gold across the snow. He looked around the camp. It was packed smooth with snowshoe tracks and littered with spruce cones and the chips of much wood-chopping. The hole melted around the ashes of the fire was big—much bigger than a one-night fire—and then he remembered that he had been here all day yesterday.

He rolled his cold and aching body from the hard-packed spruce bed and relit the fire. There were only a few *atihk* bones and hard, dry strips of hide left in the stewpot, and he started them boiling for a final carrion stew.

While he waited he took the calendar stick from the packsack. Seven notches. Niska would have eaten all of the fish by now, and most of her *oseepan* and lichen, too. If he started back today, it would be perhaps the eleventh day before he could reach her. And he had left her bark scrapings and lichen for ten. But there was no purpose in going back without *atihk* meat. Even if his body held up for the four-day journey back to the Little Ninkik, and even if he could somehow shake Taka from the back trail, he would still only be able to gather *oseepan* when he reached her, and *oseepan* without meat wouldn't keep them alive much longer.

There was the other way now—the taunting, abhorrent way of final surrender. He tried to push it from his mind, but it clung there as rock tripe clings to a boulder. It seized his eyes, irresistibly moving his gaze to the other spruce island on the bog beyond.

Taka must have arrived there late the day before, after Jacob had become convinced he wasn't coming and had relit the fire. Or perhaps it had been when Jacob exposed himself on the open bog to count the cones. In any case, he had seen Jacob in time to keep himself hidden. And he was over there now, with food, with flour, lard, *atihk* meat, tea, maybe even with some of the luxury foods like beans and raisins, for he had come from the post where the Cheechoo credit was good for all the food he would need.

Jacob could go across to Taka's camp and tell him that Niska was on the Little Ninkik, as he had intended to tell him yesterday when he put out the fire and waited for Taka to come. And as soon as Taka learned where Niska was, he would have no further purpose for Jacob. Perhaps the killing urge would become a drive too goading to resist, or at best, he would leave Jacob here without food to starve. But Niska would live, and the son of Jacob Atook within her would live, too.

Yet there was another way. The thought started Jacob trembling. He, too, could kill. And take Taka's food for himself and Niska. It wouldn't be easy. Taka had proven yes-

terday, by not walking blindly into Jacob's camp, that he
was alert to this danger. But it wasn't the difficulty of
setting up an ambush in this open land of little hiding cover
that forced Jacob to thrust the thought away with repugnance and fear. And it wasn't the memory of the sixth com-
mandment in the *Manito*'s book. It was the deeper, older,
fearsome memory of the wrath that the forest spirits always
had for the killing of man by man. Taka, with his great
pride bruised and mauled by what Jacob had done, might
kill and risk the spirits' wrath, but Jacob was afraid.

The calendar stick was still in his hand. He recounted
the notches while his memory appraised once more the
size of Niska's pike, and this started him thinking about
the multiplication again, for fish were a part of it, too. He
thought of the sparrow that laid four eggs at a time, and he
remembered the way the cones multiplied on the snow. Now
he was thinking of the pike that laid thousands of eggs in the
weedy bays—so many that it would take all the spruce
cones in the land of little sticks to count them. And he
didn't need the cones to tell him that with so many eggs
from each mother fish the lakes should soon be so filled with
fish there would be no room in them for water.

Yet the pike was like the sparrow—it never increased the
way the multiplication said it should. And a sadness came
to Jacob Atook. But it was only a small sadness, not the
deep, sharp sadness he could feel for the *atihk*. And it was
atihk meat that Niska needed, *atihk* that the *Manito* had
told him not to kill, and *atihk*, not fish, that he should
be thinking about now.

He saw the cones, scattered across the snow where he
he had thrown them when he decided that he didn't want to

do more of the multiplication and bring back the *Manito* thoughts he feared. And his mind began puzzling over the contrast between the pike that had thousands of babies every year and the *atihk* that had one, or twins. His curiosity became a compulsion. He put the calendar stick back in the packsack, strapped on snowshoes, and began picking up the cones and piling them on the toboggan. He did it slowly, because there was a reluctance still in him that the curiosity could not dispel. When he had gathered most of the cones, he pulled the toboggan out to a clear, smooth patch of snow.

He began again.

"You are not cones, you are *atihk,* a mother one and a father one. And you have the calf when the winter ends."

He was going to put a third cone down for the calf, but he stopped. It was harder to do the multiplication for the *atihk,* because the *atihk* didn't have young ones when they were one year old as the sparrows did, they had to wait until they were two years old. He tried to ignore it, and went on lining up cones on the snow, but soon he was mixed up and had forgotten which were calves, which were yearlings, and which were full-grown *atihk* that could have more calves, and finally he gave up.

But there were many cones on the snow before the confusion forced him to stop, and he was glimpsing again a truth he feared to see. The thought of the pike with its thousands of babies every year had given it a broader dimension. He trembled now at the vision, and an aching anguish filled him. Father Webber was wrong, and the sparrow hymn was wrong, because the cones couldn't lie.

It was a harsh, bitter thought, this thought that the *Manito* couldn't love all things large and small as the hymn told. Jacob had liked that picture of a loving *Manito*. There was no assuagement of love in the forest spirit ones of the *Atihk-anishini;* they were workers of evil whom a hunter had to fear and guard against, and the vision of a *Manito* of pity and love up there in the heaven had been a bracing counterbalance that had made the forest ones seem less fearsome and severe. Now that vision was gone. A great strength and comfort was being wrenched away. But in its place a new strength, a new determination, was forming.

If the *Manito* didn't love the sparrow, maybe he didn't love the *atihk* either. So perhaps he wouldn't warn the *atihk* a second time. But *had* he warned her the first time? The wind was always changing. Did the *Manito* change it every time, or did it sometimes change itself?

He thought of Niska again. Would she have started rationing her food when Nellie didn't come? Surely she would go out and collect more *oseepan* while she still had the strength that the fish would give. But it was hard to tell whether the mind was building hopes or whether it really believed. In any case, a grim resolution came. He wouldn't go back to Taka and tell him where Niska was. Not yet.

He scooped up the cones and piled them on the toboggan and took them back to the camping place. His mind still puzzled over the inconsistency of the pike that had thousands of babies every year while the *atihk* had only one or two. And he thought he might want the cones again, so he dumped them into the bottom of the packsack to save them.

He drank the last of the bone broth, took down the lean-to, and loaded the toboggan. Then he saw the *atihk* skull hanging from its tripod of poles.

"Spirit One, you only need the skull. The brains aren't any good to you."

He took down the skull and with his knife scraped out the frozen remnants inside that the teeth of the wolves had not been able to reach. When the skull was clean, he had only a good handful of brown shreds of brain, but it would be a meal, so he opened the packsack and carefully put the brains in the stew pail to carry with him. Then he raised the skull and tripod again.

He slung the gun on his back and adjusted the eye mask, because the sun was well up the sky now and there was already an incandescent glare on the snow. He looked back once more at the other spruce island.

"Taka, I'm going. You can follow again now."

He took up the toboggan drawrope and started.

The silence was a profound and pressing thing, not a negative quality, not just an absence of sound; it had substance and reality of its own. The cold was biting despite the brilliant sun, the sky was high and clear, and the land of little sticks had the acoustics now of an immense cave, magnifying every sound. The swish and creak of his snowshoes and toboggan on the dry snow, inaudible in the moan of the wind before, became a screeching now that would be reaching far out ahead of him.

He crossed the bog strip to the spruce island where the *atihk* had been, and began to follow her trail. The tracks were distinct and deep in the softer snow amid the trees, but when they moved out onto the hard snow of the open bog beyond they were shallow and blurred, because the trail was now a day old. But as long as no new snow came, he would have no difficulty following them. At this stage he could do no more than stay on the trail and wait, for the *atihk* now was warned and knew a hunter was coming. Her guard would be keen, and there would be no opportunity to close in for a kill until the wind came again. It didn't matter that the sound of Jacob's snowshoes and toboggan was sending a warning ahead, for the *atihk* now was far away.

Jacob felt strangely alone and abandoned. He wanted to pray to the *Manito* and ask for the wind to come back. But the *Manito* was an enemy now. He spoke to the *atihk* instead.

"*Atihk,* this trail has an end, and where the end is, either you or Jacob Atook is dead."

Chapter 19

THERE WAS A TORTURING GUILT in him for the day he had wasted sitting in yesterday's camp—a censuring castigation that it was not his time now, not his life, but Niska's and the unborn son's. And life for them was running out. In an effort to catch up the lost day, he pushed himself on until the silver incandescence had faded from the snow and evening shadows were making it difficult to keep the *atihk* trail in view when once more it entered another spruce island.

When he stopped at last to make his camp, the great round hoofprints reaching on ahead were still fuzzy, their edges worn and blurred. The painful knowledge came that the trail was *more* than a day old now, for at this point fear of the hunter had been driving the *atihk* on; she wasn't stopping to feed, and she had been moving here in one day as far as Jacob could travel in two.

He had eaten nothing since the last of the bone broth that morning. The hunger was a dagger twisting in his gut. He still had the meal of brain scrapings, and the temptation to eat was a racking torment, but he dug leaves from under the snow and brewed a tea, and forced himself to save the brains for morning. By now the *atihk* should have forgotten there was a hunter on her trail. She should be stopping to rest and feed. And tomorrow the wind would come back, and Jacob would have to drive himself hard to overtake her and make the kill. Yes, tomorrow. He would need the strength that the brains could give tomorrow, not now when there was nothing to do but sleep. So he drank several mugs of the tea, and the warmth of it was a soothing caress for the angry stomach, but not for long, and quickly the squeezing ache of the hunger was back again.

The sunset flared like a forest fire. When his cooking fire died down and its crackle of flames softened, the silence closed in on him, intense and cloistering, until his heart was a thumping staccato, and the normally inaudible hum that was always in his ears became a roar like a giant falls, and when he moved his head he could hear the clicking of the neck vertebrae like grinding stones.

He took off the eye mask and hung it on one of the lean-to uprights. He studied the sunset, and it was vivid and florid, but with a uniformity of smoothness because there were no clouds to give it highlights and variegations. And in the sunset was himself, for he saw again, as he had seen in that first sunset of the hunt's beginning long ago, that he was a part of the sunset and the sunset a part of him. The life force that flowed in Jacob Atook was an alchemy of sun and rain and soil, the same life force that flowed in the *atihk* and the sparrow and the pike, the same life force that flowed in them all. And the life force that was Jacob Atook today would be that of an *atihk* or a moose or a grouse in one of the tomorrows. And maybe Father Webber was a part of the *Manito*'s heaven, for Father Webber didn't have to hunt, he could buy his meat in the tins from the shelves of Mr. Fennel's store; and maybe Jacob Atook, too, would be a part of the heaven someday, but he wasn't now, he was a part of earth, a part of the life force here, a part of the *atihk* and the moose and the sunset and the rain, and it was hard to see where the heaven fitted in.

As he cut the spruce boughs and laid his bed, the compulsive fascination of the cone-counting began its gnawing again, luring the mind as a new toy lures a child. But it was *atihk* multiplication he wanted to see, and he couldn't figure out how to overcome the confusion of calves and yearlings and old ones, and he left the cones untouched in the bottom of the packsack. He was seeking again, however, down the dark funnel of the mind, hoping to raise the bush without breaking the roots still obscured below. But the deep roots of thought stayed hidden, mocking, like the dream one knew was there but had fled on waking beyond the borders of recall.

The evening darkened and he built up the fire to throw more warmth under the lean-to. He crouched over it, staring at the flames and the empty tea pail beside them, like a primitive fire maker awed by the orange life that the spark of his flint had spawned. As he stared the fire faded until only the blackened pail remained sharp and clear, and then his vision shimmered, and the pail was no longer a tea pail, it became a gigantic bucket, full to the brim with water, overflowing. He closed his eyes, blotting out what remained of the flames and the leaping shadows, but the huge bucket stayed—obscured, yet recognizable still. And as he watched now, a great rain began falling out of the heaven, and the rain coalesced until it was a single gushing spout of water, all of it pouring into the bucket, and all of it instantly overflowing, vanishing, wasted, because the bucket was already full.

The vision of the bucket dimmed, then passed away, and only the blackness of his tightly closed eyes remained. He knew it was the way of the spirit ones to speak in dreams, and sometimes to guide a seeking mind in that manner. But this was no imagery of the sleeping time, for he wasn't asleep, only the eyes were closed. And the spirits never sent their visions to a waking mind.

He opened his eyes. The orange flames leaped again. The tea pail still stood by the fire, empty as before.

He cut another notch in the calendar stick, and that was eight. Now the stick was full, with notches to its end, because he had cut it short, confident the hunt would not be long. It should not have been long, it should be ended now, but it wasn't, because the *Manito* moved the wind and frightened the *atihk* away before the high lung shot was there. Or did the wind move itself?

Eight. And maybe five days now to get back to her with the meat when he got it, for he was traveling deeper into the land of little sticks. But to go back would only lead Taka there.

The cold of night sharpened, and he put more wood on the fire. He checked the match tin and rifle, took off his moccasins and trousers, lay the rifle in the bed, and pulled the bedding over him. The darkness dropped around him, and the stars came near. But Jacob didn't pray.

⁋ ⁋ ⁋ ⁋

The snow was still gray in the murky half light of the dawn when he awakened and made the fire and melted snow and started the handful of *atihk* brains stewing. The wind had not come back. The silence was bleak, giving the air a crystalline rigidity that seemed capable of shattering like glass. As Jacob cut firewood the ax blows rang out in a strident staccato, jarring, alien, and irreverent on the purity of air.

He ate the brains—all of them, because there wasn't enough to bother saving for another meal. A red crescent of sun was just beginning to appear as he set out again on the *atihk* trail.

It was another day of raw and stinging cold, of blinding radiance from the snow on the open stretches, and of dark, contrasting shadows where the stunted spruces grew. The sky was a blanched, pale blue-white, as if it were reflecting the snow, as the snow reflected the light of the sky. It seemed incongruous that such intense cold and brilliant light could exist together. The breath steamed from him, smoking around his face, putting a white hoarfrost on the beard hairs, and on the eye mask from which it had to be brushed periodically because it added to the searing glare that was reaching his eyes.

For the first several hours of that day Jacob walked with a firm, fast stride, because the morning meal had put a vigor in him once more. But by midday the new-made strength of it was waning, and the hunger was kneading his stomach again as Niska had kneaded the bannock dough in those times long ago when there was still flour in the tent on the Little Ninkik. And he tightened the stomach muscles in an effort to hold back the pain, and he pressed on—a bent, creeping mote of black shadow, puny and dwarfed by the shimmering immensity of white that was the land of little sticks. On, across the dazzling radiance of the bog strips, through the shaded prominences of spruce island after spruce island, on, twisting, meandering, wherever the *atihk* trail led. And there were only a few spots where the *atihk* had stopped to dig for lichen, and the track surfaces were rough and granular, the sharp cut of freshness long since eroded from their edges. The *atihk* still was far ahead, far away.

⁊ ⁊ ⁊ ⁊

It was as old as life, this pitting of hunter against hunted. Its birth was in the Cambrian seas where the earliest specks of living began, and the hunted's striving to escape the hunter became a major inducement in luring life ashore to populate the land. The epochs came and went. The hunters diversified and took myriad forms, and one of them was man. When man the beast became man the hunter, he was already a tracker, and his tracking lore came with him out of the primordial shadows as man's first and most ancient skill, older than stone-chipping, older than fire making, older than speech. And the skills and instincts born of those pre-Stone Age beginnings possessed Jacob Atook now.

For two days he had been living with all his senses concentrated on the she-*atihk*'s trail. They were one now, hunted and hunter, joined by the wispy thread of hoofprints that had become an umbilical cord of communication along which Jacob's mind was projecting itself ahead, instinctively and unbidden, letting him think and feel as the hunted one too would be thinking and feeling. There was a sadness in this oneness, for it meant that when the kill came

he would be killing something of himself. But there was a
confidence too, a confidence now of grave assessment, not
the *Manito*-based confidence that had betrayed him before.
Because the linking of hunted and hunter, the thinking and
feeling as one, was telling Jacob that the hunger he felt was
not just his own; he was feeling the hunger of the *atihk*'s
belly, too, hunger sharpened by the *keekishkawasso* that was
also there. She was a strong and noble one, this *atihk*, Jacob
was feeling that, too, but the trail could not go on tomorrow
as it had for two days now. Tomorrow the food need would
supplant all else. Tomorrow the trail would show that she
had been stopping for much digging, feeding and resting.
Tomorrow she would not travel far, and Jacob would overtake her, and the rest of it would be easy, because the wind
would be back by then. Yes, the wind would be back.
Tomorrow.

↟ ↟ ↟ ↟

He awoke several times that night, coming awake sharply,
listening, hearing no wind, letting himself sleep again. The
next day was still, and the windless hush was once more a
stifling quiet across the land of little sticks.

He melted snow and drank warm water. He took to the
trail without food, without even the bog-bush tea. The
temporary strength, the few days of respite that the *atihk*
bones and scraps of flesh and brains had granted, were
used up; the knife-edge sharpness was gone from the
hunger pain and once more it had become just a gnawing
ache as it had been before the raven led him to the *atihk*
remains. And now, as it crept back with sluggish stealth in
the first new hours of that new day, Jacob could feel again

the all-body weakness and flaccidity spreading through him, displacing the immediacy and sharp delimitation of the stomach pains.

He began finding numerous feeding craters, as he knew he would that day, for hunger had started slowing the *atihk* here. But the craters were crusted, and the tracks were growing fainter, for as the *atihk*'s flight slowed, the chase of Jacob Atook was slowing, too.

Chapter 20

"WORK, LEGS, WORK. Don't stop. There'll be rest when the sun sets, and *atihk* meat tomorrow—yes, tomorrow."

Now he was far past the point of knowing hunger. The ultimate starvation, the final yielding capitulation, was always near but never quite there, for the will that was fed by the ever-haunting memory of Niska was a power that kept him going on.

He was gazing down at his legs, because it was hard to keep the body erect, it was easier to stumble on this way with the body stooped and the eyes down. And the legs were long, reaching downward, on and on, as though his eyes were at the top of a tall tree and his feet at the bottom. The moccasins and the snowshoes with the snow crust on them were far away, blurred as in a fog, detached. Were they his? They were, because there was a burning pain in the calves and ankles, and the pain belonged to him.

"Work, legs, work. Niska, you should have married Taka Cheechoo. Our father in the heaven who sees the little sparrow fall . . . he wouldn't have listened, Niska. Taka wouldn't have let that *atihk* go last fall. Give us this day our daily bread. Amen. And this is the prayer of Jacob Atook."

The twisting nexus of hoofprint disks stretched on interminably—the lure, the only link with life that remained. Then he remembered the other link—the unseen presence somewhere on the trail behind. And the memory taunted with its reminder that there was food back there on Taka Cheechoo's toboggan, as well as at the end of this *atihk* trail far out ahead.

But he thrust the thought of Taka away and staggered on, turning automatically and unthinkingly when the *atihk* trail turned, his misted eyes cast down and seeing nothing except the chain of shadowed hollows advancing across the snow. There was no need to lift the eyes, to search the bog and island patterns ahead, for the tracks were old, and he was getting no nearer to the *atihk*. And as long as this crushing silence lay across the land, Jacob could do no more than follow, retaining contact while he waited for a wind to come.

"Work, legs, work. Tomorrow . . . there'll be *atihk* tomorrow, and you'll drink the hot blood and the strength will come back fast then."

And he tried to believe, but in his sporadic moments of rationality the smothering weight of reason became a relentless dissuader dragging down the buoys of hope. Reason told him that the winter-end time of *seekwan* must be near. He had no calendar as Mr. Fennel and Father Webber had, but he had the sun; it was far up the sky now when it was at its noontime high, and the days were lengthening, so spring could not be far away. And reason told him that spring was a time of thaw and rain, and not a time of wind.

He stopped early for the camp, because the tiredness and the weakness made the camp chores harder, and he had to rest frequently while he dug the snow hole and raised the lean-to and cut the bed boughs and firewood. And he fought desperately the urge to skimp in the camp making, knowing the danger that was there. One night with a snow hole too shallow, a bed too thin, or inadequate firewood, could bring the freezing and the silent end. If the flagging body failed before the hunt could end, it would probably come that way, not on the trail in the blazing light of day, but tranquilly and unknown in the hours of sleep on the first night that he could no longer make the camp as it should be made.

He cut strips from the *atihk* skin of his bed, scraped the hair off, and boiled them in the stew pail. The pieces of skin swelled and softened, but not enough that they could be chewed up and swallowed. He could only grind them with his teeth, rolling them in his mouth, pressing them with his tongue against his palate until the leathery taste was gone. Then he spit the pulpy lumps back into the pot to boil again. And he longed for *oseepan* and rock tripe—the despised foods of the hunt's first days that would be luxury foods now.

He made a rack of sticks beside the fire and raked a heap of hot coals under it, then lay on his back on the bed with the ankles raised on the rack's crossbar, the warming coals a few inches under his calves. Half his life he had spent on snowshoes, and he had never suffered from the pain of the calves before, for the *mal de raquette* was a complaint of the old ones, not the young. But the pain was sharp in the lower legs now, and Jacob knew it was not put there by the drag and weight of the snowshoes alone; it was a signal of the muscles' wasting. He lay for a long time, the legs raised on the wooden form as he had seen the old ones do in winters before. The soothing heat of the coals penetrated them, slowly driving out the pain.

He got out the calendar stick, filled now with its eight white notches. If he had cut another stick and put more notches there, it was forgotten and lost, for there was no second calendar stick in the packsack now. The days had been running imperceptibly together, the sunsets, camps, and sunrises no longer impinging sufficiently on his torpid senses to keep the days separate and remembered. This was the tenth day, or maybe the eleventh; it was impossible now to be sure. He didn't let himself think about how far it was back to Niska.

He made tea and chewed its sediment of twigs and leaves. He didn't count the cones, he didn't even seek the deep roots of thought to which the cone-counting belonged. When the tea was finished, he burrowed into the bed in the lean-to's warmth, and the night came, and with it, soon, the peace and mending of sleep.

⁌ ⁌ ⁌ ⁌

It was like a canoe in a heavy sea. The snow seemed to be pitching, tossing, making it difficult for him to keep his balance and continue moving on. He was hunched far over and the dizziness made it seem that his head was detached and whirling around his stooped shoulders. The snowshoes had become ponderous weights at the end of the stilt legs far below, dragging, tripping him, no longer gliding easily on the crusted snow.

"Work, legs, work. Niska waits."

His shadow was long. The day was growing old. He would stop for the night soon. Soon. The lowering sun filled the *atihk* tracks with smears of shadow, and the shadow edges kept growing fuzzier, and it wasn't the misting of the heavy-lidded eyes that made them appear that way. Even in the fog that grayed the mind, the knowledge was there, stark and irrefutable: he had not traveled far since morning, the *atihk* was moving still farther away.

"Work, legs, work. We'll take the *atihk* meat from the packsack when we make the camp, and tonight we'll have the nose and lips, because that's the best, and we'll have the liver, too, because there's much strength in the liver, and we'll roast the bones and suck the marrow, and we'll make a big bannock, and we'll put a lot of jam on it, and sugar in the tea, and milk, not the flour, we won't thicken it and spoil it and make it pasty with the flour. And legs, we'll put raisins in the bannock, a whole big fistful of raisins. . . ."

He could taste it all, and he wasn't sorry he had let the mind talk that way. Because maybe the legs would listen, and maybe they would be fooled and believe and work harder then.

He was staggering, almost falling. But the tracks led on, and where they led Jacob Atook must also go. For at the end the *atihk* waited, waited to be killed when the wind would come and fill its ears. His head was giddy, detached again. It was like the time he found the jug filled with the brew of the kind that the old ones made when the trapping was good and there was credit at the store to buy the yeast and raisins. The jug was hidden in the bushes by the Wapanishee shore—the shore where he walked with Niska. . . .

"Joe said today I'll be the wife of Taka Cheechoo. . . . Taka shot the moose for him . . . the wedding feast will be in six days. . . . Niska, we'll go and stay for the winter . . . man and wife . . . on the Little Ninkik, Niska . . . no one hunts there. . . ."

He had taken long drinks from the jug. They burned his throat and his head became giddy. As the head was giddy again now.

A snowshoe struck a snow ridge and Jacob fell for the first time. He lay quietly. There was a luxurious comfort just in getting the weight of the body off the paining legs. The snow molded to him, soothing and soft, not lumpy with jutting boughs as a spruce bed was. He lay for a long time until he realized with a start of fear that the cold was beginning to penetrate his clothing, then he shook the lethargy out of his mind and forced himself to move.

It was always difficult when one fell in deep snow with snowshoes on. The rising was hard, even in normal circumstances, because the snowshoes made it impossible to fold the legs underneath, and the arms were no help, for when one pushed a hand down to raise the body, the hand just sank into the snow.

Jacob reached behind him and tried to draw the toboggan up, but it had stopped on a snow ridge, and now it tipped onto its side and wouldn't move. He would have to take a snowshoe off and use it to give his hand some support on the snow. He removed the mitts and reached down and began unbuckling a snowshoe harness. His fingers were weak and clumsy and worked slowly. The leather harness was snow-caked and stiff with cold. He tried to hurry because bare hands would freeze quickly, especially since there was still a film of sweat on the palms from the exertion of the trail. The buckle loosened and he slipped his foot out of the harness and drew the snowshoe back beside him. He pushed a hand down on the snowshoe and came to his feet. The rising put the giddiness in his head again. He swayed and his vision fogged for several moments.

He was stooping, fitting his foot into the snowshoe harness, when the rifle on its sling across his back slipped around his shoulder. He grabbed it to keep it from falling and plugging the barrel with snow. A sharp pain stabbed his hand.

"You're a stupid one, Jacob Atook! Taka Cheechoo couldn't be that stupid. Taka Cheechoo wouldn't grab his gun barrel with a bare hand."

He slipped his foot out again and knelt with one knee on the free snowshoe. He supported the rifle across the other upright knee, pulled his tired eyes into focus, and stared dismally at the hand now frozen firmly to the cold steel. He tried to open the fingers. The skin pulled, stretched, clinging as though welded to the gun barrel. He could tear it away, but it would leave the skin frozen to the metal, and the hand bleeding and torn.

The lethargy came back, restful, balmy. His head sagged until his chin was on his chest. The pain was leaving his hand and he could feel the numbness spreading through it. He jerked his head up, forced the eyes to focus and look at it again. It startled him, for he hadn't looked at a hand closely outside a mitt for a long time. The skin was cracked, scaly, dry, like a snake's. It was all knobby knuckles and sharp ridges of tendons, and the fingernails were black crescents of caked dirt. The fingers were gaunt and long, skin over bare bones. He counted them. Thumb and four. He counted again, because their slenderness made it seem that there should be more than four. And he saw the white area of frostbite creeping outward from the steel, around the fingers, around the palm edge toward the back where the tendons and the blue veins ribbed the skin like the hand of an old man.

His head sagged to his chest again.

"Jacob Atook, are you going to stay here and die?"

He became aware again of the paining pressure of the lower abdomen. It had been there for some time before he tripped and fell, and he had held the pain there, delaying the easing of it, because it was always wise when the body needed all the heat it could produce, to hold the warm urine inside as long as one could. Now he came to his feet stiffly, lifting the gun. And he fumbled at the trousers with the fingers of the free hand, working them through the thick padding of underwear beneath. He let the steaming yellow stream trickle slowly down the gun barrel and under the frozen hand. In a few seconds the skin came free with no tearing or bleeding. The gun dropped to the snow.

He dried the hand on his trousers, opened the parka, and jabbed both hands down the trouser tops, beneath the underwear, into the warmth of his crotch. Softly he rubbed the frozen hand. There was a pain like jabbing thorns for a couple of minutes as the frostbite eased out. He worked the fingers, limbering them, bringing the circulation back. Then he pulled them out, fastened the clothes, put on the mitts, and picked up the gun.

His hands were clumsy and weak, the oil on the gun had thickened with the cold, and he had a hard time turning up the bolthead and sliding the bolt out so that he could sight down the barrel. There was no snow in it. The bolt went back stiffly. Its headlock stuck, and his vision blurred from the effort of forcing it over its stop. He wound up doing it more by feel than by sight.

He slung the gun to his back again, strapped on the snowshoe, took up the toboggan drawrope, and pressed forward anew on the *atihk* trail.

All sense of time had gone. He didn't know how much later it was when he stopped for the camp, but it could not have been long, for the sun had been well toward the west when his hand froze to the gun, and now it was still perhaps two hours high.

As he took off the gun and laid it on the toboggan in preparation for making camp, he sensed that somewhere a familiar detail was missing from the clouded picture his eyes were forming. He studied the packsack, the tick. They looked normal. The ax handle protruded in its usual place at the packsack's upper corner. He stared at the gun, and suddenly fright and despair tightened his body. The bolt was gone. He couldn't have got the head locked, and the bolt must have jiggled out while the gun was on his back. It could be anywhere along the trail back to the point where he had taken it out to sight down the barrel for snow.

The fatigue was a massive weight, but he started back at once to retrace the back trail, forcing the eyes to a searching sharpness, a frenzy of desperation reviving him. But he didn't go far. He stopped, took the knife from the belt sheath under the parka, and dropped it from waist height so that it would strike the snow on its long, flat side. He fished it out of the snow and dropped it again. The snow was hard, but the knife still sank a handbreadth each time so that snow fell back on top of it, hiding it from view. The rifle bolt would have done the same.

The newfound strength suddenly drained out of him. He turned, stumbling, the snowshoes dragging, and staggered back to the spruce island where he would make the camp.

⁋ ⁋ ⁋ ⁋

That night when darkness came Jacob scanned the back trail repeatedly, hoping now, wishing another fire would be there, yet knowing it wouldn't be. For Taka would be staying well behind, taking no chances on blundering into Jacob's camp, as he almost had before. Then Jacob stared at the boltless gun on the toboggan with its crushing and irreversible indictment that there could be no *atihk*-kill now, no matter if wind did come, no matter what happened, and a grim decision formed. For Taka *would* come eventually. It was inescapable now.

He built up the fire to give him more light, and withdrew a charcoal-tipped stick from the ashes at the edge of it. In bold black strokes he began drawing on the white surface of the flour-bag tick that covered his bed. He drew the long and slender outline of Mahkwa Lake, with the river flowing northward out of it, straight at first, then with many bends where it reached this land of little sticks. On the lake's eastern shore he sketched a small cabin to indicate the Cheechoo winter camp. He printed the name on the lake, using their syllabic native alphabet, then wondered if Taka could read even that, so he drew a picture of a bear beside it, because *mahkwa* was their word for bear. Then he put in the Ninkik River, flowing westward from its source near the southern tip of Mahkwa Lake, and finally the Little Ninkik, with its name, too, and the sketch of an otter under it because *ninkik* meant otter. Taka would be able to read the name Niska, so he printed it in big letters, and circled it for emphasis, and drew an arrow from it to the spot on the Little Ninkik shore where their camp was.

He didn't take the rifle to bed with him that night, he turned the toboggan up on its side and with a choking sob left the gun in the snow where it fell.

He studied the big sprawling lines of the map. It was crude, but it would tell its message. And he got into bed and pulled the tick over him, spreading it smoothly so that Taka would be sure to see the map when he found the frozen body underneath.

◄◄◄◄◄◄◄ Chapter 21 ◄◄◄◄◄◄◄

DEATH WAITED, baiting him, mocking, and Jacob Atook awoke to the radiance of another dawn, his body stiff and cramped, yet feeling again a trace of the succoring revitalization that sleep could always bring.

He broke the camp and started out once more, not knowing why, sensing only that this must be his last day and that the *atihk* trail still led on. The trail had been the lodestar of hope too long for his mind to accept now that its hope was gone.

The snowshoes snapped the brittle snow. Whenever he stopped to rest, often now, his heart filled the void of silence with its thumping in the ears. Behind, lashed to the packsack on the toboggan, was the gun, its empty breech caked with snow—another dead, nonfunctioning weight as the mind itself had become.

But the physical effort of the body was working its strange alchemy and slowly releasing the mental fetters of the mind. Niska was dead . . . no, not yet, not quite, but she would be before he could get back to her. Useless thought! Because he *couldn't* get back to her. There was no strength in

him now for the long trek back to the Little Ninkik. And
even if there was, there was Taka, waiting, clinging leech-
like behind. Yet there was no purpose, no hope, in just lying
in the camp, letting the long sleep come. The dogged knowledge persisted that if a shred of hope lay anywhere, it could
only be here on the *atihk*'s dimming trail.

Then an angry denial began to form. For he had been
traveling only an hour or so, and already the brief morning
strength, the taunting, hollow succoring of sleep, was used
up. He was stumbling again. The sun was whirling in the
sky. And surely there was no hope in this going on—how
could there be, for a dying hunter who no longer had a
gun?

The anger was suddenly a rending pain, chilling him as
the outside cold had never done before. He saw it now in
an agony of bitter self-castigation. He should have gone
back days ago and told Taka where Niska was. Taka could
have saved her then. Why hadn't he? It was pride, the same
vain pride he despised in Taka, that had held him back.

But was there a chance that Taka still might save her—a
frail, remote possibility that Jacob's bungling might yet be
overcome?

He stopped, the shoulders hunched, trembling, eyes staring at the distant feet below. Then he started again, the
strides firm and body erect, and he circled and headed
back, retracing the way he had come.

The sun ceased its erratic whirling in the sky. And a
strength returned, now that he had an attainable goal, because Taka was not a day or two ahead as the *atihk* was, or
days behind like the Little Ninkik; Taka would be near

enough that if Jacob could keep himself going, they would meet sometime late this same day.

But even this grim hope quickly receded. For soon the head was lolling on the shoulders, giddy as before, and the feet were stumbling again. His legs grew numb. There was not even the burning pain of the *mal de raquette* now. He tried to wiggle his toes in the moccasins to bring the circulation back, but if they moved, he couldn't tell. And he knew now that he had waited too long to go back to Taka, as he had waited too long to begin the *atihk* hunt.

His eyes were down, fixed on the snowshoe trail he was backtracking, and he wouldn't have seen the raven if its shadow had not moved across the snow almost at his feet. His gaze darted upward, for here was movement, and movement meant life. He could see nothing at first. The sky was a blinding light that forced him to squint his eyes, even behind the mask that covered them. But the big bird moved out of the blind spot that surrounded the sun's place in the sky, and then Jacob saw it, climbing on the great black wings. It must have swooped near for a closer look, and it was this that had brought the shadow into Jacob's restricted view. Now the wings were pumping rapidly, raising it again into the vivid sky. It went high, and then the flapping stopped, and it began banking in wide, lazy circles over Jacob's head, waiting, not going away.

"Not yet, *kahkaki,* not yet."

But soon. For he could feel the life force flowing out of him, rejoining the hidden reservoir from which it came, to seek regeneration there and become the new life force of an *atihk* or a moose or a wolf. No . . . a *kahkaki,* because the raven, eater of the carrion that other more noble ones had killed, black vulture of the *Atihk-anishini* land who could grow fat when others were starving, still circled above. Jacob stared upward at it, foul blot of black wheeling on the clean and luminous blue, and his face grimaced sourly, because there was a corruptness in this waiting for death instead of being its instrument.

The snow crust caught a snowshoe, pitching him forward; he staggered, regained his balance, struggled on for a few more strides, and then stopped.

He gazed again at the sky, and now there were two ravens there.

He pulled his eyes away and looked around him, his body swaying and vision shimmering. And still the sun shone, the snow glared, the spruce trees stood in their silent, implacable way, and the tufts of tea bush cast their shreds of shadow on the snow. Old companions, partners all in the struggle that now was ending; a part of him as he was a part of them. Yet now, with the last dregs of life force flowing away, the old friends were still living on, unchanged, not noticing, not caring. And how could it be that way, when one of them was leaving? How could the world that had produced him and nurtured him so long be so indifferent and serene when one of its creations was dying? And Jacob saw the truth that was there with the same bitter sadness in his heart that the cone-counting had brought. It was all a great elemental, impersonal leviathan without heart, an interweaving of many parts, and the whole had purpose, a reason to be, but each part was nothing. He was a jot of dust in a universe of competing matter that reached

to the heaven and the stars. And he was of no more impor-
tance to it than the brown spruce needle that also dies when
its purpose is served.

"Work, legs, work!"

The legs tried to move, but the snowshoes clung to the
snow. He tripped and fell. The snow yielded and molded
to his body, and suddenly there was a blissful peace and
contentment in no longer having to concentrate on the trail
and keep the legs working. Jacob lay still, relishing the
unexpected comfort of it, making no effort to rise. Then he
remembered the tick with the map on it. Was he going to
bungle that, too? It was rolled on the toboggan with the
map inside, and Taka would never find it there. He reached
behind and pulled the toboggan up beside him. He took off
the mitts, untied the tick, and let it unroll. Then he put the
mitts back on and let his body sink once more into the cush-
ioning snow.

Since he had no need for vision now, he let the eyelids
droop to shut out the glare. They closed slowly, reluctantly,
as though fearing reprimand, but the mind could summon
no reproof, and when some of the outer brilliance still
burned through, Jacob closed them tighter until only a dull
red glimmer was left. The snow grew colder, but it seemed
a faraway, inconsequential cold, too remote to diminish this
Elysium of rest and peace. A distant voice was telling the
eyes to open and the body to rise. Another voice replied
angrily that he *would* open them, and he *would* rise, not
now, but soon, when he had had some rest.

His breathing slowed and shortened. The remnant of
glare that was still lighting the inside of his eyelids faded

from red to gray. The cold moved farther away. And then a strange luxurious warmth replaced it.

But a muffled murmur of sound penetrated the mind's torpidity and snatched Jacob Atook back. There had been such a sparsity and sameness of sounds for so long that this one came through and registered instantly. The mind groped to identify it, fighting the shackles of lethargy. It had been a whir of wings, so close over his head that he had heard the slapping of the feathers.

He forced the eyes to open, to seek. The image of the black smudges unfurled slowly. The ravens were standing near him on the snow, heads tilted, shiny button eyes peering. And now they were three.

His mind focused clearly, as the old ones said it always did when death was at hand. A full, keen awareness was back. He could feel the cold, and the glare was burning his eyes again. And he could see the night-black ravens with startling clarity as they walked stiff-legged back and forth across the snow.

"Bold and stupid ones, you would be an easy shot. I could get all three of you before you could fly away."

They flew instantly at the sound of Jacob's voice, stiff feathers clacking in the hush of air. He turned his head upward and saw them circling again in the sky above.

The mind was starkly clear. The picture of Niska that came was sharp and accusing. The Niska who might still be waiting. For now he remembered that even if Niska's food was gone, she had lots of firewood, because he had cut a big supply to save him the work of cutting more when he returned, tired, at the hunt's end. She would be in the bed, resting and warm, not weakening there as Jacob had weakened here on the *atihk*'s trail.

The will was insistent. It spoke to him of the ravens, which were flesh, and near, not far away as the *atihk* was. And it spoke the silent reminder that the *Atihk-anishini* had always been hunters, yet had not always had guns.

The fatigue was no longer a thing of the flesh, it belonged to the bones and was everywhere through him. But he fought it, rolled onto the toboggan, and stiff hands tied the tick up with the map inside once more. Then grasping the pack-sack, he dragged himself to his feet and staggered forward again.

He reached the next island of trees, and on its northern edge where the winds and the driving snow struck, he began a hurried seeking. All the exposed trees here were lopsided deformities with branches only on their southern sides, for the abrasive of wind and snow killed buds and left the up-wind surfaces of the trunks smooth. Many were bare white spikes, dry and seasoned, their barks peeled away. And most were twisted, awry, and it took much searching to find a tamarack that stood straight with no spiraling of grain. It was this one, not the hard and brittle spruce, that would have the springy recoil.

He cut the tree he had chosen, splitting it with the ax into several narrow shafts that went parallel and true, for the grain was straight. He selected the best and truest shaft from the windward side where there were no knots, and where the growth rings were crowded together, giving it strength and resiliency. He saved several smaller shafts, split the rest of the tree into firewood, and then he dug a snow hole and made a quick, crude camp. He lit a fire, for the work would be long, and his hands were weak, and he would need warmth that would let him rest frequently without freezing.

He cut the largest shaft to a length equivalent to the spread of his arms; then he worked on it with the knife, tapering it to each end, carefully equalizing the taper and tension of each half until the whole would bend in a symmetrical arc. The work went slowly, for the hands and eyes were tired, and he had to stop often, holding the hands out to the fire for the heat to limber the fingers. Mostly he worked with his mitts on, but sometimes, for fine work, he had to hold the knife barehanded, and the scrawny hands whitened and shook with the cold.

As he worked, his eyes lifted skyward repeatedly, and fearfully, for now he wanted the ravens to stay.

He considered the next problem. The moccasin laces and the drawstring in the hood of the parka were too short. The lashing rope on the toboggan was too heavy, but it was three-ply, and one strand of it might do. He unraveled a length of the rope and cut one of the strands free. Would it be strong enough? He looped the ends, then cut notches for it at each tip of the tapered tamarack shaft. He flexed and strung it, and the cord snapped taut. When he plucked it, it sang with a sturdy twang. He pulled it out to full draw and released it. The bow recoiled, thudding sharply, but the bowstring held.

Many generations had come and gone since the traders had first brought guns and the *Atihk-anishini* hunters no longer had had to depend on the arrow and the bow. But the ancient skill was still a slumbering part of their culture, for there was a period in the growing-up time of every *Atihk-anishini* boy when he waited impatiently for his first gun, and while he waited he made his own tamarack bow, to learn of its use from the old ones who had learned it from the old ones before them. Jacob Atook's bow-and-arrow playtime had been brief, for the summer school had given him other interests, and he had not yearned for the reaching of the hunting age as his playmates had. But he had had his bows and arrows, nevertheless, and now the mind went back, remembering.

He began shaving down the other shafts he had saved for arrows. It was getting harder to hold the knife, and the shavings curled away with a distressing slowness. But he looked at the sky, and he counted, and he didn't stop working until he had three arrows smoothed and rounded and ready for straightening. He had no feathers for guide vanes, so the arrows would have to be perfectly straight to fly true. He spent a long time now steaming them over the tea pail, bending the last small curves out, sighting down them, rolling them on the flat toboggan, and repeating the process again and again. When they would roll on the toboggan without a wobble, he sharpened the tips, hardened the points by charring them slightly in the fire, and notched the butts for the bowstring.

Now he gazed again at the sky and trudged out into the glare of the open snow, drawing the toboggan behind him. And his stumbling was real, but he would have feigned it anyway. He didn't look up again. They were wise, and they might suspect if he appeared too interested in them; and if a suspicion came, they could wait. But Jacob couldn't, for his waiting time was gone.

He let a snowshoe drag in the snow. He let himself trip and fall, but as he fell he jerked the toboggan up beside him. He dropped two arrows on the toboggan in front of him and quickly nocked the other on the bowstring. Then he lay still, left hand holding the slanted bow, right hand gripping the string and arrow, an elbow supported on the toboggan, ready to raise him.

They were wise. Would they sense that the life force still lingered in Jacob Atook? He waited, immobile, wanting to look up, not daring to do it.

A shadow flitted across the snow and was gone again, but for the moment of its passing he heard a rustle of feathers cutting air. Then for a long time there was no more sign that the ravens were there, no shadows, no whir of wings. Could they know that the death they awaited was not yet here? Would they outwait him? Or if they came while the life force survived, would the bow be effective? It was crude. He hadn't even tried a practice shot, for he had been afraid of losing the arrow in the snow. What if they came, but landed behind where he couldn't see? It would be hard to get the arrow away quickly and accurately if he had to raise himself first on the toboggan and then turn before he could shoot.

Slowly the mind fogged and the tortured doubts drained out of it. For a while the cold pierced, and then the body numbed and he could feel the cold no more. The heart ceased its frantic pounding. The brilliance around him grayed, the summoning of outer reality became harder, and he abandoned the effort of it, and let the grayness stay. Now the feigning had gone out of it. Dying was easy, a comfort. Why should it be feared? Only living had pain.

But again, just as hearing faded and was almost gone, there was a patter of wings behind him. The mind heard, but struggled to ignore, to cling to its soothing inertia. And now a gurgling croak sounded, but it, too, was behind, and Jacob was too tired to try to turn in the bogging snow. The eyes were closed; he wanted to open them, but they were heavy, and the lids wouldn't obey the feeble signal of the brain.

There was another rustle of wings, and this time it was close, over his head, and the hurried slapping of the landing strokes was in front and not behind. The eyes struggled open, but even opened it was hard to make them see. The gray world slowly resolved to white, and the dark blur in its center constricted, the black silhouette sharpened, and suddenly Jacob Atook was a thinking, planning hunter again. He could feel the cold reaching to the deepest bones. He could see the raven clearly, even the hint of blue sky reflected in the glistening black feathers.

The hunter instincts took command. Don't move yet. Its fear and suspicion will still be strong. Feign death a little longer. He was still propped up on an elbow, left hand holding the half-raised bow, right fingers gripping the arrow and bowstring. Now, move slowly. The bow first, a little lower, until you sight the black one over the point of the arrow. Imperceptibly the arrow tip crept down from sky to black bill to shaggy throat to breast. He began the draw. Keep it slow, as long as there is not the little bouncing bend of the legs that is the prelude to flight. The bow was stiff. He hadn't allowed for this awkward shooting position, or for the strain on the arm of a slow, prolonged draw. He should have cut the bow down and made it lighter. The arm ached and began to tremble with the strain. The arrow point was wavering. Relax, don't stiffen. Now *kahkaki* was peering curiously, and the head tilted, and then the leg bounce came. But the draw was almost full, and Jacob snapped it back, and the arrow release was clean. There was a swish of sound, but the arrow flew too fast for the eye to see against the dazzle of the snow.

He nocked another arrow and clambered to his knees, but the effort brought a reeling dizziness, the turning around was cumbersome and slow, and the two ravens that had been behind were winging strongly away before his heavy eyes could find them. He didn't try to shoot again.

He turned back. He could see the shot arrow lying on the snow, but there was no *kahkaki* with it. He rose painfully, clumsily, his lips trembling. He was certain the aim was good; surely he was too close to miss. And he hadn't seen the raven fly, but that could be because he had turned to get the other two, without waiting to see what his first arrow had done. He scanned the snow again, hoping the tired eyes had been mistaken, but there was no black carcass marring the clean expanse of white, and now the sob burst over his lips and his shoulders sagged.

The ravens would never come near enough for a bow shot again. But he could still try to return to Taka. He jabbed the bow and the two arrows under the packsack straps, took up the drawrope, and leaned into it. He started to retrieve the other arrow, then realized he would have no more use for it, and was turning away after a few strides when a thin black line impinged itself on the hazy rim of his vision. He dropped the toboggan rope and almost ran.

The black wings were still quivering when he picked it up from the hollow behind a snow ridge where it had fallen. The arrow had gone completely through.

There was a foul, carrion smell of death on the raven's feathers, but it did not deter the hunger pain of anticipation that churned now in Jacob Atook's stomach.

⫷⫷⫷⫷⫷ Chapter 22 ⫷⫷⫷⫷⫷

THE FLESH OF THE RAVEN was stringy, and pungent with a carrion rankness. He started out eating small quantities with plenty of the bog-bush tea, and after a time the stomach accepted, and the mouth learned to ignore the evil taste, and he ate greedily. The raven was fat with the gleanings of the deaths of others, but there was not much more than two pounds of meat and entrails. Jacob threw none of it away, for it was a cardinal knowledge of his people, born of long experience with starvation times, that there was a nourishment in guts and organs that flesh could not provide.

Jacob's was a body inured to hunger and hardship, with a capacity for quick rehabilitation bred deeply into it. So recovery was rapid. The numbness first changed to pain, then the pain softened and filtered away. By nightfall, several hours later, he could feel the strength trickling back, and with it, hope. By morning, after a night's sleep with a full stomach, he would be in shape to take up the *atihk* trail again for at least one more day, perhaps two.

He gazed the way of the back trail many times that evening, knowing that Taka would be near once more. So he

built the fire big to warn Taka, if he was in sight, that
Jacob was here close by. And he wanted the fire for a second
purpose—to give him light for yet another job that now had
to be done.

The vaneless arrows had served for close range, but they
would need feather guides to hold an accurate trajectory
for longer shots. He split the quills of several of the raven's
tail feathers, trimmed the halves to size, unraveled a length
of yarn from one of his spare socks, and bound guide vanes
on the arrows—three for each one. Next he cut a strip from
the canvas tarp and sewed it with yarn to form a quiver
that would hang behind his shoulder, where the gun had
hung before.

Now he stared at the arrows and frowned. The headless
arrows were satisfactory for bird shooting, but for big game
they would produce small wounds, have limited penetrating
power, and would probably shatter if they struck bone. A
headed arrow, on the other hand, would break through
bone or sheer around it, leaving a wide, deep wound for
heavy bleeding. And he did have one good arrowhead.

He held the knife out in the firelight and studied it. The
point was sharp. He would still have most of the cutting
edge if he could break the point off; and he would still
have the point, too, for piercing or awl work, only on the
arrow instead of on the knife.

He didn't deliberate further. He took the knife out to the
edge of the firelight and drove its point thumb-deep into one
of the stumps left from firewood cutting. The blade would
be warm from lying in the sheath against his body, so he
returned to the fire and left it several minutes to let the cold
penetrate and give the steel a brittleness. When he felt it

was ready, he went back with the ax and gave the knife a sharp sideways blow. It broke cleanly at the surface of the wood. He dug out the embedded point with the heel of the ax blade, picked it up with a mitted hand, and took it back to the fire to warm it, so that it could be handled without the fingers freezing to it.

He scraped gum from the bark of a spruce and melted it in the tea-pail lid at the edge of the fire. He selected his best arrow, split the end, gummed the inner surfaces of the split, and inserted the knife point. While the gum was still soft, he held the arrow vertically between his palms with the point resting on the toboggan, and then he twirled it by rubbing the palms together, eying the point where arrowhead and shaft met. There was a wobble. He adjusted the head a little, and twirled it again. The wobble had disappeared, the balance and alignment were true. Now he bound the split end tightly with yarn, painted the yarn with spruce gum to harden it, and then moved the arrow back from the fire to let the gum set.

He tested it a few minutes later. The head was tight, the feather vanes firm.

"Niska, I'm a hunter again."

For now he had an arrow that could kill an *atihk*—or a man.

⁊ ⁊ ⁊ ⁊

The next morning he had another filling meal and then set out again on the *atihk* trail. And there was enough carcass left to give him one more meal.

His snowshoe pace was firm and steady, and the stooped stagger was gone. Two ravens returned, circled, following him briefly, and then flew on and disappeared. He passed quickly over the section of trail he had backtracked yesterday, for he hadn't come back far. His old toboggan trail and snowshoe prints had hidden the *atihk* tracks, but they reappeared and went on alone where he had turned back the day before.

The trail, the beaconing hope, was fainter, another day older now. The *atihk* was as far away as she had been at any time since the trailing of her began.

There were wisps of cloud today, so high they stood still in the sky—frail, evanescent clouds, not the hard, distending ones that could bring wind. And so the silence stayed, magnifying sounds, carrying them far, filling his ears with the heart thumping whenever he stopped. But perhaps it didn't matter now. Perhaps it was too late for wind to help, even if he did overtake the *atihk* one. It would be hard, even with wind muffling the *atihk*'s ears, for a lone hunter to stalk near enough to kill with bow and arrow. Two hunters might, for there were ambush opportunities then, but not one hunter alone.

Yet he knew the mind was evading. For there *might* still be a time and way. The ugly suggestion crept like a timid fugitive from its hiding place deep in the intellect. He thrust it back with an angry repugnance, for it was an evil, sordid way from which the mind and heart recoiled.

<<<<<<<< Chapter 23 <<<<<<<<

THE STRENGTH had come back quickly, but it dissipated
again in the same rapid pattern soon after the raven meat
was gone. The body reserves were long since used up, and
there was no well of deeper strength to call upon. The raven
meals had been like green spruce boughs on a dying fire that
produce a sudden frenzied burning but provide no lasting
fuel.

He could remember only one camp since the raven one,
and now it was midday, and already the body was sinking
once more into the numbed starvation state. The lassitude
of flesh, the tiredness of the bones, and the gray shutters
of the mind were coming back. The snowshoes dragged, as
though the snow caked on them were molten stone.

The eyes were losing their sharpness; there had been
times that morning when he had lost the trail and had had
to circle to find it again. His pace had slackened to a fraction
of what it had been when the hunt began. But for all the
struggle and torment of it, the *atihk* trail was still old.

Was it useless? This driving on? He knew now that even
if he closed the gap, and even if the wind howl returned,

his fading vision and the clumsy deterioration of his stalking skills would be no match for the alertness of an *atihk* that had had a warning that a hunter still might be on her trail. Unless . . . but again he thrust the thought away, feeling a revulsion and shame, trying to force the mind to forget.

He struggled on, and now the mind was telling him again that the trail was much too old to bother following farther; but the will would not listen, nor forget the other thing.

He looked for ravens; he had better arrows now. But the ravens had not returned.

"*Manito,* why didn't you tell me to let the raven go too? Do you love *kahkaki* less than the *atihk* and less than the sparrow and less than the *keekishkawasso* that is part of me and is dead by now in Niska's belly?"

The memory of the round hard belly released new dregs of strength.

"Work, legs, work."

And the legs worked on.

Where did the limit of endurance lie? He was there, on its verge, yet not quite there, for it teased and evaded and stayed just beyond his reach, always a few paces farther on. And he wanted it, wanted to grasp and relish in that final, surrendering signal of the will that he could go on no more. But it wouldn't come. The signal was a goading instead, a chiding, wheedling exhortation that it wasn't quite yet, that he could still go on a few more paces, and then a few more after that, and then to the next line of trees, only to the next, no farther, that would be the end. And the trees came, but the limit, the finishing line, wasn't there, for there was always another line of trees not far beyond, and the will insisted that he could reach it, too.

He was waddling like an ancient gander, but he wasn't falling, for the will was commanding that he must not fall, that if he fell he would not be able to rise again. He tried not to listen, not to heed, but he went on shuffling the snowshoes carefully, avoiding the rough spots that might trip him, because the will had become a domineering master that he feared.

The hunt had distilled to a bare and fundamental essence. The enemy now was not the cold, the silence, the hunger, the *atihk*—it was simply time. For time inevitably would bring a brief period when the *atihk*'s strength and alertness would fade to a par with his own. He had recognized it at the instant of the first *atihk* sighting, and now the thought was lingering, not letting itself be driven away, as it always had before. And even as he brooded its treachery and evil, and trembled at the wrath of the spirits that such an act would surely arouse, he was studying the great round tracks for signs that might tell if the time were near. But the trail was old, and maybe, far ahead, the time had already come and passed.

His sense of space contracted; the material world—malevolent, indifferent world—dissolved until the only sentient realities left were Jacob Atook and the *atihk* trail and time. But it was a strangely truncated time, for the world of Jacob Atook had lost its yesterdays and sacrificed its tomorrows, and all eternity had shriveled to a fleeting now.

⁇ ⁇ ⁇

For a few seconds he wondered if the eyes were playing tricks, if it was a scheme of the will to keep the body working. The gray shrouds lifted and a graphic clarity leaped

back to the eyes and mind. He adjusted the eye mask and
stared; his gaze shifted sharply, farther ahead, then to each
side in turn. But it couldn't be a dream, for all the senses
were starkly clear, and there was no blurred or hidden area
for the making of delusions. And the big new hoofprints
were still there, they didn't fade away.

The new trail came almost straight across the old one
and continued off toward the horizon of the dawn. The
edges of its tracks were not eroded and rounded like those
he had been following so long; they were cut sharply,
cleanly, and the small nodule of snow kicked up behind
each track was a loose, granular dusting, not yet solidified
and welded to the crusted snow on which it lay. Even where
a hind track overlapped a front one, as they often did in
this walking pattern, the two tracks no longer merged into
one; it was possible now to separate the print of the smaller
hind hoof superimposed on the larger front track beneath
it. And the faint jabs of the front-hoof dewclaws, obscured
before, were visible again. He could even see the jaggedness
along the front edge of the foreprints, for the front hoofs
were worn and cracked from the winter's lichen digging.

It was only a few hours old.

He studied them, comparing the best examples of the old
and new prints, measuring their size and shape with a per-
ception suddenly honed to knife-edge keenness. And the size
and shape were the same. The dewclaw spacing was the
same. Even the toothed pattern of forehoof wearing cor-
responded to the memory he had of the old trail, days back,
when its tracks were fresh and the hoof wear showed. It
was the she-one still, circling back to check the back trail at
a point a day or more behind to learn whether the hunter

still followed. Where the new tracks crossed the old, they were bunched and the snow was trodden, for the *atihk* had stopped here and snuffed the old prints and found no sign that the hunter came.

Now hunter and hunted were one again, the barrier between suddenly erased, a fresh trail once more joining them. And once more the mind of the hunter could project ahead and fashion again the primeval, psychic linking of predator and prey, giving the hunter a capacity to think and feel with the senses of the hunted one. Now the distance separating them before, making the hunt seem hopeless, had become a sustaining boon, for it had let the *atihk* circle far back and still find no hunter sign. That meant her fear would be lifted, her alertness relaxed, because she would think that the hunter was gone. But even if the alertness endured, it might be of little benefit to the *atihk* now. For why, after all these days, should the *atihk* be so anxious to know whether the hunter came? And Jacob knew, for the thinking of one was the thinking of the other now.

He turned and began following the new tracks. His legs were firm, and his mind and eyes were clear, but a bitter loathing was in his heart. He wondered if he could do it— even if its opportunity came.

He had passed only two spruce islands when he came to a spot where the *atihk* had rested, and the rest had been a long one, for the hollow that her body had left was rounded and well melted into the snow. He looked for pellets or a water stain where the rump had lain, but there was nothing visible. The tracks beyond were closely spaced, crowded; she was moving slowly now. Jacob gazed ahead, searching, but there were only the merging lines of ragged spruces there.

The trail disappeared in a shadowed ribbon of trees. Jacob approached openly, directly, making no effort for stealth as he had on the time before, letting the bow still hang on his back with the slackened bowstring across his shoulder, because if the killing opportunity was to be, there would be no need in it now for stealth or haste. No testing of the hunter's cunning and skill.

Jacob entered the trees and saw a fresh feeding crater ahead, but no sign of the *atihk* near it. He moved up, and the crater was in a lee where the snow was shallow, but the *atihk* had not been able to finish it, for the gouge marks of the hoofs didn't go through to ground level. There was another resting hollow near, but this one was only a saucer-like flattening of the snow. And there were three small pellets of excreta and a tiny urine stain. Stooping slowly so as not to bring back a dizziness that would cause him to fall, Jacob examined the pellets, and they were only thinly frozen. He studied the urine stain; it was still yellow, not the water.

The trail went on and out of the trees and across another open bog strip. It twisted erratically, the strides were shortening, and some of the tracks had grooves like tails where the hoofs had dragged. Jacob could feel what he couldn't see—that the weakness in him was now in the *atihk,* too. And somewhere in him a reluctance was trying to hold him back, but the will, the unassailable fortress that wouldn't let the life force go, still drove him on.

Now there was another bedding saucer. The *atihk* was stopping repeatedly to rest. This one had furrows where the legs had stiffened and dug the snow with their straining, and it had a large crust of fresh ice that was clear, not yellow.

The next resting spot was only a few dozen strides farther on. And here the first thin streaks of frozen blood glistened pink on the snow.

Jacob hurried forward, a desperate vigor giving him a stamina that had not been in him for a long time. The snowshoes and toboggan sang crisply on the dry snow, and he made no effort to silence them. There was still no *atihk* visible ahead, for he was in an area where the strands and clumps of trees were intermixed closely with the bog openings. He followed the trail into another spruce island, letting the tea-bush withes snap heedlessly under his snowshoes, and here, where the tracks showed that the *atihk* had stopped but not lain down, there were flecks of blood again on the satiny snow. And then, a little farther, the flecks merged into a smear as large as one of the hoofprints. Tendrils of steam were rising from it, and its color was crimson, not pallid pink, for this blood was still unfrozen.

When Jacob came out to the edge of the trees, the doe was lying in the bald stretch of bog beyond—a great black hump against the luminous white of the snow. Her head was up, the antlers rising like twisted sticks, the muzzle and white ear funnels turned toward him, for she couldn't miss having heard the noise of Jacob's approach. The moment Jacob appeared, the head bobbed quickly in the *atihk* signal of alarm. She came to her feet stiffly, breaking into an ambling trot, but her gait was awkward, and after a few paces it slowed to a lumbering walk.

Jacob slipped the bow from his shoulder. His hands trembled as he flexed it and set the bowstring. He removed the mitt from the arrow hand and nocked the knife-point arrow on the string. Then, leaving the toboggan behind, he moved

forward, bow and arrow poised before him. But the *atihk*
still moved as fast as he did; the gap was not closing. Then
suddenly she stopped, the white flag of tail lifted and stood
upright, the hind legs spread, bent at the hocks, and Jacob
could see the body straining. Quickly he moved nearer. He
could see the doe more clearly—the gauntness of the hips
with the loosely hanging skin on the protruding bones, the
narrow rump with blood staining its white fur, and the belly,
big and round, the skin drawn tightly there.

The image that the eyes were engraving on the mind
suddenly changed. Niska now. Her belly big and round, too.
Her body also emaciated by the demands of the unborn
one. Was the blood flowing from Niska, too? No. Never.
The *atihk* had come too late. The tears rose in Jacob's eyes,
and spilled.

The *atihk*'s period of travail was brief. In a few moments
the tail dropped, the doe resumed walking, again moving as
fast as Jacob could. The time was not yet, but it could not
be long. And Jacob went on, and the pain that filled the
mind, the ambivalent pitting of abhorrence and wish, the
goading to do and not to do, swelled and smothered until
the pains and fatigues of the body were lost in its stifling
folds.

Then he heard, and there was no surprise in the hearing.
"Jacob, you will let the *atihk* go."

There was something of Niska's voice in it, and Father
Webber's, and his own. It was not like any one of them
alone, yet was like them all. And again it was not from outside, or above, but from within.

He lowered the bow, returned the arrow to the quiver,
and then turned and trudged heavily back to the toboggan.

He was telling himself that the *atihk* still had the strength to evade him, to keep him from getting near enough for a bow shot that would kill. If he pressed her during this waiting time, he would only drive her into the trees beyond, where it would be harder to keep a watch on her condition and harder to close in when the time would come.

"That's why I wait, *Manito*. Not because you have spoken. For you don't love the *atihk,* you only say you do."

And Jacob Atook wondered, and a part of him hoped that what he said was true, and a part of him wavered and still didn't know.

Out on the bog, the mother one had lain again on the snow, but the head was up and alert, watching Jacob attentively. Jacob's mind was a crossfire of conflicting currents. He was seeing the awesome magic of life's renewal, and he was seeing meat, two hundred pounds, perhaps, despite the scrawny thinness—rich meat that would have brought the strength back quickly to Niska, and put milk in the shriveled breasts, if it had come in time.

The *Manito* spoke again. "Jacob, Jacob, you will let the mother one go."

Somewhere a part of him still wanted to heed. If it was too late for Niska, did he want meat now? He had defied the *Manito* the other time; he would have killed the *atihk* then if the shift in the wind had not warned her and sent her away. But Niska was waiting then, whereas now the meat would be only for himself. The thought made his teeth grind in a violent shudder and brought the spilling tears again.

Yet he didn't *know* that Niska was dead.

Now the bush with the deep roots of hidden thought

came back, unbidden. Angrily he threw off the mitts, opened the packsack, and scooped up the cones that were in its bottom, dumping them on the boards of the toboggan. He glanced quickly at the *atihk*. She still lay quietly, so this time he would do the counting slowly and carefully to be sure of what it said.

He placed two cones on the snow.

"Cones, you are sparrows, mother and father."

Then he put down four and four, and that was the multiplication of the first year, and the sparrows now were ten. He drew a line in the snow, and moved along to a new spot beyond the line, and now his wrinkled, old-man hands arranged the ten cones into five pairs. He took new cones from the toboggan and he placed two sets of four above each of the five pairs. He had to count them in English because there were not words in his own tongue for numbers that high. There were fifty. He counted them again to be sure, reminding himself that they were sparrows and not spruce cones, and then drew another line in the snow.

"Now it's the third year. . . ."

He stepped back and forth, moving the cones to the new area of snow, arranging them in pairs, and putting two groups of four above each pair. He still had a long way to go when he ran out of cones. They were hard to count now, there were so many. Once he counted a hundred and seventy-six, the next time he counted a hundred and eighty-six, and he wondered what the count would be if he had enough cones to go on to the end. Whatever it was, it was a vast number of sparrows—these sparrows that could come in just three years from one mother and father pair.

He tried to picture how many there would be in ten

years, or twenty years, if the *Manito* let the multiplication go on this way. He knew they would be as numerous as the snowflakes of winter, and the *Atihk-anishini* would have to wade through sparrows the way they waded through snow.

But the sparrows didn't come like the snowflakes of winter. Where there were two sparrows one year, there were always just two again the next. Where did the others go? Did they go to the warm southland and live there and not come back? Then he thought of the grouse that laid not just four eggs in its nest, but twelve, and they didn't go to the distant southland, they stayed for the winter here in the land of the *Atihk-anishini*. Yet like the sparrows, they didn't change, didn't multiply as the cones said they should.

And what he saw was a great cruelness, a great sadness of pain and killing and dying, and it was what he had dimly seen when he counted the cones before, but he saw it much more clearly now. For now he was thinking of the weasel and the hawk and all the other hunting ones that had to have sparrows and grouse to eat, as the *Atihk-anishini* had to have *atihk*.

"*Manito*," he murmured, "why does your hymn say that the sparrow meets your tender view when it falls from the sky with the hawk upon it? Because, *Manito,* you made the hawk too. Where is your tender view when you put ten sparrows every year where only two will live? When most of them are born only to come quickly to the fright and pain of dying? You love them no more than you love the nuts that you make to feed the squirrels."

Throughout it, his eyes had shifted repeatedly to the *atihk* that still lay in the same spot out on the bog. She had been lying quietly, but now the white tail was up again, the legs stiffening, and even from this distance Jacob could make out the heaving and contractions of the flanks. It lasted longer this time, but soon the tail dropped again and the doe relaxed. There was still a waiting time.

He looked back at the profusion of cones speckling the snow. Maybe they wouldn't say the same about the *atihk* which had one or two babies a year instead of the sparrow's eight. He vaguely remembered counting *atihk* cones sometime in the tortured days behind, but it wasn't clear and sure like the sparrow multiplication, for some of the *atihk* were always yearlings that couldn't have calves, and this had made the counting muddled. Now doubts began to worry him. It was *atihk,* not the sparrow, that was the polestar in the zodiac of wretchedness that weighed on Jacob Atook now. And it was for the *atihk* that he must know with certainty what the cones would say.

He began gathering up the cones and piling them again on the toboggan. His mind was searching. There must be a way. He stared at a spruce tree near him that had the cone clusters at its top, seeing the small soft buds among them that had not yet grown into cones—like *atihk* calves and yearlings that had not yet grown into breeding bucks and does.

He took the ax from the pack. It was heavy now in his sagging arms, the blows weak and fumbling. But the tree eventually fell, and he filled a parka pocket with spruce needles and with the buds that were not yet cones. He returned to the toboggan and placed two cones on the snow.

"You are not cones, you're *atihk,* a mother one and a father one. And you have twin calves when the winter ends and the spring begins."

He looked out quickly at the real mother one that lay in the snow. She hadn't moved. The tail was down.

He placed two needles above the two cones.

"You are not spruce needles, you're *atihk* calves, and if there are twins this first year, I'll give you only one calf next year, because I think that's the way it is."

He drew a line in the snow with the ax handle and moved along.

"*Atihk,* this is the second year. . . ."

He moved over the two cones that were mother and father ones, changed the two needles to buds because they were yearlings now, and added another needle for another calf. Then he put another line in the snow and moved again.

"*Atihk,* this is the third year. . . ."

Now there were four cones, and one bud, and he added three needles because he thought one of the grown-up pairs would have twins and the other a single calf.

He moved on, switching the cones and buds and needles with an eager concentration, snatching quick looks at the *atihk* lying out on the bog, hurrying to know all that the cones could say before the *atihk*'s time arrived. By the fifth year there were eight cones and three buds and six needles on the snow—seventeen in all. For the sixth year it was eleven and six and eight, which was twenty-five, and he worked no further, because maybe six years was as long as an *atihk* could live; maybe the old ones would start dying now, so from here on the cones wouldn't speak the truth. It wasn't the big multiplication like the sparrow's, but it was still a lot of *atihk* to come in six years from a single mother and father pair. He thought of the *atihk* herds that were sometimes six and sometimes eight, and he saw that the twenty-five figure was an easy one to work with, because four of them made a hundred. And if two *atihk* could be twenty-five in six years, then a herd of eight could be a hundred in the same time.

But they couldn't multiply that way, of course, because the lichen grew slowly—he had seen the years it took to come back where *atihk* had grazed it clean—and if there were a hundred *atihk* every six years where there were eight to begin with, the lichen would soon be eaten and all of them would starve. But in any case Jacob knew that the *atihk didn't* multiply that way, for like the fish and the sparrow and all the other forest ones, where there were two one year, there were always just two again the next. And now Jacob knew why. The *Manito,* when he made the *atihk,* also made wolves and *Atihk-anishini.*

Jacob left the cones on the snow. He had seen all that they could tell him; the bush was torn from the ground, the long deep roots exposed. With everything it was the same— always the making of life went on faster than there was room for living. Always there were the parent ones, and every year a host of newborn ones, but the only ones that would live were the few required to replace the dying of the old. The rest—the multitude in reserve to be called upon if needed, the legion born for sacrifice—were just fodder for the hunting ones. And of all the killers, only man carried the burden of reflecting on what he killed.

Again Jacob saw the overflowing bucket, and now he knew what the mind had been building. The bucket was the big land, the water gushing in was life, and with the fish it was more bucketfuls each time, and with the *atihk* it was only a cupful or a spoonful at a time, but the effect was the same, because the bucket was always on the verge of being full. Most of the new water could only overflow and disappear.

Now the vision changed. It was the big tent at Wapanishee post with the table, the white and gold cloth, the book and the shining cross. And Father Webber on his knees. Father Webber saying the thank-you prayer, the one he said so often. "We thank you, God, for your loving handiwork, for the beauty and bounty of the world of nature that you prepared for us, your unworthy children. . . ." And Jacob shivered. He looked at the *atihk* out on the snow, and a sourness puckered his mouth and put a sticky dryness on his lips. Father Webber was not a hunter; Father Webber didn't know, as Jacob knew, that there was no beauty in it, nor love. That all its serenity, all the beauty there seemed to be, was a mask for a world of silent, hidden violence and killing that never ended, that couldn't end without bringing starvation to all. And the wolf would never eat side by side with the lamb, nor the leopard with the kid, for the killing was an essential part of it, like the breathing and the heartbeat, like the sun and soil and rain that made the green things grow. The abundant making of life could only go on if there was also abundant death.

Now an angry knowledge pressed on him. If it was a *made* thing, as Father Webber said, if a power to fashion and decide had gone into it, there was no reason why it couldn't have been made differently. Only a cruel one could have planned it to work this way.

If it had a beginning, the opportunity to make it a different way must have existed then. There didn't have to be hunters, because some of the biggest ones like the moose

and the *atihk* found the life force they needed without killing. And if it could be done for them, it could have been
done for all.

"*Manito,* if you wanted to, you could have given the
weasel a stomach that would let it eat seeds like the sparrow,
and you could have had the owl eat buds like the grouse,
and the wolf eat moss like the *atihk.* You could have had
the sparrow lay one egg every year instead of eight, and the
atihk have two calves in its lifetime instead of eight or ten.
And then there would only be dying of the old ones, and
there would be no need for killing and pain."

But the *Manito* hadn't made it that way. All around was
death and killing, and Jacob Atook was one of its killers.
There was no escape. This was the way it was.

Now the *atihk* came laboriously to her feet. The white
tail rose, the back arched, and the round sides heaved and
strained. She swayed and the legs buckled and she dropped
heavily, unable now to stand. The tail stayed up; the legs
stiffened, seeking a leverage in the yielding snow.

It would be a short time, only minutes now, and then the
she-one would be on her feet, capable of moving again. But
Jacob stood, transfixed by a narcosis of dread, swaying, too,
with a weakness that was both of the body and the mind.
For perhaps there could be honor in killing when it was
done the noble way, but there was only black shame in this
thing that the dogged will would now have him do—this
making of death when a noble one lay helpless in her time
of making life.

"Jacob, you will let the *atihk* go." But this time there was
nothing of Niska's voice in it, nor of Father Webber's; it
was his own, yet alien, barely recognizable, for it belonged

to another Jacob Atook of another time. And maybe it was the *Manito* speaking to Jacob Atook in Jacob Atook's voice, or maybe it wasn't the *Manito* at all.

The snowshoes crunched again on the snow. The legs were long and the snowshoes far away, like other beings, but the mind of Jacob Atook willed their sluggish effort.

"*Manito,* this is the way you made it, and this is the way it is."

The *atihk* rose, but dropped again, and Jacob walked up as he would to a chained dog. The arrow flew. The rending heart cried: "*Manito,* why?" And he grabbed another arrow from over the shoulder, but it wasn't necessary to shoot a second time. The shame was a searing anguish, but the fear was more, and he ran up and pierced the eyes with the point of the other arrow before the *atihk*'s spirit could recognize the vileness of the deed he had done, and cast the retribution that the deed deserved. But he looked without fear to the blazing heaven, for he no longer cared what the *Manito* saw.

◄◄◄◄◄◄ Chapter 24 ◄◄◄◄◄◄

HE TORE OFF a snowshoe and dug a hole where the great
antlers pierced the snow crust, so that the head could drop
and the blood could flow. Then he cut the shaggy throat
and threw himself belly-down on the snow, clawing the
wound open with his fingers, cracked lips sucking the hot
blood that gushed across the stiff white fur.

The red tide spilled across his cheeks, matting the fringe
of beard hairs; it ran down his fingers and wrists under the
parka sleeves. He let his mouth fill, savoring the hot, salty
tang of it, raised his head and gulped it down. It was like
a fiery brand in his throat and all the way to his stomach.
Its richness started him retching, but he swallowed hard,
kept it down, lowered his head for more.

Minutes later he washed his face and hands with snow,
then rose to his feet. Two strengths flowed into him as he
went back for the toboggan and returned to the laborious job
of dressing and quartering his kill with the knife and ax.
One was the strength of the *atihk* blood that filled the
stomach soothingly now; the other was a strength of pride
in the knowledge that he was a hunter again, untrammeled

with the doubts of old. He thought of the ancestors hidden deeply within, their life force a part of his. Were they proud that Jacob Atook had fulfilled himself as a hunter in the ancient way of his people, without the white man's gun? Or did they cringe with hatred at the evil way it was done?

He shouldn't have thought of the ancestors, because suddenly it routed the burgeoning strength and pride, and put a terrible pain in their place. There would be no descendants to receive their part of the life force of Jacob Atook, and to honor him as an ancestor. The hunt had been too long, and the line of ancestry was cut, back in the tent on the Little Ninkik where the body and the other small body within it would be.

He loaded the meat, hauled it back to the trees, raised a tripod of poles, and slung the antlered head high under its apex. Maybe the *Manito* saw, maybe he didn't; Jacob no longer cared.

His thinking shifted to Taka. Did it matter now if Taka followed him back to the Little Ninkik? The mind was fuzzy and couldn't decide. But he made the camp on the side of the spruce island that faced the back trail, where Taka would see and stay behind. Whatever was to come, the body was too weak for it now.

But as chunks of *atihk* liver began stewing on the fire, he went to the quiver and snatched out the arrow that had killed the *atihk*. He had cut it out of the carcass heedlessly, not thinking he might want it another time. He studied it, rolling it in his hands. Its knife-point head was firm, the shaft unbowed, the guide feathers unbroken, unfrayed. It could kill again.

⸙ ⸙ ⸙ ⸙

He started back with the first light of morning, heading into the rising sun to return to the Mahkwa River by a route that would avoid the back trail, because in the tangled confusion of thinking, one idea persisted—if there was to be a meeting with Taka, the time was not yet.

The toboggan was much heavier than before, and for that first day the drag of it was a fatiguing strain on his legs, and he didn't travel far.

By the second morning the strength of the *atihk* was becoming the strength of Jacob Atook. He could feel the new stamina bracing him even before he rolled from the lean-to bed. And that was not the only difference that morning, for the dawn was a strange and contrasting one from the vivid crimson dawns there had been since the hunt in the little sticks began so many days ago. There was no sunrise. Where the sunrise should be there was only a pallid saffron streak piercing a mantle of turbid cloud that reached across the sky.

He had been on the trail only a short time when the snow began falling, and he gazed up into the white-flecked opaqueness of sky with a sour anger chilling him. For it was too late—there was no need to hide his trail now. In any case, it was a thin, dusting snow that wouldn't hide his trail from a hunter with eyes like Taka Cheechoo's. Jacob had not traveled far yesterday. Taka would simply close in and keep the trail in view.

But the snow brought a new thinking. Or maybe it was just that as the body strengthened, hope strengthened with it. Somewhere the same will that wouldn't surrender to reason was struggling again to be heard. And what it said was that fearing wasn't knowing, and until the proof of knowing came, there was still a place for hope.

But the implacable and dispassionate voice of reason took control again. Niska's body, with the *keekishkawasso* sapping its fading strength, couldn't have waited this long. To let the will persuade the mind otherwise was a cruel self-torture.

Yet the power that had refused to let the life force go when reason argued that the *atihk* was too far ahead to trail any farther now wouldn't let the hope go, either.

"Niska, did you go out and gather more *oseepan* when there was still time?"

The will had known, when the body and the reason wanted to give up trailing the *atihk*. Maybe the will knew again.

He stopped and looked back. The view behind was veiled by the sifting snow. He could still see at least a mile, for it was not a heavy snow, but the flakes were puffing out, growing larger, and perhaps the fall was thickening. Back there, not far now, Taka would be hurrying, his eyes concentrated on the dimming trail.

Jacob turned and went on. Ahead was an island of trees too large to go around. The spruces were sparse and scattered where he entered, but they clumped and thickened on the far side a hundred paces or so beyond. He stopped again in the center of the island and for a minute or more he studied the pattern of trees ahead, his eyes shifting, calculating. There was one round, dense spruce with lower branches that drooped so that their tips were anchored in the snow. Within and beneath those branches, there would be a hidden hollow where the snow hadn't reached.

He moved forward again, veering a little so that the trail would pass close to the spruce with the drooping branches, and then he continued straight out across the bare bog beyond.

Several minutes later he turned, went far out to the side, then turned again, circling back. And he hid the toboggan in a spruce clump at the island's edge far along from the point where his original trail passed through.

⚹ ⚹ ⚹ ⚹

Jacob was crouched, legs folded tightly beneath him, because there was little room under the overhang of spruce branches. His legs were cramped and aching. He couldn't take the snowshoes off, which would let him stretch out more comfortably, because there wouldn't be time to strap them on again.

The wait had gone on interminably. Long ago the cold had stabbed through the parka, and now he trembled uncontrollably, and he hoped the trembling was just from cold. He gazed again at the bow beside him, ready, strung, the arrow nocked, and he wondered if the stiff fingers and numbed arms would be capable of drawing it.

He studied the opening behind him, where he had broken branches away to let him crawl out quickly, and he remembered that he must do it carefully and not snag a snowshoe on one of the broken branch ends. He turned to the other opening where the spruce twigs were bent back to make a tiny window facing the back trail. The snow was still sifting down. His snowshoe tracks were perhaps two hours old now and the snow was blurring them.

He couldn't see much of the trail, because trees hid it. He should have selected a point facing a broad stretch of bog where he would have had plenty of warning of Taka's approach. Here, Taka would almost be on him before he came in sight.

Maybe Taka was farther behind than he had calculated, and had already lost the trail. Maybe he was guarding against ambushes like this by not following directly on the trail, but off to the side instead; or maybe he was circling the spruce islands, avoiding tree cover, picking up the trail each time around on the other side. And if he *had* gone around this island, had he found the tracks of Jacob's circling back, or the toboggan where Jacob had hidden it? Was it too much to expect that a hunter as cunning as Taka could be outwitted with a ruse as simple as this one?

He heard the swish of snowshoes and the creaking of the toboggan before he saw him. For a few taut seconds he wondered if his ears were teasing. Then Taka appeared. Jacob had had no doubt for a long time that Taka followed, yet perhaps a shred of skepticism had lingered, because now his vision grayed and his head swayed giddily, and it all had an overlay of unreality. It was hard to accept that he was near a man again, after so long alone. But he steeled the trembling body, and he willed the vision clear. And Taka still came.

The stocky figure, dark against the snow, had appeared among the trees at the far side of the spruce island. It was hunched forward against the drawrope of the toboggan, the eyes down, fixed on Jacob's trail. It came rapidly; Taka was hurrying, as Jacob knew he would be. The face was shaded and had a ghostly look from the white rime of frozen breath that clung to the shaggy eyebrows and to the rim of the parka hood.

The rifle was slung by its carrying strap on Taka's back. The toboggan that followed behind, like a part of him, was laden with three fat packs—the food that would have saved Niska and the *keekishkawasso,* if Jacob had done what reason wanted him to do, and told Taka where Niska was.

He raised the bow, horizontally, because there wasn't space among the branches over his head to hold it vertically as it should have been held. Taka was only a few toboggan lengths away, coming almost straight toward him. It would be easy. He couldn't miss. He drew the bow to full. The arrowhead crept up from Taka's legs to his chest and steadied there. Jacob's hands and arms were firm, there was no trembling, for he knew this wasn't yet the crucial time. He had no intention of killing, and never had, unless Taka left him no other choice. And the new snow was offering another way. But the bow arm had to be ready for instantaneous response in case the plan went wrong. He let the bow's tension ease, then drew it full out again, working the stiffness out of his drawing arm.

There was a stinging flick against his cheek beneath the eye that sighted along the arrow. The bow recoiled with a muted thud. The arrow dropped free. And he gazed in shocked panic at the frayed ends of broken bowstring dangling from each tip of the bow.

Jacob's body was gripped now by a spasm of convulsive trembling.

The thud of the bow had not been loud enough to reach Taka and penetrate the parka hood that covered his head. And Taka passed now, no more than a toboggan length away, his eyes not lifting from Jacob's trail. He strode on, and out onto the open bog beyond, his back to Jacob now.

Jacob had to act quickly, for in a short time his trail would lead Taka around and back here to the hiding spot. The broken ends of bowstring were too short to knot together, and there wasn't time to return to the toboggan and improvise another. He must not let Taka get much farther away.

He rose, bent low beneath the spruce branches. His legs tingled and almost buckled as the blood coursed back into them. He waited a few more seconds for the legs to strengthen. Then, grasping the useless bow and arrow, he scrambled out through the opening in the branches and came erect outside. The trembling ceased, his body steeled. He raised his arms and bow and arrow to shooting position.

"Taka!"

Jacob saw the sudden stiffening and the shifting of the feet as Taka started to swing around.

"Don't turn! Face ahead!"

Turning was difficult on snowshoes. It took several seconds, because the snowshoes had to be shifted around a little at a time to keep them from snagging on each other. And if Taka turned his head it would give him at best only a partial view, because the head would pivot inside the parka hood which projected like blinders on each side of his face.

Taka had stopped the swing around. He stood stiffly now, not trying to turn.

Would he know that Jacob didn't have a gun? He would have seen the discarded tamarack shafts and the split raven feathers back in the camp where Jacob had made the bow and arrows. Or if he had been following close enough behind, he would know there had been no rifle shot when the *atihk* was killed. He might even have found Jacob's rifle bolt.

"I've only got a bow and arrow, Taka. But it killed an *atihk*."

Taka would know that, for the great red stain of the killing place would be impossible to miss. But he might turn his head enough to get a glimpse past the parka hood's rim, and recognize that the bow was dead and useless now, although the snow was coming more thickly, pricking the eyes, keeping them blinking, impeding vision. Jacob kept the bow raised and his right arm cocked by his ear, hoping it would look as if the arrow were ready to go.

He moved up to the rear of Taka's toboggan, then crouched behind the packsacks. The rifle was still slung on Taka's back.

"Drop the toboggan rope, Taka."

Taka lifted the rope over his head and dropped it behind him. Jacob studied the broad back for signs that might tell whether Taka obeyed from fear, or whether he was getting the rope out of the way for the turning and unslinging of the gun. But there was no evidence of the trembling on Taka's back that Jacob hoped to see. After the first surprised stiffening, Taka now looked relaxed and calm.

"Taka, my bow is full drawn. The arrow is headed with the point broken from my knife. Remember? I think you taught me to make arrows that way. I learned better than you thought I did. It's aimed at the spot between your shoulder blades. If you start to turn . . . it only took one arrow—*this* arrow, Taka—to kill the *atihk*."

He had to pause and wait for the husky edge to leave his voice. One hint of fear, one suggestion that his threat might be a hollow one, could embolden Taka and change it all.

"Now . . . unsling the rifle and stand it in the snow beside you. Then get moving. Don't stop, don't turn, until I tell you to! And stock down in the snow, Taka; don't try to plug the barrel with snow. . . ."

He was too late catching it. The words were said. Would Taka guess from that that Jacob must have the gun in firing condition? He was talking too much. Would all the talk, and the fact that Jacob hadn't killed him immediately without warning, make Taka begin to suspect that he was bluffing? And what if the gun wasn't loaded? But he was committed to it now. There was no other way.

"The rifle . . . down in the snow! If you make me, I'll kill you, Taka. It'll be safer that way. Then I'll be sure you'll never find her."

But Taka still didn't move.

"Now, Taka! The gun!"

Taka raised it slowly over his head. Now he was holding it canted in front of him. He spoke for the first time.

"It isn't loaded. Put your bow and arrow down."

But Jacob heard the snap of the releasing safety lock over the sound of Taka's voice that had been meant to cover it.

"I'm not putting the bow and arrow down. And I'm shielded behind your packsacks, so if you do manage to swing around and get a snap shot away ahead of my arrow, the shot will probably hit a pack. I'll have plenty of time to make sure the arrow has good aim."

It was better to tell him, because Taka might turn and get a glimpse past his parka rim and see Jacob crouched behind the packs. And telling him in advance might steer off Taka's guessing the real reason for putting the packs between them. He moved the bow in close to the rearmost packsack, so that only the arrow and upper half of the bow showed above it.

The bottom of the bow was braced on the toboggan. The arrow was in shooting position. Half of the broken bowstring was still attached to the upper tip, and Jacob had its loose end looped around his right hand. He was drawing down on it, putting an arc in the top of the bow visible above the packsack, making it look as if the bow were drawn.

Taka was shifting his weight, spreading his snowshoes farther apart.

Jacob shouted. "Don't try it!"

But Taka pivoted at his waist, the rifle swinging around at hip level, and the shot was instantaneous, shattering the silent air and echoing back almost instantly from the spruces behind. Jacob flinched, stiffened. His crouching body was thrown off balance and almost fell sideways. There seemed to have been impact somewhere on it—a sudden, wrenching jolt; but there was no pain yet. His arm was weakening; it was hard to maintain the tension on the upper half of the bow. He waited for the pain, not knowing where it would be. For a moment there was a reeling of vision, and then the eyes were clear again. And still no pain.

At the instant Taka turned and shot, Jacob had realized that Taka's right eye was seeing just past the furry rim of his parka hood. But the hood had shifted back, blinding him; he wouldn't know where his shot had gone. Taka was flinging his head sideways, trying to see around the hood again. The gun was still low, at his left hip, aimed far off to the side. It was an awkward position in which to work the bolt for a second shot. To get enough leverage, he would have to lower the barrel a little. And the barrel hadn't dropped. Taka, for those few seconds, was working frantically to get an eye clear of the parka hood, instead of shooting blindly again.

Jacob's arm trembled as it strove to hold the tension on the bowstring. Suddenly the lower tip of the bow, braced on the toboggan and taking all the strain of the draw, slid sideways with a jerk until it came against the toboggan side pole, throwing his body momentarily off balance—as it had before. And now he realized why there had been that wrenching jolt, but no pain of a hit, when he flinched at the blast of Taka's shot.

"It was wild, Taka. Nowhere near me . . ."

His voice quaked with fear. He stopped and tried to control it.

"But you've scared me. . . ." The breathless tremor was still there; it wouldn't be controlled. Maybe Taka would think that a frightened man was more to be feared than a calm one at a time like this. So he continued, not trying to hide the fear.

"I won't give you time to shoot again. You might be luckier another time. If that hand makes one move on the bolt . . . ! Put the hand over your head, Taka. Up! Fast! Away from the gun!"

"All right, Jacob. Don't shoot." But the voice was composed and placid, and Jacob would have felt more at ease if it had had a tremor of fear in it like his own.

Taka's right hand lifted slowly from the rifle. It paused beside his head.

"Don't touch that hood!" And Jacob drew down on the bowstring again, arcing the bow tip above the packsack, in case Taka did snatch another look.

But the hand and arm snapped upward, high. Taka turned, faced ahead. The left hand that held the gun lowered it, jabbing its butt fiercely into the snow. He started walking forward, leaving the gun behind.

"You won't get away with this, Jacob."

Jacob ran up and grabbed the rifle, quickly working the bolt, lifting a cartridge into the chamber. For just a moment he let himself glance with a fleeting smile at the old, splintered stock.

Out ahead on the bog, Taka was coming around, and now Jacob let him turn.

"Stay there." Jacob swung the rifle toward him.

"Are you going to leave me here without a gun?"

"I'm going to leave you with less than a gun. But I'll leave you my bow. How'll that be? In return for the bow I'll borrow some of your food."

Jacob stepped back to the toboggan, stood the gun near, and began searching through the packs, glancing up every few seconds to make sure that Taka didn't move.

"You won't miss a little. And I'm hungry for some bannock."

He set aside a twenty-five-pound sack of flour, some lard, tea, and baking powder, and put it all together in one of Taka's packsacks. Then he took the rifle, leveled it at Taka, and moved out nearer to him. For the first time Taka's face showed a little tightening of fear.

"No, Taka, I'm not going to kill you. That would be your way, but not mine. I'm just going to make sure you stay here for a while. Take off your snowshoes."

Taka didn't move. Jacob jerked the rifle up to his shoulder.

"I'd sooner kill you. And be rid of you for good."

Taka bent slowly. He removed his mitts and began unbuckling one of the harnesses.

"Faster!"

The fingers worked more rapidly.

"Step off them, and toss them over here to me."

Taka stepped away from the snowshoes and sank to his thighs in the snow. He threw them, one at a time, and Jacob picked them up and started back toward the toboggan. He turned his back casually on Taka now, for without snowshoes Taka could only struggle clumsily through the clutching snow. Jacob strapped the snowshoes to the food pack he was taking.

"Take the food but not the snowshoes. Without snowshoes it'll take me a day to move a mile."

"You've got a knife. Make new ones. Cut up one of your *atihk* skins for webbing. But I'll borrow your ax to make sure it takes you a few days to cut and make the frames."

Taka's voice hardened. "When I get back and tell the old ones this, they won't let you stay in the tribe."

"Tell them, Taka! Tell them that Jacob Atook got an *atihk* with a bow and arrow, when all the others were running back to the post for store food. And tell them that Taka Cheechoo let Jacob Atook disarm and overpower him with a bow that couldn't even shoot! Tell them that, and they won't run *me* out of the tribe, they'll laugh *you* out!"

Taka's jaw dropped. A perplexed frown came.

"Here. I promised not to leave you unarmed."

He tossed the quiver of arrows toward Taka, then the bow. The bow landed close to Taka's feet. Taka stared sullenly at the frayed ends of broken bowstring. He didn't speak again.

Jacob shouldered the pack, picked up Taka's ax and rifle, and without glancing back he walked along the edge of the spruce island to where he had left his own toboggan. He lashed Taka's packsack to it, beside the big frozen chunks of *atihk* meat. Then he took up the drawrope and started again.

The snow was stinging his face, falling heavily. It would hide his trail in an hour or two. But it would end before he could reach the Mahkwa cabin, and Taka might still try to pick up his trail there, days from now. So as soon as a spruce island hid him from Taka, Jacob turned southward to avoid the Mahkwa. Somewhere this way he would come to Ninkik country that he would recognize.

He had left Taka with a feeling of haughty pride. For the last hour or so the mind had been too occupied with the immediate crisis to have room for other things. But now it could think again. And he stared ahead to where the Ninkik country was, and the haunting dread came back.

⪻⪻⪻⪻⪻ Chapter 25 ⪼⪼⪼⪼⪼

JACOB COVERED THE LAST MILE along the shore of Little
Ninkik Lake at a jogging trot, despite the heavy toboggan
and the new soft snow that impeded the snowshoes. But
when he turned in toward the screen of spruces that hid the
tent, a great weight came, dragging at his legs until it took
superhuman effort to keep them moving at a slogging walk.
He wanted to run, but a frigid dread held him back. He
trudged up through the shoreline alders, stopping, peering
ahead, then moving slowly on, like a hunter stalking game.

He reached the spruces, crouched, scanning under them.
There was no tent visible. The heart pounded, but the body
was suddenly cold. He narrowed his eyes, pulling the vision
sharp, searching the patchwork of snow, trees, and shadows.

The faint gray triangle of tent front gradually emerged.
The rest was hidden by the snow that banked around it and
over the sagging slopes of the roof.

As he forced them to move again, the snowshoes dragged
like great stones, even heavier than on the last delirious
days of the *atihk* hunt. In the past few hours he had been
trying to reconstruct how long it had been, striving to recall

and sort out the night camps, for each camp was different and they were what lingered sharpest in the hazy memory. As close as he could figure, the hunt had gone on fourteen or fifteen days, and there had been five days after that settling with Taka and getting back here. It had been twice as long as he had expected it to be—twice as long as her food was meant to last.

Now, none of the wood he had cut and piled remained outside. No smoke rose from the stovepipe chimney. There was no fresh trail to or from the front of the tent, and the pit where the steps should be, leading down to the tent door, was rounded, smoothed, half filled with snow. He shuddered. At least the wolves had not yet come.

He tried to call. The voice faltered and died on his quivering lips, and only a whisper came.

Then the will that wouldn't surrender spoke—fainter now, hesitant, but still demanding attention. The snow that was starting when he ambushed Taka had continued to fall lightly until early the previous day. So at least the absence of tracks at the tent door spoke only for the last two days.

A fragment of hope revived. And now the voice breached the barrier of terror that blocked his throat.

"Niska?"

He stopped to silence the snowshoe noises, pushing the parka hood back to uncover his ears. The echoes came again and again, as though the spruces were mocking. Then they died, and the stillness plunged down.

"Niska!"

It came then, at once. Muffled by the snow that covered the tent, but strong enough to rise clearly over the new echoes. One word.

"Jacob."

He threw off the drawrope and lunged forward, leaving the toboggan behind. He snatched at the tie strings on the front of the tent and dashed in without even taking the snowshoes off. It was dark inside, because his eyes were constricted against the outside glare, and little light was penetrating the snow that covered the roof. He had to grope his way to the bed. His fingers found her and began stroking the hair and the grooved cheeks. A trembling enchantment shot through him as she raised her arms and clutched him in a feeble embrace. She sobbed softly.

"I have an *atihk*," he whispered against her ear. "There's food now."

Her face moved back. Jacob's eyes were sharpening in the gloom and he could see her now. Her cheeks were wan, thinner, the lines around her mouth were deeper, but there was a vigor still in the sudden smile.

"I knew you would, Jacob. And I'm a good hunter, too. When Nellie didn't come, I chopped out the ice hole with the ax you left and put the net back in the lake." A teasing gleam came into her smile. "It caught a fish. Only one. But a big one."

Her hands crept up and drew his face down again. Her lips brushed his cheek, seeking, found his, and pressed in a long, hard, quivering kiss. It was a pain to draw his lips away, but he burned to tell her more.

"And not just an *atihk*, Niska. Flour and tea, too."

Her head tilted back. The eyes questioned.

"Later, Niska. Later on I'll tell you how."

He was afraid to ask the one paramount question that pained and seethed within him. Her avoiding of the subject was its own grim answer. She needed food. He must save her the torture of telling him until the food had started to build strength in her again.

He pushed himself away and went back outside. As he brushed snow from the tent with a spruce bough to let the light in, he heard her stoking up the fire inside. Was she stronger than he thought? He thrust its hollow hope away.

He drew up the toboggan and took meat and Taka's food pack inside. She was back in the bed, but she had combed her long black hair. He stared, his breath catching, for even with the gauntness her startling beauty shimmered still. Was it all an evil dream? Was he freezing now in the snow beside the *atihk*'s trail, while the dying mind built fantasies? But she smiled again. And he knew a dying mind couldn't reconstruct a smile so beautiful.

His eyes moved down to the mound of bedding at her waist, and the chilling fear came back, and he couldn't smile in return.

As he made bannock and cut meat for the stew, he told her of the hunt. In the ecstasy of homecoming and finding her alive, it was already becoming difficult to remember the hunt's long pain and despair. He told her of how the raven's flesh had saved him when he had given up and was going back to Taka, of how the *atihk* turned back on its own trail, making the kill possible, of the snowstorm and the ambushing of Taka with a broken bow, and of the food he took from Taka's toboggan.

"You are a good hunter, Jacob," she murmured, and a pride glinted the dark eyes.

His lips couldn't speak the angry denial that rankled in his mind. He hadn't told her of the evil way in which the hunt had ended, and now her words brought a sudden surge of pained and cold remorse. But the rest of the hunt's story, its crux and core, thrust forward, erasing the remorse, demanding voice.

"Niska, there is more I must tell. . . ." His throat tightened. How could he tell her? She hadn't seen it in the cones as he had. But he forced the words to come. "It's all wrong! He doesn't love the sparrow, or the *atihk,* or anything else. Tomorrow I'll show you why I know . . . with cones, Niska. The cones can tell. . . ."

He stopped and gazed at her. The smile, the pride were gone; her face was blank, emotionless.

"He doesn't care about us!" Jacob declared.

The blood left her lips and her eyes hardened.

"Who brought the *kahkaki* just when you needed it?" she asked.

"They always come when a hunter is dying!"

"Who turned the *atihk* back?"

"They always circle back at calving time."

"But the time didn't have to be right then. And who brought the snow so that Taka isn't trailing you now?"

"There are always snowstorms. There have to be . . ." But his voice had faded, and the last words were almost inaudible. He was staring at his feet, and rubbing one moccasin slowly against the other. Then the voice came back, firm and undaunted again: "Yes, and *who* changed the wind and scared the *atihk* away when I could have killed it way back when the hunt was starting? Niska, maybe there isn't a *Manito* at all!"

Her smile had returned, but it was mischievous and teasing.

"Jacob, come to bed with me."

He wanted to, passionately, but he held back, fearing the thing that it would reveal.

"Come," she insisted.

He drew back the bedding and lay beside her. The hand moved, unwilled; he was powerless to stop it. It slid beneath the heavy underclothing and the fingers spread on the swollen flesh where the thicket of hair began.

Now all was gone—the pain and shame and the great tiredness; the taunting thoughts about the *Manito;* now all was a numbed insensateness and everything that was Jacob Atook flowed and flooded and dammed and waited in one kindled, burning palm. The wait became long, and the fear became a terror. A sob gurgled, almost strangling him. The *keekishkawasso* was hard, like stone, and still. And the knowledge flowed back from the palm, permeating, possessing, filling all the interstices of mind with its scourging condemnation. The meat of the evil attainment had reached the stewpot too late.

But Niska still smiled. She snuggled closer against him, lifting a hand from over his shoulder and pressing it on his mouth to silence his sobbing. Then her hand moved slowly down to his, and shifted it to another place on the taut, warm flesh.

"There. You've forgotten where."

He waited while the sobbing stopped but the strangling stayed. And the belly quivered, and for the first moments he thought it was the tremor in his own hand; then it came again, a sharp thump, unmistakable.

"And who kept *it* alive, Jacob, when you were sure it was dead?"

He groped for an answer, reaching deeply again down the dark cavern. But no answer was there. Instead, the bush was back, with the deep roots of thought that the cones had revealed. Only now, were there deeper roots, unknowable, still hidden beyond? He didn't know.

But he did know that he was hearing again the arrow's thud in the helpless flesh, and now he was hearing without pain. For death at the hunt's end did not destroy, it was only an exchange of fleeting flesh amid life's permanency. And the fleeting flesh murmured in the stewpot on the stove, filling the tent with its savory fragrance, and the new being stirred again under Jacob's hand—this death and living, but without contradiction or negation, a warp and woof of the same inseparable cloth. For that was the thing the gods had made.